RecruitZ

Afterworld Series #1

KARICE BOLTON

ISBN-13: 978-0615946429
ISBN-10: 0615946429

DEDICATION

To my husband and mother. Thank you for all of
your support and encouragement as I talked endlessly
about the Afterworld.
Love you both so much!
And to my dad who's up above enjoying the show.

ACKNOWLEDGMENTS

Cover Artist: Phatpuppy
Photographer/Wardrobe Styling: Teresa Yeh
Model: Taylor Smith
Leather bracelet and holster: Chris Anderson

And I want to say a simple thank you to Amazon and all of the other avenues available for the indie publishing world. It allows the art of storytelling to continue to flourish in unexpected ways

Revenge fueled me and anger drove me. That combination was all I had left to remind me that I was still human—that I was still alive. What I'd become wasn't what I was born to be, but it was what the world needed.

CHAPTER ONE

I sat in the passenger seat horrified, but I didn't dare drag my gaze away. The world had been told zombies no longer threatened human existence. Yet I was staring at an onslaught of them taking slow, deliberate steps toward our vehicle. We had barely pulled into our driveway when the horde descended out of nowhere.

I managed to slide my fingers along the door to the electric lock. I didn't know why I thought that would save us. The undead had never let a lock deter them before. I looked around our house and it looked untouched. These creatures were only in our yard, coming for us at a most vulnerable time.

Gavin attempted to take the car out of auto-drive, pressing the buttons frantically and commanding it with voice controls. The car only responded with words. We didn't control it. The car controlled us.

"Pedestrians within minimum safe distance," the car said, acknowledging Gavin's attempts to drive us out of danger.

No shit! We want to run the pedestrians over.

Tiny beads of sweat began forming at my hairline as I watched Gavin repeatedly engage and disengage various controls. Nothing would let us override the car's safety features.

Gavin's foot pressed on the accelerator trying to override the computer system, but the car still refused to budge. His foot slid off the pedal, and he quickly replaced it.

Damn these self-driving cars!

The engine red-lined with each attempt from Gavin's override, but the brain of the car overruled Gavin's actions with every rev of the motor. Gavin kept shaking his head as his finger slid up and down the dashboard. He glanced at me, his green eyes connecting with mine. I didn't want to believe what I saw behind them so I turned to look out the window.

I gripped the console as I watched the twitches and spasms of the zombies' movements closing in on us. They were everywhere...the grass, the sidewalk, the driveway. There was no mistaking the rotting, grey flesh that exposed the muscle and bone of the undead. They were something I'd run from countless times, but this time we had nowhere to run. The undead had us trapped. They would rip us to shreds in an instant.

"I think some of 'em are new," I said, turning my attention back to Gavin.

There were some clean-looking zombies staggering toward us, their flesh mostly intact. That made no sense. The outbreak had been contained for months.

There should be no freshly infected roaming around. Everyone had been vaccinated. The only stragglers evading capture had been around awhile, so their bodies were beat up badly by the time they were caught. Not these.

"Let's hope not," he murmured, not bothering to look out the window to confirm nor deny my suspicions.

"We can't run. They'd totally get us before we got away," I said, hoping he'd correct me, tell me that we had a chance.

He didn't.

He slammed his fist into the steering wheel and looked over at me. When the outbreak happened, we never looked back. We were always on the move, running from the disease that took our families and friends. That was the key to survival. Never stay in one place. Always stay on the move. Now we had nowhere to move. I glanced over at Gavin and saw the fear in his eyes. Even with everything we'd encountered, his eyes had never held this amount of terror.

"Babe, whatever happens…"

"Knock it off," I said.

"We have nothing to fight them with, and a horde this size needs a distraction."

"Don't you dare," I hissed, shaking my head. The fear was pulsing through me at an unstoppable rate. "We didn't live through the outbreak to die now."

I gritted my teeth, grabbed the civilian anti-zombie kit from under my seat, unzipped it, and looked for anything inside that might help. We were instructed to drop these kits off at government collection stations. I was grateful we never got around to it.

Gavin held down the ignition and reverse buttons at the same time in a vain attempt to override the safety sensors.

"Damn it," he muttered.

"Try rebooting the car. Turn it off and take the key out. Give it a few seconds and slip the key back in. Maybe if you pop it in reverse before the car can sense the zombies, it'll let us reverse," I directed.

He nodded, biting his lip, and turned off the engine allowing the moans of the horde outside to be heard. I took a deep breath and looked out my window that was now completely blocked by tattered shirts and non-oozing wounds pressed against the glass. It would only be a matter of time before they began to break through the glass. The moans turned into a chorus of humming.

"One-Mississippi-two…" Gavin's words wrapped around me.

I prayed silently to the same God I'd prayed to many nights before. He listened then and I hoped he'd listen now.

I grabbed two knives that were in the kit and flipped the blades open, locking them in place. The anodized orange handles were larger than the actual blades. Not comforting. I handed one to Gavin.

"There's still a Louisville Slugger on the floor behind us," Gavin said. His brown hair was cut short. That was one of the first things he did after we were vaccinated. A haircut and a shave to celebrate our survival. He still looked young but not as young as we both did before the outbreak.

I slid toward the center console, crawling as far from the passenger window as I could get. Gavin's breathing was heavy, and I felt the heat rolling off him as he continued to struggle with what we were facing.

I dug around in the bottom of the bag for the zombie deterrent. My hand clasped around the ADD, also known as the Audible Distraction Device, and I dropped the kit to the floor.

The car rocked back and forth as the number of beasts grew on both sides, creating a trance-like rhythm that was terrifying.

"Grab the bat," Gavin instructed, his voice low.

I slid my hand to his knee, squeezing it hard before I reached behind us and grabbed the wooden weapon.

The challenges we faced living off the land paled in comparison to what we faced confined in this car.

Gavin turned the engine on and sunk it into reverse, only to be stalled right where we were.

"Pedestrians in minimum safe distance," the car warned again.

"Shut up!" I shouted at the car's inhuman voice.

An oily residue smeared against the glass all around us from their bodies touching and gliding along the surfaces. They were crawling on the hood, metal pops sounded with every dent created. Their bodies slowly snaked up the windshield as they climbed toward the roof. Their mouths opening, jaws clicking as they tasted our scent. That was all we had separating us from zombies—glass. It would be only a matter of time before they mangled the metal above us and shattered the glass around us.

"If I get out of the car, I can distract them and you can run. I need you to run," he said slowly, his eyes locking on mine.

"No way. I'm not—"

The glass shattered, interrupting my objection. The

shards of glass crumbled down the door and into Gavin's lap. Several mismatched arms shoved their hands through the nonexistent barrier, reaching for Gavin as I let out a scream and lunged with the knife in hand.

"Don't watch what happens, babe. Promise me you'll look away," his voice pleading, as he struggled against the fleshy fingers that twisted and pulled at his shirt.

I reached across Gavin and began breaking off fingers and slicing hands and anything I could connect with that was attempting to gouge at Gavin. Pieces of flesh tumbled into the car.

We'd been vaccinated.

We'd be okay.

The stench of the decaying flesh filled our small car with every crack of a bone and tear of the skin. Gavin and I were shoving the arms, bodies, and heads back the other direction, but they kept pushing through the small driver's window. Gavin grabbed the bat, shoving and poking the zombies through the window. The space was so small it was hard for him to hit with any force.

It wouldn't be long before they broke the other windows. The first thump on the roof made me jump and then the second. The metal was crunching with every step above, and I looked up to see the roof dipping in places.

The moans grew louder as more arms pushed through the opening, scraping and digging at our flesh. Fingers with calloused skin grazed my face, poking at my eyes and scraping my cheeks, but they would fall from my face almost instantly in search of Gavin. Why Gavin?

Gavin propelled the bat into the crowd with such velocity that he managed to run it through the stomach of one of the beasts, spreading the group out momentarily. The zombie collapsed, but the swarm returned, descending on us again.

I jabbed the knife directly into the neck of the most insistent intruder and pulled it out, severing the head from the neck. The head toppled into the car as the body slumped outside against the door. There was a brief hesitation as they stepped back, and I grabbed the ADD, removing the pin and flipping the lever. I threw the ADD out the window, but it bounced against an undead girl in the back of the crowd. It dropped to the ground with a thud. My heart sank with the realization the zombies wouldn't be running anywhere.

Broop-Broop-Broop

Maybe I was wrong.

Once the ADD sounded, the zombies peeled away from our car and turned toward the device, but there wasn't enough distance to open the door or escape through the window. They'd get us in a heartbeat. The deafening sound made it hard to think. I watched as each zombie turned back toward the car and shoved their arms back at us. A set of hands latched onto Gavin's neck, and I slashed clear through the zombie's wrists—bone and all—, stopping only because the blade encountered the softness of Gavin's throat.

"They're not going to stop until they get what they want," he whispered, punching back at the beasts.

The windshield began cracking from the weight of the bodies. The ADD siren stopped blaring, and I was almost completely positioned in Gavin's lap, stabbing at anything and everything in the opening. Hands had broken through all of the windows. The passenger side window had arms flailing as bodies attempted to squeeze into the narrow opening.

"I don't know what to do." My yell could only be heard as a whisper of desperation above the noise of the horde.

"Becca, there's some research in my folders from the campus…" his voice trailed off. His eyes began to cloud over, and I dropped my gaze. Dodging rotten, fleshy fingers and elbows, my hands ran protectively over his chest as I fought the undead. There was nowhere for us to hide.

"Don't start saying goodbyes," I commanded, noticing blood on my fingertips, lots of blood. Where was this blood coming from? There was no pain beyond the scratches on my arms. I felt no pain. Elbowing the beasts, I looked at Gavin. His eyes on mine—locked on mine—as his lips curled up slightly.

"What are the odds?" he whispered weakly.

A cry wanted to escape my lips as I watched Gavin blink slowly. His breathing became shallower with each passing second. I searched feverishly, gliding my hands along his chest and stomach. My fingers fell into his wound.

The zombies had torn through his shirt, through his abdomen. Blood was pooled on the seat, blood was everywhere, and I watched the hands of the undead still stirring and grabbing pieces of him. I swallowed my horror. A gasp wanted to escape my lips, but I was stronger than that. We were stronger than that.

I continued slapping the hands away but none were after me. They only wanted Gavin.

"I've loved you since your sixteenth birthday," he murmured, closing his eyes.

"No!" I screamed, grabbing him, attempting to move him from the window.

But it was too late. Several arms had wrapped around Gavin's neck and chest, hauling him through the window. I grabbed his body but he told me to let go. I couldn't let go. I wouldn't let go.

My hands slid from his waist…to his thighs…to his knees…to his ankles. I was holding on so tightly, but it wasn't enough. Only his feet were left inside the car, and I held on with a strength I didn't recognize as my own. As they pulled the last of him out the window, I followed right through the opening, collapsing on the concrete driveway. None of them attempted to attack me beyond the accidental push or scrape. They weren't after me.

I watched in horror as the love of my life was torn to pieces and thrown about. Why didn't they take me too? Why were they leaving me alone? My screams did nothing. I wasn't sure I was even screaming. The zombies huddled together, and I forced my eyes away from what was left of my husband.

"Please, kill me too," I whimpered.

Two unmarked, black vans came barreling down the street, stopping right at our driveway. The back doors flung open and the killers vanished inside. That wasn't possible. I couldn't trust my own eyes.

I was hallucinating.

The last of the undead stepped inside the vans, and the doors closed before the van peeled off.

"Is there anyone out here? Can't anyone help us? Please? Can't someone help us?" I sobbed, crawling toward what was left of Gavin.

I heard the screams of the neighbors as they ran toward us, stopping just short of our driveway. Their mouths dropped open, speechless. There was nothing anyone could do. The sobs and cries for help continued, and I didn't know if they were coming from me or from everyone else. I was numb. I heard apologies about not coming out when they heard the ADD, but it wasn't their fault. The ADDs were the equivalent of fireworks nowadays. Everything was in slow motion or people were moving slowly. I slumped over Gavin, holding the remains of his torso, listening to the ambulance siren make its way down our street. I wrapped my arms around him tightly for the last time.

That's what I remember from that day—and that I never told him I loved him.

CHAPTER TWO

I unclipped the black leather holster from my jeans, unloaded the pistol and placed it in the locking drawer. Thankfully, peasant tops were in fashion now, and they hid the bulge beautifully when I was out and about. I grabbed the notebook that had the address of the bar I planned on visiting tonight and shoved it in a drawer. The place was a dive bar in the far end of town that might reveal what I was hoping to find, but I wouldn't know until I checked it out. From all accounts online, it was a hotbed of underground activity and exactly how I might gain access into the unsavory side of society. All I wanted was answers but for some reason those were very hard to come by.

I briefly let my mind wander to happier times. Looking around our basement, I thought back to how thrilled Gavin was when I told him I was totally fine with turning the space into a media room. He'd also managed to build a safe room inside.

We'd only been married a matter of months, and it

was an incredible time. I'd never let go of those memories.

Ever.

After surviving the outbreak, we knew exactly what we wanted, which was each other. Like most college students before the outbreak, we imagined our time would go on forever, and we'd get to everything at some point. After the outbreak, one of our many mottos was to never again waste another minute given to us, so we got married right after we got vaccinated.

The leather recliners Gavin had chosen for the media room had been shoved against the far wall. After the outbreak had been contained, one of the main priorities of the government was to get commerce going again. With the large payouts that were disbursed to the remaining citizens, the government recognized there was money to be spent. And they wanted to ensure there was a place to spend it. Makeshift stores began popping up everywhere as manufacturing plants revved back up. Out of all the issues our country—and the world—faced, I found it odd that guaranteeing we had a place to buy furniture and electronics was a top priority. But I guess they felt we needed a sense of normalcy.

I was willing to buy into that dream until Gavin was taken from me. We'd barely finished the remodel when it happened—when he was killed. There my mind went again, wandering back to Gavin.

God, I missed him.

Looking around the space now, it looked like some makeshift army command post with maps and photographs pinned to the walls.

The doorbell rang through the house. It was time

to play 'let's pretend' with Abby, who was one of my many friends I'd managed to ignore since everything happened with Gavin. The world was supposed to be a safer place now, and there was an evolving sense of community if a person chose to participate.

I did not.

The epidemic had been stopped, or at least that's what the general public was told. We were all vaccinated and to the government that was enough. Yet, here I was without my soul mate, hiding from my friends, and attempting to understand what happened.

I locked the basement door behind me and did a double jiggle of the lock to ensure she didn't accidentally wander down there. I was sure it would just be another bit of gossip that my friends would toss around for awhile before approaching me to perform an intervention. That was something I could really do without.

"Hey," my voice sang out as I flung open the front door. "So good to see you."

I hoped my acting skills were up to par.

Abby sailed through the door and gave me a quick kiss on the cheek. She was dressed in grey yoga pants and a navy sweatshirt. She had straightened her normally wavy, blonde hair, and she looked really nice and healthy. That was a look of progress I enjoyed seeing. Most of us had gone without for so long during the outbreak, a gaunt appearance was the norm.

"Ready for dinner?" Abby asked, holding up two brown bags.

"Sounds good to me," I said, realizing I wasn't even sure when I'd eaten last. "Let's spread out in the family room."

"You look amazing, Becky," she complimented me. My brown hair hit just below my shoulders, which helped to hide how skinny I'd become, or at least I hoped it did.

"Thanks. You're not looking so bad yourself," I said.

"It's amazing what a constant food source can do for a person. I'm filling out again in all the right places."

"I'm sure Caleb is happy about that," I laughed, following her down the hall toward the family room. I turned my eyes away from the wall where all of the photos of Gavin and me hung. After the outbreak, anywhere we went I made him take a picture of us. I was just so excited to be participating in life again— even our first trip to the grocery store was documented. I was grateful to have those photographs. Nevertheless, I usually avoided this route to the back of the house.

The family room was one of the first rooms Gavin painted when we got back in my family's house. A gnawing sensation in the pit of my stomach crept up as I thought about that day, how much fun we had. I glanced around and saw the bright, cheery yellow walls. Back then it seemed fitting somehow... Now, not so much.

Once I flipped on the lights, I noticed that every surface had a thick coating of dust. I never really came in here unless I was grabbing a book off one of the shelves.

Oops!

The ivory curtains were closed along with all of the drapes in my house. After seeing the dust on the furniture, I could only imagine what a good shake of the curtains would release.

"What do you have to drink?" Abby dumped the bags on the coffee table, ignoring the tiny dust particles that floated around. That's what good friends were for.

"I've been specializing in beer, coffee, and more coffee."

"Sounds good and in that order." She plopped on the couch and began looking around the room as I went to the kitchen to get our drinks.

"Where'd all of your art books go?" she yelled from the family room.

Shoot! I didn't expect her to notice that.

I grabbed a bottle opener and walked back to where I'd left Abby. She was staring at the farthest bookshelf, which now overflowed with books and manuals on weapons, surveillance techniques, tactical planning, and nano-technology. Nothing like what I used to enjoy reading, but these gave me a purpose. And to wake up every morning, I needed a purpose.

"I put them all up in the attic. I can always pull them out when I need them," I muttered, sitting next to her on the couch. I handed her a beer and the bottle opener, hoping to distract her enough to move on.

"Kind of a sudden switch of interests," she mused, raising a brow at me.

"Meh." I shrugged, taking a sip of the beer. I turned on the television, and she grabbed the remote from me and began channel surfing.

"Not that I don't trust your wonderful taste," she said, before I could object.

Okay, so the twenty-four-hour news channel wasn't everyone's idea of a good time, but I liked it.

"What's Caleb doing tonight?" I asked.

"He's at the library doing research for some paper." She gave me a pouty face. "I think they should give us all a pass and an honorary degree for all we've been through."

"Ditto."

She took another chug of her beer, and I noticed a flicker of sadness in her eyes. Like everyone, her family wasn't what it once was. We all managed to think we had put the savagery behind us, as if we could pile the grief somewhere. What we were all coming to realize was that sorrow couldn't be ignored, and we could never predict when a piece from the pile would come tumbling down for others to witness.

We ate our teriyaki, catching up on things about her and Caleb and our other mutual friends. Caleb and Abby were finally planning on getting married. I think Gavin's death had something to do with the sudden change of plans for them. Previously, neither of them had any interest in marriage until after they finished school and started their careers. It was hard to think we might start living in a world with careers again. That seemed so far off.

I melded into the rhythm of our conversation, answering some questions and dodging many more, as I attempted to suppress the restless energy that was beginning to fill me. I had a place to be in less than an hour and I didn't want company.

"You seem like you're doing better. More focused," she offered.

"I'm beginning to see my purpose in the world again," I confirmed, feeling the ghost of a smile surface on my lips. I didn't really want to divulge what

I thought that purpose was.

"Hey, are you coming back to school?" she asked, folding her legs under her.

"I don't think so. Not yet." I shook my head and glanced at the television.

"I think Gavin would want you to keep going," Abby said quietly.

My stomach clenched as soon as I heard his name.

"I'm going back. Just not yet. I've got some stuff I need to take care of," I replied.

Abby brought her beer to her lips and slowly sipped. I could tell she was going to start the lecture again. It was the one conversation I could count on with her whenever we got together. It also explained why I didn't get together with her very often.

She placed the bottle back down on the table and I waited for it. Abby narrowed her eyes at me and took a deep breath in and exhaled.

But she didn't say anything.

"So what classes did you sign up for?" I asked, hoping to dodge an unpleasant conversation.

"Environmental Chem, an English Comp class, and Globalization in the Afterworld," she said flatly. She was pissed. She didn't even look at me when she answered.

"The Afterworld? Is that what the academics are calling it now?" I shook my head. Gavin would've gotten a kick out of that. "Sounds like a heavy load."

She shrugged her shoulders and looked at the television.

"I can't even pretend to imagine what you went through," Abby started.

I turned and stared at Abby. Her blue eyes connected with mine. I arched a brow and leaned back on the couch waiting for what she really wanted to tell me. I knew all my friends were thinking it, but it was only Abby who had the balls to say anything to my face.

"But you've gotta let go. Quit pursuing something that doesn't exist," she said.

"So now you don't believe me? What I saw?" I whispered, leaning over the table.

"The other witnesses never saw any vans pull up, Becky. I just think with everything that you experienced, you may've thought you saw something like that, but..." her voice trailed off as her eyes filled with tears. She looked over at the bookcases and then looked back at me.

That wasn't like her usual lecture. Nope. It was completely different. She was dropping me off in the crazy bin and possibly not planning on picking me up again.

"I know what I saw." My words steadied. "It was a planned attack. I'm not the only one who's experienced something like it, either."

Her gaze dropped from mine, and she crumpled a napkin in her hands.

"Don't you see what you've become?" Her mouth pursed together disapprovingly, and I wanted to shake her. Snap her out of whatever delusional fairytale she was living in. I wasn't the one with the problem.

"What's that?" I questioned, watching her fingers tear through the napkin.

"You've become completely obsessed with conspiracies and things that aren't true. I mean look at your reading material." She pointed at the bookshelves.

"So you think I've become some wacko?"

She just told me everything I needed to hear. I now knew I had to walk a fine line, even with my friends. There were places for people like me, and no matter how much I hoped my friends wouldn't volunteer me for one, I was no longer sure.

"It's not that. I just think that you've become obsessed with a possibility that's unrealistic." She looked away. "The government's trying their best to capture the rogue zombies, but their first mission was to get everyone vaccinated. We all know that a zombie floating around here or there isn't that abnormal, and unfortunately, they can still rip us apart."

"So Gavin was just another casualty of war?" I questioned, ignoring her statement about a rogue zombie. We had a horde attack us, not a straggler.

Her eyes softened and she reached for my hand.

"I think you know the answer to that."

"I know what I saw." I pulled my hand away from hers and wrapped it around my beer bottle that was unfortunately empty.

"You're wasting your life. He never would've wanted this."

"Then tell me… why wasn't I killed? Why did the zombies leave me alone?" My pulse was racing. "Why was there a horde of zombies and where did they all go?"

"Sometimes bad things happen, and it doesn't mean anything beyond the obvious." She turned her face to look back at me. "I'm only telling you this because I care about you."

"Our histories are being constructed right now, and I want to ensure my story is heard," I said, kicking my legs out in front of me.

"And what story is that?" she asked.

I glared at her.

"It's the story of truth. Not just what some want represented. If we don't start acknowledging the things that are going on around us, history will repeat itself, and the next time, it might not be possible to stop. What I witnessed was unstoppable. They were on a mission. It didn't matter that we were vaccinated. They used their strength, not their disease. I lost my best friend, my world, Abby." I gulped away the tears. They wouldn't help. Only the truth would help.

She shook her head and moistness formed on her lower lids.

"I care about you. We all do."

I needed to watch my step. I had to maintain control and that was even more evident with every one of her pity glances. I had to change my tactic.

"I get it." There was no point in arguing. All I could do was discredit the naysayers. It was unfortunate I had to add my friends to that list. I nodded and plastered a pretend smile on my lips.

"I've upset you. I can tell. I'm just so happy to be able to visit with you. I didn't mean for it to go this way." She patted my knee and let out a sigh. "How about if I take off…if you promise to meet with me again soon."

"Sounds perfect. Are you busy Friday?" I asked.

A huge grin spread across her face. "Really?"

"Yeah. Totally." I stood up and tossed the pillow I had been holding back onto the couch. "You're right. I need to start participating in life a little again. It's what he would've wanted."

I was surprised how easily the lies slipped out.

"Maybe a little of the old Becky is coming back,"

she said, hopping off the couch, hugging me.

Impossible.

"So does the afternoon sound good on Friday?" I asked, smiling.

"Absolutely," she said, and gave me one last hug.

We walked to the front door and with every step the anxiety began turning to excitement. I was ready to start my evening.

I waved goodbye as she climbed into her car and drove off. Closing the front door, I locked the deadbolt and ran to the basement door, almost giddy with the prospect of tonight's adventure.

Let the games begin.

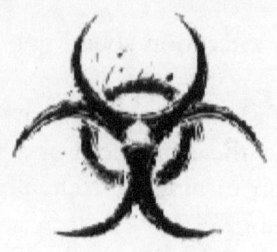

CHAPTER THREE

I stood in the dark alley, staring at the blinking red and blue open sign across the street. At an attempt of Afterworld humor, there was also a blinking 'No Zombie Vacancy' sign flashing underneath. I leaned against the brick wall, watching and waiting. I'd been staking the place out for over thirty minutes, and I was fully willing to admit to myself that I was only attempting to buy time. I didn't really need to keep staring at the front door. I knew everything I needed to know. First, I was at the right place, and second, the crowd looked rough. I only had one shot at convincing them I belonged, and I didn't want to screw it up with a case of bad nerves. I looked down at my hands and commended myself on the fact that I had gotten them to quit trembling. I wore my diamond wedding band and my mom's diamond tennis bracelet along with some silver bangles. I was hoping that if I ran into the right sharks, they'd think I was one of the many survivors spending their survivors' checks on frivolous things, ready to play whatever they wanted to offer that would help take away the bad memories.

The bar across the street was the only business that had reopened in the block, which only made it creepier. The isolated location made it perfect for illicit activities. This once bustling end of town was now full of empty shops and restaurants waiting for owners who would never return. It was one more reminder of the devastation big and small towns everywhere had experienced.

Just as I got up my nerve, a guy in a black leather vest and tight jeans exited the door, letting death metal drift out, along with a bunch of shouts and laughter. A shiver ran up my spine, and I almost talked myself out of crossing the street, but the first raindrop landed on me. Even the Gods were telling me to get the show on the road.

I took a step out from behind the shadows and caught the attention of the guy who'd just lit up a cigarette. He gave me a quick nod and walked down the sidewalk to look at the line of bikes.

I slowly walked to the curb and glanced both ways before dashing across the street toward the bar's entrance. I pushed on the door to be greeted by a bouncer who was at least a foot taller than me. He had a shaved head and a goatee that was down to his chest.

"Welcome to Shackles." His voice boomed over the loud music and yelling of intoxicated patrons. I wasn't surprised that he didn't card me. Ever since the outbreak, drinking rules had gone out the window.

Taking a deep breath in, I smiled at him and

scooted through the doorway. The smell of stale beer and fried food floated through the air. I spotted the bartender flipping some brightly colored bottle in the air and made a beeline to him.

One drink wouldn't hurt. In fact, as I scanned the crowd, I thought it would be the only way to make it out without losing my mind. I pulled a worn black leather stool from under the counter and sat down.

"I've got ten on that one," a man shouted. I looked behind me to find a guy holding up cash in the air, flipping it between his fingers. He wore a red thermal shirt, and his grey hair was slicked back. His leather jacket hung over the chair, and he was staring at one of the screens above me.

"Double or nothing, Tommy. That's it. You know that," a woman's voice sang from two barstools away.

"Is there something I can get ya?" the bartender asked.

"Greyhound." I turned back around to face the bartender. His eyes were striking, a sea blue mixed with green, and they were kind. Far kinder than anyone else in this bar, that was for sure.

"That's old-fashioned." He grinned at me, sliding a coaster in front of me.

I shrugged. "It's what I like."

"Comin' up."

"Oh, come on. I'm going in blind on this batch, Brenda," Tommy argued.

"Marcus is the best trainer around. You know you'll come out just fine, Tommy," she laughed. "It's double or nothing. Take it or leave it."

Things were looking up.

"This is how I make my living," Tommy grumbled.

I glanced quickly to my side to see the Brenda person in a tight fitting, red halter. She was smiling widely, but her blue eyes were cool, calculating as she watched Tommy. Her black hair was cut in a short bob, showing off the sharpness of her features.

The bartender slid me the Greyhound and watched me carefully as I stirred the drink and took a long sip from the tiny, red straw.

"You've never been in here before." He grabbed a bar towel and began wiping down the dark, cherry counters.

"Not recently," I lied.

"Not ever," he countered, smiling.

"Maybe that too." I grinned at him and turned my attention back to the two arguing about something that sounded far too perfect to miss.

"You can come out tomorrow an hour before and take a look at the stock. If you want to switch your target before, that's fine, but the batch can't be changed," Brenda said.

"I got it. I know," Tommy replied.

I watched Brenda hop off the stool. When she returned, she had a wad of cash tucked in her halter.

"Anyone else?" she asked, eyeing the group around me.

Everyone stayed quiet.

"What about you, sweet thing?" she purred, looking directly at me. "You want in?"

"In on what?" I asked casually.

"You know very well what," she laughed and crossed one leg over the other.

I shrugged my shoulders and shifted my gaze away from hers.

"It's not my thing." Not wanting to raise suspicion

by acting too eager I turned to look at the television over the bar.

"Have you ever tried?" she cooed, sliding off her stool.

"I like to keep my money." I smiled, turning toward the bartender.

"It looks like you like to enjoy splurging a little." She stood next to me and traced her finger along my bracelets, the tennis bracelet and sterling silver bangles hanging on my wrist. The bangles had been my high school graduation present. A sign of happier times, I suppose.

"I wouldn't know the first thing about it," I muttered.

"If the girl doesn't want to do it, leave her alone," the bartender said, his voice warning Brenda.

I threw him a smile and watched as she leaned over the bar counter and swatted at him.

"You're bad for business," Brenda replied playfully.

"How does it work, anyway?" I asked, raising a brow.

"See now? I knew she was interested."

"You've heard of cockfighting, right?" Her eyes gleamed wickedly.

I nodded.

"Well, replace the roosters with zombies and you've got a hell of a show."

"Seriously?"

"Now you're interested, aren't you?" She narrowed her eyes at me. "I can tell you, it's very gratifying watching these beasts get ripped to shreds."

My eyes dipped to the floor. I was close to getting a pass and didn't want to screw up.

"I just don't think it's my thing," I replied, after a few seconds. "I don't want to spend that kind of money."

"Nuts?" the bartender asked, scooting me a bowl full of cashews and peanuts.

I think he was honestly trying to protect me from Brenda.

"Is that what's stopping you?" she asked.

"Partially," I replied.

"Tommy's a professional. You don't have to go in that deep. Isn't that right, Tommy?"

I glanced back at Tommy, and he nodded and smiled, throwing back another sip of his beer.

"I'll make you a deal. Come out tomorrow, check out the facilities, and I'll let you enter for half the usual entry fee. I'll even throw in my two cents on which zombie you should bet on." A young guy came up behind Brenda and tapped her on the shoulder.

"I'll be back in a sec, and you can let me know what you've decided," Brenda said.

I smiled and nodded, turning back to my Greyhound. So far so good.

"What's your name?" I asked the bartender.

He was dressed in a black t-shirt and jeans and his dark hair was shoved back. Judging by his forearms and shoulders, he could crush anyone in here if they misbehaved. His chiseled features were offset by his gentle expression. It was an intriguing combination, especially for a place like this.

"Preston. Yours?"

"Rebekah. Have you ever done this zombie fighting thing?" I asked.

"A few times. Made a killing, actually. But it's not really my thing," he paused and eyed me carefully.

"It's pretty brutal."

"I can imagine."

"The ring…" his voice trailed off when a customer tapped on the other end of the counter. "I'll be back."

I sipped my drink, letting the cold liquid trickle down my throat. I wondered how much longer I should play this card before accepting the invite from Brenda.

Preston returned and noticed my empty drink.

"Another?"

"Nah. I'm good. So about the ring?" I prodded.

"Yeah. Right. The Zombie Pit is in the center of the room and even people that are all the way in the back of the crowd get dirty."

Queasiness began climbing from the pit of my belly up to my throat, and I forced it down. This was my ticket into the world of underground trafficking, and I needed to take all emotion out of it. It was the only way.

"Dirty," I repeated and then sighed. "Sounds fantastic."

"So what's the verdict?" Brenda reappeared quicker than I expected. I caught her shoving more cash down her halter.

"I think it might be just the release I'm looking for," I lied, avoiding Preston's penetrating stare.

"Great. Here's the address for tomorrow's event. Come early, and I'll get you set up, show you around." She shoved the card in my hand.

"I'm Rebekah by the way," I started, but she had already walked away to recruit her next payday.

"Don't go there with much money," Preston whispered. "And don't go there unarmed."

I looked up at him, and his blue-green eyes locked

on mine. I heard Brenda's spiel in the background and exhaled slowly.

"I'll take another Greyhound after all."

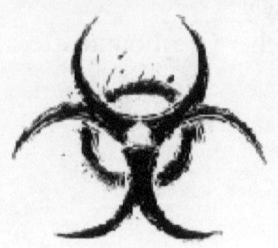

CHAPTER FOUR

It was late afternoon and I was on my way to the Zombie Pit. The address was out in the sticks, and I'd already been on the road for what seemed like forever. The rural areas were hit as hard as the cities during the outbreak, but fewer people returned to the outlying areas when it was all over, leaving everything pretty much in ruins. It was trips like these that made me realize how much rebuilding our world faced.

I'd always felt like Washington was protected from the disasters the rest of the country faced. We didn't have tornadoes, hurricanes, or blizzards to constantly deal with. Sure, we had the occasional earthquake, but that somehow seemed better than the other options...at least until the outbreak. The West and East coasts were hit first, and then the virus traveled inward to the rest of the country. It certainly burst my bubble of living safely in the Northwest.

I tapped the steering wheel of my '77 Ford truck to the beat of the music. It was as close to anti-autopilot driving as I could get. I would never get in one of those cars that drove themselves again. This thing didn't even have power steering. It was perfection. Gavin and his dad lowered it, put in a plush bench seat and laid a dazzling cherry red paint job on it, along with a stereo that could make a person's ears bleed. We used to take it camping, and there were a few times we got it stuck in the mud, but it was worth it. Between how much it cost to fill up the tank and the cost of parts to keep it running, we considered it our splurge. If only we'd been driving it that day. I shook the images from my head and focused on the rumble of the engine. I enjoyed hearing the roar that most cars lacked these days.

I was listening to electronica to psyche myself up for what I was about to encounter. To say I wasn't looking forward to watching zombies rip each other apart would be an understatement, but I might be able to find out how they were manipulating these creatures. And I had already gotten the name of one of the trainers—Marcus. That was a start.

It was amazing how quickly some humans turned back to their greedy, power-hungry selves. Once the vaccines were administered, apparently this underground stuff started popping up readily. It was cowardly, but so typical of human nature to exploit one another even in times of tragedy.

Feeling the adrenaline pumping a little too hard, I flipped my player to another song. One that was a little more soothing. In the distance I saw a large estate with a beautiful scrolled wrought-iron fence surrounding the pasture, but the closer I got, I realized it had also fallen victim to the world we now lived in.

The sprawling home's front door was busted in, and all the windows were shattered on the lower floor. There was a ladder propped up against the side of the house, beneath a bedroom window, with only shreds of clothing hanging from the steps. A shiver ran up my spine as the blood soaked fabric blew in the breeze. Apparently the owners would never be coming back.

"Destination in 3 miles," the woman's electronic voice instructed. I silenced the GPS and kept alert for anything out of the ordinary. I doubted that they did the fights in the same area as the training, but one never knew.

I saw a line of cars parked on the side of the road, and my pulse quickened as I drove up to the club's acreage. There was a long driveway to the right with more cars parked up and down it. Wanting to always have an escape plan, I drove past the driveway and down the road, probably a quarter-mile or more away. I clunked the transmission into park and stepped on the emergency brake, taking in a deep breath.

I flipped down my visor and adjusted the clip-on mirror that Gavin had bought just for me. I reached in my bag, grabbed the red lipstick and colored in my lips. I puckered my mouth around my index finger and pulled my finger out, allowing the excess red to bleed onto my finger. There! Now I'd avoid the dreaded lipstick on the teeth syndrome. One of the many reasons I wasn't into wearing lots of makeup.

I reached under my seat and grabbed my Betty holster holding the Beretta Tomcat .32 that seemed perfect for the occasion. I clipped the holster inside my jeans' waistband, securing it in place. I didn't want to take a chance on giving anyone a glimpse of my

Beretta, so even though this holster was a little more uncomfortable than some, at least it was easy access and almost invisible.

Remembering Preston's words of wisdom, I wore tight black jeans and a black sweatshirt that I didn't care about. My brown hair was slicked back in a bun, and I slid my sunglasses up on top my head.

I began walking down the road when a black sedan came driving up, slowly coming to a halt next to me. The passenger window rolled down, and the driver ducked his head so I could see him. The man had dark hair and was wearing a flashy gold Rolex and a suit. Must be his first time here too.

"Is this the place for the—"

"Think so. First time here," I interrupted and kept walking.

I heard the car drive on behind me, and then the wheels hit the gravel as he parked. I sped up my stride to avoid having to chitchat with anyone who would actually enjoy being a spectator at an event like this.

I made it to the driveway and was shocked to see how large a turnout such an event brought. There had to have been at least three or four people to every car I'd seen. There was a large, newly constructed barn. It was painted brown with the decorative beams a nice shade of green. The lawn looked freshly mowed and sported a few large, white canopies where people congregated, holding their drinks tightly. This was in complete contrast to all the deserted homes I'd passed on the way here. There was life for starters.

I saw several buckets with beverages placed all over the yard, along with an assortment of finger foods. The surroundings here had such a different vibe than the bar I visited the night before. At the moment, it almost felt like I'd arrived at a nice fall wedding.

I made my way to the closest tent, which seemed to be filled mostly with men and grabbed a bottle of water from a bucket. I found a seat at one of the tables and began looking through the sheets of paperwork that were displayed. There was a cup full of pens in the center of the table, next to a beautiful floral arrangement.

"There you are," Brenda's voice rang out. I half turned in my chair to see Brenda trotting up behind me. She was dressed in a black halter this time and a pair of khakis. She was wearing a black cap and looked completely in her element.

I nodded. "Hey."

"I wasn't sure if you'd really make it out."

"Yup. Well, here I am," I said, standing up, grabbing my water.

"I'll give you the grand tour. We've got an hour before the first showdown."

"Great," I replied, my voice accidentally catching in the back of my throat.

She caught my gaze and narrowed her ice-blue eyes on me.

"There's no need to be nervous. We've got enough armed guards around to take out any fighters who get out of control. It's never happened though. Not with our trainers."

I shook my head, trying to grasp what she implied, and followed her out of the tent across the lawn. As we walked by a large tent, I saw a chain-link ring in the center of it with a few bleachers scattered around the tent. It didn't look like there was much seating at all.

"It turns into standing room only," she said, as if reading my mind.

"I heard it gets a bit messy even for the crowd."

"That it does," she confirmed, stopping in front of a steel building.

"What's this?" I asked, looking at the secured metal garage door.

"This is where we keep the fighters before the events." Her eyes gleamed with an intensity I'd seen before, but it generally never led to good things. "I want you to meet one of our trainers."

"Inside?" I arched a brow, pursing my lips together as I scanned the building noting the lack of exits.

"You'll be fine." She entered a pin onto the keypad, unlocking the door.

The clanking of the metal door retracting forced me to shove my fears deep inside. I stared at the ground and twisted slightly at the waist to get the Beretta to stop pinching my skin.

"Right this way," she said, flipping on both the lights and a large industrial fan that began whirring. I heard her lock the door behind me and an uneasy feeling spread throughout my body.

Still refusing to look up, I saw that the floor was sawdust. The air was heavy and unpleasant to breathe. I moved my arm up to my nose and began breathing into the crook of my elbow before looking up. A sudden crashing of metal got my attention, and I looked up to see a horrifying sight.

There were rows and rows of chain-link kennels, completely enclosed. Each one contained a single zombie. The kennel directly in front of me was shaking violently as the zombie's fingers wrapped around the links. It pressed its face against the fencing, etching brand new marks into its decomposing flesh.

I looked away but not fast enough. The creature's tongue was hanging out of its mouth, and it was difficult not to vomit as the bile rose up in my throat. I was looking at someone's father or husband who was now being exploited for profit.

"Let's get going. I want you to meet Brad." Brenda's words brought me back to reality and into the role I needed to play.

I glanced behind me at the zombie who was still mesmerized by my presence and noticed its tattered suit and polished work shoes. We walked along the side of the building. A metal wall was on my right. The never-ending stock of zombies was to my left.

There was an office in the corner that we were walking toward. I couldn't imagine how anyone could possibly stay inside these walls with these creatures, but as I got closer I noticed the office had thick bulletproof glass, and a door leading directly to the outside. The blinds were closed on all the windows but one, and I at least understood that. I guess that made it better.

Wait! No! That didn't make it better—ever! I wouldn't want to look out to see a flock of the undead, staring back at me. Who did that?

Brenda rang a buzzer near the door and a guy hurriedly opened it up.

"Right on time," he said, bringing her into his arms and letting go quickly once he saw me.

"Who do we have here?" he asked, quirking his lip slightly.

"I'm Rebekah," I said, extending my hand.

"Nice to meet you. If Brenda didn't tell you, I'm Brad." He ushered us into his small office and closed the door, locking it. He took a seat behind his desk and joined his fingers together. He was wearing a sweater and jeans, and, if he held any other profession in the world, might be considered good looking with his brown eyes and shaggy, blonde hair.

"So, what brings you here to check out the goods?" he asked.

"Uh. Just new to everything," I said, looking over at Brenda cautiously. "I'm not totally convinced that this is the hobby for me."

The guy started laughing and leaned back in his chair. The entire wall behind him had an arsenal of automatic rifles, pistols, and shotguns.

"It can take some getting used to. That's for sure." He shook his head and put his weight on his elbows.

"It doesn't look like you're totally used to everything with that amount of weaponry behind you," I said, pointing at the wall.

"I just stack the odds in my favor." He smiled. "Now what can I help you with?"

"Who do we have tonight that you feel certain about letting her place her money on?" Brenda asked.

"What bracket's she in?" he asked.

Brenda looked at me and raised her brows. "Well?"

"What are the options?" I asked. "What's the least amount of money?"

"The entry fee is five-hundred, but I told you I'd knock it in half for you. The lowest wager is two-hundred and fifty, but the return just won't be there," Brenda said. "I don't recommend it."

"Of course you don't." Using Brenda's technique,

I reached into my bra and grabbed the cash and threw it on the desk. "I only brought seven hundred so that should cover my entry fee and then place the rest where it needs to be."

"That puts you in the base bracket, but your return will be solid. I'll make sure of it," Brad said. "Wanna see the fighter you'll be betting on?"

"Sure," I said, standing up.

Not really!

"All right. Follow me." He grabbed a sawed-off shotgun, and I followed him back out the door to the herd of undead.

We went on the far side of the building, and the creatures all around us were seething and twitching in distress from being confined. I hugged the wall until we stopped at a kennel where the infected creature glared at me with dull eyes, snapping his mouth at the vacant air. My palms began sweating, and I wiped them on my jeans. He would've been my age if the vaccine had only gotten to him in time.

"We call him Jared," Brad said, jiggling on the door. I watched the zombie swipe at him, gashing his own fingers against the metal, causing gouges in his rotting flesh.

He wasn't as fresh looking as some of the ones that attacked Gavin, but he certainly didn't look that old, which made no sense at all.

"Why the name Jared?" I asked.

"Thought he kind of looked like the Subway guy from years ago," Brad laughed.

"He's certainly quicker than most," I offered, backing up against the metal wall as Jared continued swiping at air.

"That's why it's in the bag for you." Brenda

winked at me, and Jared seemed to be getting more wound up the longer we stood in front of him.

"I think I've seen enough. I feel good placing my money on him."

"Right this way then," Brad said, walking back toward the main metal door that Brenda and I had walked through only minutes earlier.

I shuffled past several crates when my eyes caught one of the infected gripping the chain-link, licking the air. My heart stopped when I looked directly into the grey eyes of the zombie and realized it was Gavin's older brother, staring right back at me.

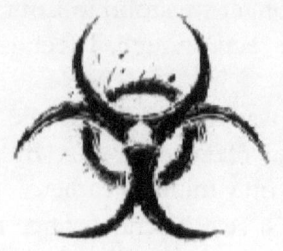

CHAPTER FIVE

I could barely catch my breath as I wandered outside of the building. Brenda left me alone so she could deal with the constant stream of guests and take any last minute bets, which was perfect because I needed time to get hold of myself.

How could Gavin's brother, Peter, be here? This had to be a mistake. It couldn't be him. He went missing almost a year ago during the apocalypse. We assumed he was bitten when the rest of Gavin's family had been turned. And our suspicions were verified when we went over the burning lists. The thought of the lists made me cringe. The hurt and anguish those lists caused for millions of survivors was sickening. The lists were initially called the T9m lists but quickly became known as the burning lists because that's what they did to the bodies. They burned them.

A shudder ran up my spine, remembering the torment that Gavin and I felt as we searched for our families' names. It was such a horrible time. On the one hand, we were celebrating the fact that we had survived. But on the other, we were coming to grips with the reality that most of our family hadn't. Survivors' guilt took on an entirely different meaning for us then.

And now? I wouldn't call it guilt. Just rage.

Standing beneath a large oak tree, I looked at the crowd of people that continued to grow. This was the only way into this underground world. I knew that. I thought I had prepared myself for it, but to see greed firsthand as fellow survivors bet on beasts that had left most of our world in shreds was something else. The evil that sprang up from this type of activity was far more apparent in person.

A shiver ran up my spine as my brother-in-law's lifeless eyes flashed into my mind.

"*I won't ever give up on finding the truth,*" I whispered to Gavin. The familiar ache rose in my chest as I thought about him. "*I love you, babe.*"

"Am I interrupting?" a man's voice from behind the oak startled me.

"Uh, no," I said, taking a step back. "Just babbling to myself."

"Happens to the best of us," he rumbled, his voice now familiar as he took a step out from behind the tree.

Even though they shouldn't have, my nerves instantly calmed at the sight of him.

I felt a slight smile touch my lips as I watched him take a step forward. "I thought you didn't hang out at these events?" I asked.

Preston, the bartender from the night before, just shrugged his shoulders and smiled. There was something commanding about him, soothing possibly. His broad shoulders filled out his sweatshirt and his baggy cargos fit him well. Judging by his wardrobe choice, he was ready to watch the events this afternoon.

"Preston, wasn't it?" I asked.

He nodded and slid his hands into his pockets.

"So what brings you here today?" I asked, raising a brow.

"Thought you might like some friendly company, since it's your first time," he said, narrowing his eyes.

"And that's supposed to be you?" I asked, crossing my arms.

"Indeed," he laughed, and took a step closer at the same time I took a step back.

"Thanks," I muttered, looking down at the grass.

"You look like you saw a ghost. Are you okay?" he asked, his eyes fastening on mine.

I nodded. "Totally fine. I just wasn't prepared for what I saw in the building." I couldn't tell him who it was I saw in there or how, I was second-guessing my decision to ever come to a place like this. I had to make my entrance into this underground world as non-personal as possible, at least to insiders.

Preston narrowed his eyes at me and grabbed my elbows, slowly bringing me into him. My heart started beating rapidly as a mix between fear and hostility began to pump through me. What was he doing? He had no right to hold me like this.

Bending his neck slightly toward my ear, he whispered, "I think there's something more that brings you here."

I jumped back from him, pulling my arms away to keep a safe distance.

"I don't know what you're talking about," I snapped.

His gaze fell to mine, and I caught a glimpse of sadness behind his eyes. The same type of sadness I felt every moment of every day.

"I think you do," he said softly, taking another step toward me. "You're wrecked, and so am I."

Feeling completely exposed, I shook my head and looked toward the tent. I swallowed hard, pushing the lump back down my throat. I hadn't broken down in front of anyone and wouldn't be doing that anytime soon, especially at a place like this.

"Aren't we all? Aren't all survivors wrecked?" I said, turning back to face him.

"Some more than others," he said, pressing his lips together.

He stood quietly in front of me, watching my reaction.

I gave him none.

"It doesn't look like you took my advice," he said, cocking his head.

"What advice was that?" I asked.

"Coming armed."

"I wouldn't be so sure of that," I said. "Which means you should watch yourself."

Throwing his hands in the air. "Will do. But remember not everyone is…"

"Is what?" I interrupted. "Anyone who is here is scum."

"Present company excluded, I hope?"

"Doubtful," I replied.

The announcement calling all spectators came over the loud speaker, disrupting my intended verbal assault on Preston. Preston actually looked relieved by the interruption.

I turned around and began walking toward the white tent. Preston was right on my heels and as much as I hated to admit it, I was pleased. I glanced at all the people making their way to the tent and wondered how many of them were fathers and mothers betting their family's allotment on a horrific event like this. Too many.

Music was turned up as we made our way into the tent. The blaring bass of Dubstep filled the tight quarters. The once spacious tent now felt like it was the size of a closet as everyone attempted to fit inside, shoulders and elbows knocking into one another. In the center of the room, there was a cage made out of chain-link fencing and barbed wire. There were a few metal benches framing the interior walls of the tent, but something told me not to find a seat there. I wanted to be close to the exit.

In each of the corners, I saw a square metal perch of some sort with a ladder leading to the empty platform. A man dressed in a black suit was standing in the far corner, underneath one of the platforms. His overcoat was draped over his arm, and he sipped champagne out of a flute as he watched the crowd assemble. People continued to filter by me as I stood watching my surroundings. I wasn't sure what answers I expected to get from participating tonight, but I prayed there were some for having to endure this.

A man spit on the sawdust floor next to my shoe. He began laughing as he caught my look of disgust and leaned over.

"You don't look like you belong here, darlin'," he said, coughing into his hand and wiping it on his pants.

A shudder ran up my spine as his eyes took me in. Preston slid his arm around my waist as he took a step forward, landing right next to me.

"Is there a problem?" Preston asked, his brows pulling together as he stared the man down.

Preston was a good six inches taller than the spitter, and I could see how his presence would be overpowering to weaker men. The spitter slinked away.

"Thank you. But I can take care of myself," I said, facing Preston.

"I don't doubt it for a minute," Preston said, lowering his voice as he glanced around the space. "But sometimes it's better in pairs. The odds of survival increase exponentially."

"Not always," I said, glaring at him.

The door closed, the music softened, and the lights were extinguished as my heart began beating at a rapid pace. What was going on? Right before panic began to set in, bright blue and green lights flashed on and danced off the walls of the tent, faintly lighting the space up. Some spectators began making their way to the benches while others gathered closer to the cage. I remained anchored exactly where I was, which was about fifteen feet from the tent's opening. If I needed to escape, I'd be able to get there in seconds.

My eyes connected with the man in the corner, and he gave me a slight nod before continuing to scan the crowd. His stare was fearless.

"Who's that in the corner?" I whispered to Preston.

"I thought you could handle this yourself?" he asked, his lips turned up slightly.

I ignored him and turned around to watch the events unfold. We had to be getting close to the first fight. Loud voices of excitement and intrigue were traded for whispers and hums as the crowd prepared for what was about to occur.

Footsteps marched outside to the beat of a man's command, and the panic returned as the footsteps came closer. Were these the fighters?

"Hup. Hup," a man yelled outside the tent opening.

I glanced back at Preston, and he placed his hand on my shoulder and leaned in so I could hear him. "It's show time."

The door opened up to reveal a line of men dressed in tactical attire carrying assault weapons. They all wore identical, black uniforms, and each appeared to be equipped with a bulletproof vest, an exposed hammer with a large head, several strategically placed knives, and a baton with a serrated edge.

I had to get that baton for my arsenal.

I watched the group of men march through the crowd, and I noticed white lettering emblazed on the back of each jacket reading TRAC.

"What is TRAC?" I asked, watching as the men divided into groups and headed toward empty platforms.

"It's a private security company," Preston whispered. "And the man you asked about is the owner of the company."

"What's it stand for?"

"Tactical Reinforcement and Capture," he answered.

I nodded and watched the men climb the ladders

to oversee the event. As soon as they reached their perch, they took their stance—weapons at the ready—and peered over the crowd of anxious gamblers. The only problem was that I wasn't sure who the TRAC members were really being paid to protect, the zombies or the crowd.

"Does he have a name?" I asked.

"Marcus Lordan," Preston said. I noticed the sound of hate peppering each syllable.

"Ladies and Gentlemen, it is without further adieu that I'll introduce our first two fighters," Brenda's voice boomed over the speakers. I glanced around the tent briefly, trying to spot her. She was standing on the far platform in between two TRAC team members.

Dubstep was traded out for solid drumming, and I glanced around the tent as I watched the audience members close to the cage begin to pull plastic ponchos over their heads.

My stomach turned.

"Z1AY2, otherwise known as Curly will be fighting Z1AH9. You will notice Z1AH9 listed in your pamphlet under the section New RecruitZ. We are counting on you to give us a nickname for him once the fight is over, if he is still standing that is. Let's hear it for Wave One in tonight's lineup," Brenda said into the microphone before the crowd began going wild.

A group of men promptly moved the crowd aside and placed portable chain-link fencing from the tent opening to the cage. I heard the clank as the metal was set in place, and the men scattered into the crowd. My heart started pounding as I realized there was no way out as long as that walkway for the fighters was in place.

"It is very unusual for the new ones to make it through their first round alive," Preston said loudly, over the crowd.

I wondered how long this had been going on...how many champions were there to fight another day?

The music began blasting through the space again as the tent door opened up to reveal the first fighter, Curly. I understood his name now. His hair was long and blonde with cascading curls. He was dressed in a tattered, blue t-shirt and baggy shorts. I looked away quickly as my imagination began wondering who he used to be, what he used to do? I shoved the thoughts away as soon as they came. I needed to remain strong, and to do so, these fighters—these zombies—could claim nothing more than disgust inside of my mind. For my own sanity, I couldn't allow for more. In my mind, they needed to be nothing other than beasts and fighting machines, not humans...never humans. I looked around the room at all the spectators and attempted to hide the displeasure I felt as I witnessed them cheering as the excitement level rose with each passing second.

"Whenever a fighter wins his or her first fight, they tend to turn into the champions of the arena," Preston continued. "They live to fight another day."

I snapped my head in his direction as the green and blue lights continued to revolve around the tent, stirring up pandemonium among the crowd.

"I wouldn't call it living. Would you?" I asked, gritting my teeth. "It sounds to me like the real winner of these matches is the loser."

Curly had six chains attached to him, one on each

wrist and ankle, and two leading away from his waist. He was in the center of the aisle, and the chains dripped over the top of the chain-link fence, held on the audience side of the fence by three burly men. I watched as the zombie moved with the certainty I had recognized only one other time in my life. The day Gavin was stolen from me.

"Those are the guiders," Preston said quietly, as the last of the men walked by as they led the fighter into the center of the cage.

"Are you ready for Z1AH9 ?" Brenda shouted into the microphone.

The crowd erupted once more, and all heads turned toward the opening. A man stepped in front of me, blocking my view. I tapped his shoulder, but he ignored me. A low chanting began around me and Preston joined in, which surprised me. He leaned down to me and whispered, "You better start acting like you belong before they figure out otherwise."

I locked my eyes on him and he gave me a knowing nod. I closed my eyes and strained to understand what they were saying, what Preston was saying. It only sounded like a hum of mumbles that meant nothing. I heard the chains clinking against the fence as the guiders led the new fighter down the path, and the words became clear.

"Flesh Eater," I began to chant as the new fighter was slowly led down the corridor. I only saw the feet slowly marching in as the guiders walked by. Instead of tapping on the guy's shoulder who was in my way, I pounded on it. He let out a grunt and stepped to the side, allowing me to see my worst nightmare unfold in front of me. Gavin's brother was the new fighter.

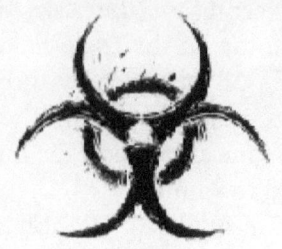

CHAPTER SIX

The crowd was going insane as both fighters appeared in the ring. My screams couldn't be distinguished from anyone else's as I fought my way through the crowd.

"Peter," I hollered. I was only ten or so feet away from the cage. I could make it there with just a few shoves. I elbowed the man to my left as I heard him insult my brother-in-law.

"What was that for?" the man yelled, but before I could respond, Preston came up behind me and cupped his hand over my mouth.

"Not here and not now," he hissed in my ear.

He slowly guided me back through the mass of people so that the crowd swallowed me into the safety of obscurity.

"Let the match begin," Brenda hollered, as I worked to get away from Preston's tight grip.

"Don't do it," he whispered. "They're watching you."

His words went off like a stick of dynamite in my psyche. I had to get a grip. I straightened up and began cheering, but I was unable to take my eyes off Peter. I watched as the guiders released the chains, signaling the start of the show.

"This is considered to be the oldest spectator sport," a drunk guy next to me slurred. He winked at me and burped.

"I think you're thinking of cockfighting," I replied, not taking my gaze off the ring.

"Same thing. Just with a modern twist," he laughed.

The green and blue lights switched off, turning the tent pitch black. Preston's hand ran down my arm and into my hand. I glanced at both zombies who stood motionless—hunched over—in the shadows. Nothing was happening. What were they waiting for? Just as I silently asked my question, red lights flashed quickly on and bounced off the sides of the tent. Apparently that was what the zombies needed. The crowd went silent as Curly reached his arms out for my brother-in-law; his mouth looked like a gaping, soulless cavern as my brother-in-law dodged his attack. Zombies weren't thinking beings.

But that took some thought.

My brother-in-law reached for Curly and grabbed his neck, ramming him into the chain-link fence. My stomach turned as I watched shredded pieces of Curly fall to the ground. But at least it wasn't pieces of Peter. I cringed at the last thought and began not-so-silently rooting for my brother-in-law.

This was what my world had become.

"Rip into him," I yelled. "Don't let him get away."

Curly reached up and grabbed Peter's shirt. His

fingers clung to the fabric as Peter pushed Curly to the floor. My stomach was in knots as if my brother-in-law was actually fighting for his life. I had to get ahold of myself. My heart desperately wanted to believe it was Peter, but my mind knew better as I watched Peter punch his fist into Curly's chest. My eyes moistened and I blinked back the tears.

A wave of nausea rolled through my body, and I turned away as Peter stood up holding something in his hands and then threw it at the crowd. Pieces flew through the fencing, and the screams from the crowd rivaled a rock concert. I didn't know how much longer I'd be able to last.

Peter grabbed Curly's hand that was attached to his shirt and squeezed it so tightly, I heard cracking noises drift over the speakers. The audience roared in delight, and Peter turned around slowly, gazing at the crowd of people on the other side of the fence—his mouth open, jaw slack.

For a fraction of a second, I locked eyes with Peter. I wanted to believe more than anything that I saw a flicker of recognition behind his grey stare, but I'd be lying to myself. And that was too dangerous. I watched him turn back around and dive into Curly, evidence of his victory splashing into the crowd. I turned away in disgust, and listened to the crowd's recount of the next several minutes of Peter's victory as I attempted to steady my breath, body, and sanity. Preston's hand was still in mine and I didn't let go. The red lights were exchanged for the blue and green lights and the fight was over.

My brother-in-law won.

He would live another day to fight to the death.

That was today's victory.

That was tomorrow's defeat.

"Let's give a round of applause for our newest champion," Brenda's voice broke over the speakers.

The crowd erupted into applause, and I felt like my world had gone into slow motion as the people around me pulsed their fists into the air. Was this what humanity was left with in the Afterworld? I thought back to Abby and how simply she looked at our new world. But maybe that was what she had to do to survive.

I had that choice this very moment. I could turn my back on finding out what was going on, or I could continue to fight for the truth—Gavin's truth. He deserved that and so did his brother.

A familiar tingle began in my fingertips as I thought about how good it would feel to expose what was going on. I wanted to find out how these zombies were being trained to behave like this. Something in my gut told me that Gavin's death and this were related, and it was time for a little retribution.

"What should we name the victor?" Brenda continued, scanning the crowd.

Men and women began shouting names as the guiders reattached the chains to lead Peter out. And that's when something inside of me snapped. I couldn't be like Abby. I couldn't act like this wasn't happening in our world. I needed answers. I needed payback. I squeezed Preston's hand and let go.

"Payback," I hollered into the tent.

The crowd went silent as Brenda followed the voice to me. She smiled and her brow rose slightly as she considered my offering.

"Payback," she cooed into the microphone. "I

think we have a winner. What do you all think?"

The crowd cheered and began chanting Payback.

If only they knew.

"That's right. This is payback to all the vicious creatures that stole our loved ones away," Brenda said, playing the part of a mournful citizen as she scanned the audience. "This is the people's Payback."

No, bitch. This was my payback. I smiled back at Brenda and felt Preston's gaze on me as I stood taking the scene in. I would take this down, somehow, someway.

Brenda continued igniting the crowd, fueling the hatred, pumping more money from the audience members as she spoke. That was how they were able to play on these people. They were making the vulnerable feel like they had a say in the fate of these creatures…as if they had power over the situation.

I watched Peter slowly walk down the path as the guiders led him back the way he came. I fought the lump in my throat when I realized I might never see Peter again—my last connection to Gavin. But what saddened me even more was that I wasn't sure I wanted to.

"You okay?" Preston asked. "You look like you want to kill someone."

"I just may," I shot back, watching Marcus speaking to Brenda as the arena was prepared for the second fight of the evening. My fight was next and I didn't even care.

"Have a drink with me later," Preston said, grabbing my arm so I'd look at him.

"No."

"I'm not asking," he replied, his eyes flashing between Marcus and me.

I shook his fingers off my arm and crossed my arms as I turned to glare at him. "I'm not sure what you're after, but I don't have time for it."

I heard the rise and fall of the audience as Brenda turned back to the microphone. "Ready for Wave Two?" she asked the crowd.

In a daze, I watched as the two zombies were moved into place. My bet, Jared, was one of them. Even in the shadows, he looked as agitated as he did earlier in the cage. The lights changed to red and once again, the zombies began their assault. This fight was more vicious—messier—as the zombies tore into one another. I took a step back as flesh and bits sprayed into the crowd. Thankfully all the large men in front of me blocked me from the mess.

I couldn't actually tell which zombie was winning. Only so I could get my money back, I hoped Jared was in the lead, but I really didn't care. I felt a set of eyes on me from the far corner and lifted my gaze to see who was watching me. It was Marcus. Discomfort lodged into my gut as I turned my attention back to the fight. I needed to get out of here as soon as the fight ended.

"Better step up your game," Preston murmured. "Or you risk exposing more than you realize."

I had no idea what Preston was talking about, but his tone told me one thing. I wasn't alone. I threw my fist into the air and attempted to shout at the correct times and cheer my bet on. I watched the zombies with careful consideration and one thing was for sure. These weren't anything like the zombies that we had grown to fear during the apocalypse. These held something deeper and more mysterious for us to fear. I just wasn't sure what.

Jared wrenched the head off the other zombie, ending the match, and I looked away as I tried to regain some sort of stability. But my mind flashed to Gavin as he was hauled out of the car, and I couldn't catch my breath.

I needed air.

A victor was declared.

I needed out of here.

Intermission was announced as Jared was led out of the tent and the chain-link barrier leading him away from us was torn down.

"About that drink?" I asked Preston.

He nodded and led me out of the tent.

"I need to go get my winnings," I whispered.

"You bet on Payback?" he asked.

"No. Jared."

"Too bad. Your payout would have been huge on that new one."

My stomach twisted into knots as he spoke about my brother-in-law. There was no way for Preston to know, but it didn't make it hurt any less.

He guided me to a tent that I hadn't noticed before.

"Where is everyone?" I asked.

"Most continue to bet up until the end and don't cash out until then," he answered.

I gave my ticket to a woman who was standing behind a makeshift counter. She nodded and glanced at my outfit.

"First time here?" she asked, counting out my winnings.

I nodded.

"What did you think?" she asked.

"Don't know if I quite have the stomach for it."

She counted out the small stack of hundreds. "Twelve-hundred."

"That might make me learn to love it," I lied, flashing her a grin.

"Always does," she said, recounting the stack in front of me.

"Thanks." I grabbed the money and stuffed it in my bra.

I noticed Preston's gaze drop to follow my fingers, and then he looked away quickly.

As we made our way out of the tent, Brenda was already outside making the rounds, drumming up business for the second half.

"How'd you like it?" she asked, waving at us.

"I don't quite have the stomach for it, but I might learn to love it."

"That's the spirit." She winked at Preston. "You two leaving?"

"I think it's best," I said. "I don't want to become the main event when my stomach turns."

Brenda laughed and nodded in agreement. "Don't blame you. It takes some getting used to and that last one was pretty rough. Gotta get back at it, but I'm glad you came out tonight, Rebekah."

"Thanks."

I watched her walk away and waited for Preston to say something. He didn't. Instead, I followed his gaze and saw Marcus talking intently to one of the TRAC members.

"Well, you ready? I'll pick the spot and you can follow me there. Not that I don't trust you but—"

"I get it," he said smiling, returning his attention back to me. "You like to take the lead."

I rolled my eyes and walked down the driveway

with Preston by my side.

"I just like to stay alive. Where'd you park?" I asked.

"To the right. You?"

"Same."

"So are you going to let me in on what you're really doing here?" he asked, his voice low as we walked onto the street toward our cars.

There were no streetlights so this section of roadway was quite dark until Preston turned on a flashlight.

"Where were you hiding that?" I changed the subject.

He grinned and pointed the way with the beam of light. "This is my truck. Let me walk you to your car."

His truck was an older model like mine, but I couldn't tell the color, other than it was dark.

"I have an old truck too. Not a big fan of the autodrivers."

"I'm not keen on depending on much of anything besides myself either," he confirmed as he followed me to my truck. "We might actually have something in common after all."

I opened my door and turned around to face him. His eyes held the kindness I recognized that first night, and I wanted to trust him. I really did.

But I couldn't.

Not yet.

If ever.

"Okay, well, follow me to town. My friend's working the late shift at a great place with cheap food and even cheaper drinks."

"Sounds like my kind of place," he said, slamming the metal door with a thud. He waved and walked back to his truck as I started the ignition and pulled onto the road, doing a U-turn.

I passed by him as he switched his lights on, and he turned around to follow me. I flipped on the radio, hoping the images of Gavin's brother would drift away as the music played. Nothing of the sort happened. Instead, I was plagued with new feelings of grief and desperation. I had already mentally laid Peter to rest once. Seeing him here tonight drove my anxiety level through the roof. I was barely hanging on as it was, and now I was leaving tonight with many more questions than I'd arrived with.

I drove down the long country road, passing by vacant home after vacant home, and every so often, my headlights bounced off the broken windows of the abandoned homes. I wondered if there'd ever be enough life on the planet to fill up the vacancies left by so many. If tonight had been any indication as to where humanity was headed, I'd guess no.

Preston flashed his high beams at me, and I looked around in front of me to see what he was pointing to. I didn't see anything except a turnoff leading to a private road. If he thought I'd turn off in the middle of nowhere with a man I barely knew, he had another thing coming. We passed by the road and he flashed them again. This time, I caught a blinking light off in the distance where the road led. Trying to make out what the structures were from the road, I slowed some and craned my neck as I passed them. They looked like water towers or silos of some sort. One more thing I could ask him over drinks, I supposed.

Still on edge from the night's events, I was relieved to see the first working stoplight in town. Even though I'd become somewhat of a hermit, I enjoyed the idea of civilization…from a distance. I turned right at the second light I hit and pulled into a busy parking lot. Preston parked his truck next to mine as I slid off my bench seat.

"That's the place," I said, pointing across the street. It was a three-story brick building with apartments on top and a bar on the corner. There was a blue awning lit up by the floodlights that surrounded the entrance. It used to be a bank. But we needed fewer banks and more places to drink in recent times, or at least that's what the governments believed. They actually had special loans specifically for bars.

"Never been here before," he said, walking over to me.

"My treat," I said, patting my pocket. "The sooner I get my winnings out of my pocket, the better I'll feel."

He smiled at me and shook his head. "That's not how it works. You'll still feel like shit, even after you spend it all."

"Thanks for that," I said, walking across the street.

"Just sayin'." He shrugged his shoulders. "Did you get a glimpse of those buildings on the way here?"

"The ones that you almost blinded me over with your high beams?" I laughed. "Yeah. I saw 'em. Are they old water towers or what?"

"Something like that." He opened the door for me, and the flood of music and sounds of conversation wrapped around me.

I glanced over at the bar and saw my friend, Baily. She waved at me and noticed Preston standing behind me, her face lighting up.

I pointed at a corner booth and she nodded.

"Over there okay?" I asked Preston.

"That'd be great."

We walked past full tables as people rehashed the day's events, and all I wanted to do was forget them. I slid in the booth just as Baily came over with two menus.

"Greyhound?" she asked.

"Yes, please. A double."

"That great of a day, huh?" she teased, turning to take in Preston. "What can I get for you?" Her eyes fell to Preston's mouth, and I watched his reaction as she ate him up. He didn't seem to notice or care—maybe both.

"I'll take whatever your specialty is," he said.

"Okay. One Lame Brain coming up," she said, laughing.

Preston's jaw tensed and he nodded. "Sounds fine by me."

She turned around and headed for the bar.

"I wonder how long places will insist on naming everything after zombies?" Preston asked, spinning the coaster in front of him.

"I'd say at least a decade," I laughed.

He nodded in agreement and glanced back at the bar.

"Her name's Baily," I offered. "And she's single."

He brought his attention back to me and grinned. "Am I supposed to care?" he asked.

"I just figured," I said, shrugging.

"How about you?" he asked, his brow arching. "You single?"

My heart started pounding. I hadn't expected the line of questioning to shift to me. I shook my head.

"And he let you go to this thing tonight alone?"

Preston's voice lowered as he leaned in closer. "Or did you not tell him. That seems like something you'd do."

"It's not like that," I said, shaking my head and dismissing his questions.

He shifted back in the booth as Baily brought the drinks over.

"Then what is it like? What are you searching for?" he asked, sipping his drink. He cringed as he swallowed it, and I couldn't help but chuckle.

"The old standbys aren't looking so bad now, are they?" I laughed, sipping my grapefruit vodka mixture.

He wiped his mouth and returned his gaze to me. "I saw something in you that night you landed in my bar. Something that scared me—"

"Ha," I said, louder than I expected. I couldn't imagine what he was talking about.

"Scared me for your *safety*," he corrected. "I get the sense that you don't think you have anything to lose. And that type of thinking is the most dangerous."

"How so?" I narrowed my eyes.

"Because if you're not afraid of getting killed, it leads to carelessness."

"Everyday is a great day to die. I'd rather embrace the inevitable, do what I need to do rather than…"

"That doesn't sound like a woman who's thinking of her partner," he interrupted, his voice calm but determined as his eyes focused on mine. "It sounds like a woman hell-bent on revenge."

"I think of my husband every single second of every single day," I replied coldly. "But that's all I can do is *think* of him. Because he's dead. Now why did you demand I have a drink with you tonight. What was it you were so worried about me exposing in the arena today?" I glared at him as I awaited his answer.

"Me," he replied simply.

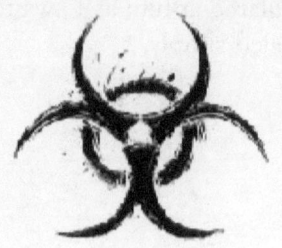

CHAPTER SEVEN

"Trust isn't something you hand out freely, Rebekah. I understand that," Preston said, his eyes fastened on mine. "But I'm begging you to trust me."

"Why should I?" I asked, picking at the chips that Baily delivered to our table. "What's in it for me?"

Preston dipped his head as he thought about his answer. I wondered what was so hard about that question.

"Because, like you, I lost someone I loved *after* the outbreak. My sister, Sophie," Preston stated. His eyes filled with the same sadness I recognized. "She was targeted."

"How can you be sure?" I found myself questioning him just as my friends doubted me.

"I was with her when it happened, and they left me alone—completely alone," his voice caught. "I couldn't save her. I tried to distract them. I attempted to lure them away from her by sacrificing myself. It didn't matter. They had their sights set on her, no matter what I tried."

I glanced down, attempting to shield myself from him as my eyes filled with tears. I wasn't crazy.

"I know it happened to you too. I saw the look in your eyes that night at the bar and then again today. It's a different type of sorrow from others who lost loved ones from the outbreak."

"Others have reconciled their losses as part of the war. I haven't," I whispered in agreement.

"You haven't because our loss was *not* part of the war, *not* part of the outbreak. We both know it," he said.

I let out a deep breath as I thought about what he was saying. I hadn't found anyone who'd believed me, and now that I had, I was contemplating whether or not to give him the benefit of the doubt. How ironic.

"I've been following the underground movements longer than you. I think we can help one another," he tried again.

"When they took my husband, they didn't just take a piece of me, they took all of me," I said softly. "I'm nothing more than a shell of a human, so what you recognize as carelessness or a death wish on my part, I see as nothing more than trying to remind myself that I'm still alive. I walk around feeling empty every day."

Preston reached out for my hand and I pulled it away.

I looked around the bar, trying to ground myself in the present, because I was feeling like I was about to be swallowed back into my past. I watched Baily flirt mindlessly with her customers as she made drinks behind the bar. I watched two couples talking and laughing amongst themselves in the middle of the bar, near the pool table.

I looked back at Preston, this time with a deeper understanding of what created us, what drove us both.

"I think my friends are on the verge of reporting me," I muttered. "At least one of them."

I was shocked by my admission. I was already embarrassed that my friends didn't believe me, but after the dinner with Abby, I realized there was a chance that she might report me as delusional.

"You understand that once you go in for assessment, you won't be coming back out?" he asked, his eyes pained.

"Very much so. Do you know anyone who has been sent away for treatment?"

"I know that I've never heard from them since." He took another sip of his drink, this time with no expression. "My mother was one of them."

I glanced at Baily who gave me a quick wave. I waved back not missing the growing paradox between our two worlds.

"Before we start working together on anything, we have to change how your friends view you. That's the first step."

"How do you propose we do that?" I asked.

"I have the sheet they use during the initial assessment. It's always what they use to investigate initial complaints from family and friends."

"Isn't that confidential?" I asked.

"Absolutely."

"Then how'd you get it?" I took in a deep breath not sure I wanted the answer.

"I used to work for the agency that oversees the program, the MHA."

Interesting, but I wasn't sure I believed him.

"I'd like to think my friends wouldn't report me, especially since—"

"I'm sure they'd only do it because they care about you, but they don't understand that what they say will haunt you forever," he interrupted.

"And I'm not crazy, just observant." I smiled, attempting to shift the awkwardness of the moment.

"I know that," his voice softened. "If we ensure you're not exhibiting any of the traits, even if they do report you, there'll be nothing for the agency to move forward with. But my hunch is that if we can show them a lighter side of you, the old Rebekah, they may not be so quick to judge you any longer. And truthfully, it's best if your name never appears on any of the paperwork that agency handles."

"I couldn't agree more, and I'll work on that," I said.

"We'll work on that," he corrected.

I narrowed my eyes at Preston. "How can you be so sure that I'll be an asset to you?"

"Your husband went to the university," Preston stated.

"How did you know that?" I asked, my blood curdled.

"He had a notebook," he continued, "that gave you lots of information that is impossible to decipher."

My pulse started escalating as I watched his eyes darken. He looked around the bar and then at me. "My sister was in the same department at the university as your husband and she had a folder."

"I haven't told anyone about that folder," I said, my mouth completely dry.

"It was only a hunch. I'm full of them," he assured me.

I didn't believe him.

"You already knew my husband was dead, didn't you?" I accused. The table of customers next to us glanced over at me, and I lowered my voice. "Didn't you?"

Preston shook his head. "I wouldn't play that kind of game with you. I'm not that cruel. Since my sister died, my world has been full of nothing but observations, gut feelings, and finding reason where it doesn't exist. But I promise you, I didn't know. I only guessed."

"So tell me about Marcus," I said, sitting back in the booth.

"He's as crooked as they come. He's got a network established for underground fighting all across the country. Honestly, I wouldn't be surprised if it was global. He's got his hands in many pots. The private security company he founded is filled with retired Special-Ops. It's one of the three top private security companies that our government uses."

"So you think he's involved with your sister's disappearance?" I asked.

Preston shook his head. "I think it goes further than just Marcus, but I don't know what makes me think that."

He drained the last of his drink.

"Do you hear that?" he asked.

A loud diesel vehicle was driving past the building, vibrating the old structure as it passed. It wasn't unusual for supply trucks and military vehicles to be on the streets at night so I wasn't sure where he was going with it.

"Have you noticed an unusual amount of buses with blacked out windows driving around in the early morning and evening?"

"Can't say that I have," I confessed. "I might need to get out of my basement a bit more."

"You know the towers I wanted you to notice on the way here?" he asked, his voice lowering.

I nodded and scooted toward him.

"I've followed the busses there. It's heavily guarded with TRAC units so I've never been able to see anything past the first set of barriers."

"It sounds like a field trip is in order," I said, smiling as the spike of adrenaline hit.

"Not so fast," he said, putting his hand up. "I haven't worked this long putting the pieces together to jeopardize everything by rushing into something."

"How did you know about my husband attending the university and what department he was in?" I asked, hoping my abruptness would throw him off. I was never one to accept the first answer I was given for things and certainly wouldn't start now.

"The pendant around your neck is the same one my sister wore."

Relief crept in as I touched my pendant. Of course! I forgot I was wearing it. It was the department's logo.

"Like I said, it was just a hunch. And those hunches are based on observations. The problem is that I'm coming up with lots of observations and no way to connect them all," he said.

"We will," I told him, reaching my hand across to his. "And we'll make everyone involved pay for what they've done."

Preston nodded and a hint of a smile shattered the

stern look on his face.

"Now let's come up with a way to make my friends remember the old Rebekah," I said, motioning for Baily to come over.

"Why don't you tell me about her so I can help?" he asked, his eyes lighting up.

Baily walked over to take our order. Before she left the table her eyes connected with mine, asking for permission. I knew what she wanted, and he was sitting right in front of me. I smiled and laughed, nodding at Baily, as I glanced at Preston. Poor guy. He didn't have the slightest clue. He was definitely attractive and quite attentive if the situation called for it, and his strength was very impressive. His lip curled up slightly as he watched my gaze wash over him, and I turned beet red.

"So let me hear about the old Rebekah," he started again.

I shook off my embarrassment and tried to reach in for the old me. It seemed so long ago. I thought about who I'd been pre-outbreak—even during the outbreak—and realized that was the same person. I didn't actually change until Gavin…

"I was an art history major," I began. "I wanted to work at a gallery when I grew up." I curled my fingers in quotes around the last phrase and smiled. "I didn't have a care in the world beyond getting through school and talking my way into bringing Gavin to every family function and vacation we had. We met in junior high," I stopped myself as Gavin's last words slammed into me, "loved you since my sixteenth birthday…"

"Going down memory lane isn't really working for me," I said, locking my gaze on Preston's. "I'd like to hear about the old you..."

"My brother and father were killed during the outbreak. I was able to keep my mother and sister alive, only to have them stolen from me after the outbreak," he stopped himself and sighed, realizing he wasn't able to separate yesteryear from the present year either.

"Not so easy to talk about the other life is it?" I asked softly, twisting my lips.

He shook his head, "Seems almost impossible."

We both sat quietly, each wondering how to start a new friendship based on an unidentifiable history. I wasn't even sure it was possible. If the only thing uniting two people was something as horrendous as what was behind us, was it even worth it?

"I used to love peppermint ice cream. I could outdrink any guy in college. Halloween used to be my favorite holiday. I loved twinkle lights. I hated to cook, but I loved to bake. I used to love to read. I used to spend my afternoons daydreaming. I loved taking long walks on the beach," I teased, as I glanced at Baily who was bringing over our food.

She set our plates down and handed Preston an extra napkin. I spotted her scribble on it and chuckled internally. Preston set the napkin aside. I wasn't even sure if he noticed her number.

"Why don't you try listing everything again and this time make it present tense," he said quietly, as he stared at me intently.

I took a shaky breath in and began again, " I love peppermint ice-cream. I can outdrink any guy in college. Halloween is my favorite holiday. I love twinkle lights. I hate to cook, but I love to bake. I love to read. I spend my afternoons daydreaming.

And I absolutely hate taking long walks on the beach."

It felt like a huge weight had been lifted off my chest, and I had no idea why.

"I think I would've liked the old Rebekah," he said, smiling.

"Me too," I replied.

His eyes flicked to mine. "So you are or aren't into long walks on a beach?"

I smiled and laughed. "Not my thing, unless I'm chasing something."

"Is that the new or old Rebekah talking?" he laughed.

"I think in that instance it's one in the same."

"Fair enough." He smiled. "So I think you should work at Shackles. I think it would be a good cover."

That completely took me off guard.

"Really?" I crossed my arms.

"I do. And I happen to be in charge of hiring so you're hired."

"I don't know how to make any drinks," I protested.

"It's not rocket science," he laughed. "Besides, it seems people will drink anything nowadays. Pour it heavy, slap it with a zombie name, and you're in." He pointed at his empty glass and I laughed. "I bet your friends would also be relieved to see you with an outside interest. It's a twofer situation."

I took a bite of my hamburger as I thought about his offer. It would get me around the people I wanted to find out about. And it would look somewhat normal to my friends, proving that I wasn't turning into a complete hermit. But the thought of showing up at Shackles, especially if Preston wasn't around freaked me out.

"What's holding you back?" he asked.

I didn't want to lead him on. I was in no place for any type of a relationship—platonic or otherwise—but I didn't want to work there unless he was there on the same shifts as me.

"I don't want you to take this the wrong way." I set my burger down. "But I wouldn't want to be there with any other bartender. I'd only want to work the shifts with you."

"That can be arranged," he agreed. Unfortunately, I also noticed a glimpse of satisfaction appear behind his eyes. I would have to set him straight. "So is it a deal?" he asked.

"I think it is," I said, surprised.

"Good. Show up on Saturday at four o'clock and you've got yourself a job. I'll teach you who's who in the scene, and we'll go from there. Another set of ears on the floor will be perfect."

I nodded and debated about asking him one last thing. If I was going to persuade my friends that I was okay, like really okay, I could use Preston to my advantage.

"I'm meeting Abby for coffee on Friday. That's the one who I'm—"

"Say no more," he said, nodding.

"You'd do that for me?" I asked.

"Absolutely. If we act like you're into me and the reason you've been avoiding all your friends because you've been wracked with guilt…"

"Huh?" I interrupted, bewildered. "That's not what I meant."

"Well, what did you mean?"

"I just thought you could show up and talk me up

or something."

"I think my idea is more believable."

I sighed and pushed my empty plate away. He was probably right, but just the thought of it made me feel like a traitor to Gavin.

"I won't over do it," he replied, grabbing the napkin with Baily's number on it. I watched him wipe his mouth with it and started laughing.

"For someone who's supposed to be observant…" I raised my brow and stared at the napkin he tossed on the plate.

He glanced at the napkin and leaned forward. "What makes you think I didn't see it?"

CHAPTER EIGHT

I woke up to the sunlight spraying into my bedroom, which resulted in me tugging on the comforter to cover my head. I had no idea what time it was, but it felt far too early to be up. I didn't have to meet Abby until noon and had hoped to sleep in until at least ten. Last night hadn't been kind to me. Between waking up from nightmares and the neighbors playing their music too loud, it was a miserable night. My mind slowly escaped to the muted dream world that I so often craved. It was a place that only held pre-outbreak memories, and there were so many days where I wished I could stay there. Some days, I did. My breathing shifted as images of Gavin smiling and gliding from the tree swing outside his home drifted into my mind. I smelled crushed pine needles as I sat on the ground underneath the tree, peering up at him.

And then the phone rang.

I let out a sigh and pushed my comforter off my head. So much for going back to sleep.

I glanced at the screen and saw Preston's name. I wanted to be annoyed, but I wasn't.

"Hello?" I asked, in the best non-sleepy voice I could muster. I didn't want him to think I slept all day.

"Shit. I woke you."

"No, you didn't," I fibbed.

"Rebekah, I can tell. Your voice is all hoarse. I'll call you back later."

"Wait. It's too late now. I won't fall back asleep. It was actually the sun that woke me, not you."

He laughed. "So I take it you're not a get up and watch the sunrise kind of girl?"

"Definitely not. I'd much rather watch the sun be traded for the moon any day," I laughed.

"I'll make a note of it," he teased. "Just wanted to make sure we were still on for today. Noon was it?"

"Yeah. Abby's usually late so if you don't get there on time it's totally fine."

"I was actually wondering if you wanted me to come pick you up?"

"Sure, that'd be fine." I glanced at the clock, which read seven o'clock. "Do you usually get up this early?"

"No. I'm a night owl too. I haven't been to bed yet."

"Seriously?"

"Seriously."

"You need to sleep then. Don't worry about today," I told him. "That's not healthy."

"I'm totally fine. I'm sure everything else I do will get me first," he laughed.

"Point taken."

"I'm gonna get some shut-eye when we hang up.

Promise," he said.

"Are you sure?"

"I am. So where do you live, and what time do you want me to come to the house?"

I gave him my address and ended the call. I thought about curling up in bed again, but I knew I wouldn't be able to fall asleep. Instead, my mind drifted back to the towers Preston showed me the other night. My curiosity was killing me. I wanted to see them in the daylight. I let out a deep sigh as I pushed the covers all the way off and stood up. I wouldn't do anything to jeopardize us. I just wanted to see them from a distance. I wouldn't even pull off the main road. A jolt of adrenaline shot through me as I hopped under the warm spray and quickly showered. I toweled off and pulled on a pair of jeans and a sweatshirt. I was staring at myself in the mirror, trying to untangle my hair, when I heard it, a loud thump downstairs. I froze in place, closed my eyes, and listened intently as I steadied my breathing.

Another thump and then another.

I ran to the back window and looked outside, but I didn't spot anything. It didn't sound like the noise was coming from inside, or at least I hoped the noise wasn't from inside.

The pounding was becoming more persistent, and if whoever wasn't inside yet, they would be soon. I grabbed the lockbox from my night table and rapidly entered the code and grabbed the pistol out of it. I walked down the hallway and slowed my speed as I approached the stairs, which would lead me directly into the family room. Exactly where the sound was coming from.

I paced myself with each step, not wanting the

adrenaline to cause me to do something I'd regret.

The thump hit hard again, and this time I was able to identify the location. It was the far wall of the family room. Why would someone be thrashing against the siding of the house? I walked slowly toward the noise, and as I reached that section of the wall, the noise moved to the sliding glass door. Instead of the deep thump of wood, I heard the banging transition onto the glass. Not exactly what I was hoping for. The curtain was closed, but I needed to know what was out there. I slid along the wall, not wanting to cause shadows, and slowly lifted the edge of the curtain.

The sight was absolutely gruesome, and I let go of the fabric. Part of me was relieved and the other was sickened by what I saw. It was a straggler walking into the glass over and over again. That must have been what it was doing to the side of the house. I wasn't sure how it got into the backyard since Gavin had fenced it in completely.

I let out a deep breath, walking quickly to the kitchen. I placed my pistol on the counter and picked up the landline phone. Every occupied home was now equipped with a phone that dialed directly to the authorities who were in charge of picking up the rogue zombies. It was a great idea in theory, but there were loopholes. For one, cell phones weren't part of the program, and the system would drop calls immediately if they came from cell towers.

"What are you reporting?" a woman's voice picked up after the second ring.

"There's a straggler in my backyard. He's continually walking into the slider. I'm not sure how much longer the glass will hold."

"Can you move furniture in front of the opening to block the intruder in case he breaks through?" she asked, her voice monotone. She was obviously bored with these calls.

I glanced at the family room furniture and realized I could move the sectional in front of the door as well as the coffee table. But I knew if I answered yes, they wouldn't make me a priority. And I wanted to be a priority.

"No. Not really. It's just me in the house, and I don't think I could manage," I lied.

"Okay, ma'am. Dispatch has been notified. Someone will be there shortly. Stay locked up until you hear their sirens and a knock at the front door."

"Thank you," I replied and hung up.

I walked over to the sectional and tugged and pulled on the arm until I was able to slide the large couch in front of the slider. As I positioned it, the curtain caught and pulled to the side slightly, revealing the zombie staring back at me.

It was definitely a rotter. I couldn't guess how long this one had been roaming, but it looked to be a very long time. Its flesh had darkened to a bluish-grey from the level of decay, and the clothing was mostly tattered and frayed to bits. I shivered as I saw the hollowness in its eyes. I recognized the emptiness. I felt the emptiness. Only I was supposed to be alive.

I tugged on the curtains as if that would block out the dark thoughts that were invading my mind. I wanted to kill the straggler. I wanted to point my pistol directly at its head and pull the trigger. I didn't want to be that person who enjoyed the thought of destroying these creatures or any creatures, for that matter, but I was that person. I often found myself hoping to come across one in a parking lot or some random place where I would be legally allowed to knock it off. But as long as there was no threat, discharging weapons in civilized areas was a crime and worthy of a trip to jail, and that wasn't how I wanted to spend my Friday.

I paced back and forth until I heard the sirens barreling down the street, stopping in front of my house. The zombie was still continually thumping into the slider, and I was just relieved that they'd arrived so soon to dispose of my problem.

The stragglers were easily corralled. They were normal zombies. Normal zombies.

From the living room window, I watched two officers wrangle the zombie into the back of the truck. I glanced at the clock. Nine o'clock. I could still take my little drive. I heard a light tap on the back slider and made my way there, shoving the couch away from the door. Opening the slider, I poked my head out and greeted a female officer.

"The straggler's been captured. For some reason, it got the idea to bust down a portion of your fence. I'd have someone fix it for you right away. Once there's a trail from one straggler, others tend to pick up on it." She pointed to the side of the house.

I took a step onto the patio and saw the hole in the fence. Images of Gavin building the fence flooded through my mind, and I felt as if I was going to be swallowed by grief.

"Ma'am, are you okay?" the female officer asked.

I nodded and leaned up against the house as my eyes fell to the splintered wood along the ground. "Thank you for coming so fast."

"Anytime," she said. "Anything else we can do for

you?"

I shook my head and watched her walk away as I slid my body down the wall. I needed to regain control of my emotions. I'd been doing so well at channeling my grief into anger that the tears that threatened completely destabilized the façade I'd attempted to build. I looked up at the blue sky and stared as if I halfway expected a sign of some sort but none came. I let out a deep sigh and stood back up. I walked over to the hole and peered into the field that was next to our home. Gently kicking aside some of the debris, I turned around and went back in the house. I was starting to crack and that couldn't happen. Checking out the towers could wait. It was time to go blow off steam.

I darted up the stairs and changed into my workout gear. I wrapped my hair into a tight ponytail and pushed my feet into some sneakers. I glanced at the clock and figured I'd even have time to grab some coffee. It wouldn't hurt to treat myself twice today.

I was out the door by nine twenty and on my way to my favorite espresso stand and then to the gym.

Wow. That sounded halfway normal. I hopped in my truck and started the engine. As I turned onto the main road, I noticed how vacant the roads were. I guess rush hour didn't exist any longer. I hadn't been up this early to find that out. A shudder ran though me as it dawned on me what that really meant. There weren't enough people left to fill up the roads.

I saw green garbage trucks parked down alleys, and construction workers tearing down buildings that had been condemned. The level of devastation was still difficult to comprehend, and it literally changed from street to street. Some streets were completely unscathed, while others looked as if a bomb went off. It was the strangest of things, really. It's like the home I'm living in now. It was actually my parents' home. After the outbreak, homes were turned over to whoever was the closest living relative. In many cases, that left several pieces of property to one sole survivor. That was what happened in my case and Gavin's. We both inherited several houses each. How sick was that?

I drove up to the drive-through window at Crazy Beans and ordered my iced-latte. The moment I felt the cold liquid trickling down my throat, I was immediately better. And I knew the moment my fists connected with a punching bag, I'd be back to my new self in no time. There was nothing like the feeling that came with beating the shit out of something.

I pulled into the parking lot and noticed only a couple of other cars, which was perfect. I'd have the run of the place. Glancing in the mirror, I yanked my ponytail tighter and hopped out of the truck. The door opened in front of me and Frank peered out the opening.

"Becky," he said, grinning. "What a pleasant surprise. I don't have you on the schedule."

"Nope. Just stopping in to let off some steam. Had a straggler in the backyard this morning."

He nodded, his expression full of understanding. Frank owned the MMA gym and was the instructor who first got me hooked on the sport. I took countless private lessons from him, and I still popped into the gym every so often to keep up my speed.

"Rough morning," I mumbled, as I walked into the gym.

It looked the same as it always did. There was a

boxing ring on the far left side of the gym. I shivered when my eyes landed on the fighting cage that was to the right. I'd never had a reaction like that before. Then again, I'd never been to the zombie fights before either. The thought of going inside the cage freaked me out, which told me that was exactly what I needed to do.

"Anything in particular you want to work on?" Frank asked, as I stood staring at the metal frame.

"Maybe cage work," I said.

"You've never really focused on that," Frank said, scratching his goatee. "Any particular reason you want to start now?"

I shrugged and walked over to my locker. "Not really. Just feel like changing it up." I taped my hands and slammed the locker shut.

"Let me know if you need anything," Frank said, walking back into his office.

"Will do."

Opening the latch on the cage, I walked inside and let go of the door, hearing the clank behind me as it closed. Standing in the middle of the cage, I looked around the ring slowly. My heart rate sped up as I continued taking in the enclosed space. My mind drifted back to Peter and the fight. He was in something just like this but without the mat flooring.

With gritted teeth I ran toward the chain-link and leapt toward the metal, entwining my fingers through the loops. My toes lodged into the squares, and I began scaling up the side. I didn't know what was pulling me to experience this but something was. I swiftly climbed up the fence and reached for the dangling metal rings. My fingers slipped off and the rings began swinging back and forth.

Once I got ahold of them, I wasn't even sure if my upper body strength would be enough to hold me above the cage, but there was only one way to find out.

Keeping my toes secured in the chain-link, I waited for the rings to stop moving and stretched for the rings again. My left hand made contact, and I wrapped my fingers around the cold metal, squeezing until my nails dug into my palms. I grabbed the other ring with my right hand and gripped as tightly as possible. I looked down, trying to calculate my risk before dislodging my feet from the fence. I was perched about twenty feet up so I was pretty sure if I slipped, the landing wouldn't be kind to my bones.

My upper arms began burning from the angle I was hanging—arms stretched up and toward the center of the ring—while my legs were still splayed to the side, hooked into the fence. I took a deep breath in and unhooked my feet from the fence. Now or never. The weight of my body tugged on my hands as they desperately clung to the metal rings. My body swung above the mat, sailing through the air as if I suddenly had wings. I had always been afraid of heights but forced myself to keep my eyes open as my body swung over the mat.

With every moment that passed, my courage soared and my muscles adjusted. I was actually surprised that I was able to hold my body weight. As I dangled from the rings, I took a deep breath in as I surveyed my way down. I could swing and hop from the rings, hoping I'd hook my hands through the chain-link in time, or I could swing to the metal bar across the cage and attempt to lift up my legs and hook them over it, kind of like a trapeze artist. The thought made my hands sweat. This was a really bad situation to be in. I didn't need to slip off and crash to the ground, twenty feet below. I needed to take baby steps. I worked my body back and forth to create the momentum needed to touch the side of the fence. It worked exactly like a swing only it was my hands holding on for dear life, and my legs controlling the direction of my body.

My feet banged against the fence time and again, but I realized the fear mounting inside was literally paralyzing me. I didn't want to let go of the rings. I would rather dangle for hours than sail through the air, hoping to grab the chain-link in time. I let out a deep breath and slowed my movements away from the fence.

Gavin popped into my head and I started laughing. I was sure as he watched from his seat in heaven, he was laughing at me and wondering why in the world I was so determined to get myself in these situations. I was beginning to wonder that myself.

As crazy as it sounded and looked, the safer option was the trapeze. Once I could get to it, if I could hang from my knees, I'd be able to swing to the fence and ensure that my fingers were holding onto the chain-link before I disconnected from the trapeze bar. There would be no freefalling or chance of not connecting with the fence. The only problem was that I had no idea if I had the core strength to work my legs over my head.

There was only one way to find out. I began pumping my legs in the opposite direction and once high enough I kicked my legs in unison toward the bar. The tips of my toes shoved the bar away, and I brought my legs back down in defeat, my body still dangling above the ground. My abs felt like they'd just been stretched over a large barrel or something, but they were still usable. I could do this. I waited until the trapeze bar stopped moving and began pumping my body again. The ache in my stomach muscles soon turned to a burn, but that didn't stop me.

"One, two, three," I whispered, as I flipped my legs into the air, my hands holding tight onto the metal rings. My stomach muscles pulled and tightened while my knees bent inward, and my body glided toward the bar. My arms were shaking while I continued to stay in the fetal position until the time was right.

And the time was right.

I extended my legs out and up on the last upward motion, and wrapped my legs around the bar. The moment the bar was tucked behind my knees a wave of relief washed through me. I did it. My body was now arched across the ceiling of the cage. My hands securely fastened to the rings and my knees locked onto the trapeze bar. The only thing left to do was release my fingers from the rings and hang upside down from the bar before swinging over to the fence. It really didn't seem this complicated when I was standing on the mat.

Just as I was about to release my fingers, the front door sprang open with a large crash against the metal wall.

"You in here, Frank?" a man's voice boomed through the mostly empty space. I heard more footsteps come in behind the man. Something shifted in the gym as the man's voice got increasingly agitated. "Frank."

I heard the two fighters in the ring mumble

something to one another and snap the ropes as they exited the ring.

"Do you know where Frank is?" the same man yelled at the two fighters.

"Probably in his office. We don't want any trouble," one of the fighters said.

"Let these two gentlemen out," the man directed.

I heard the men's footsteps scurry out of the building as my pulse began pounding in my ears. I was stuck.

The way I was positioned made it impossible for me to see who was at the front entrance.

"I don't have what you're looking for," Frank stated. He took a few steps backward, and he came into my view.

Who were these people? What was going on?

"Don't you mean who?"

There was silence.

"The girl? Have you seen her?" the man asked.

"No. She hasn't been in for weeks."

Girl? As far as I knew I was the only female with a membership.

"I can tell when you're lying, Frank," the man said. Several pairs of footsteps shuffled toward Frank, bringing into view five large males, all dressed in black.

"Let's try this again. Has she been in here recently?"

If it was me they were looking for, Frank could easily point toward the ceiling and the charade would be up. But he didn't do it. Instead, his voice remained steady and his eyes fastened on whoever was in front of him.

"Screw you," Frank said.

"Then why's her truck parked outside?" the man asked.

Frank said nothing.

The sound of the safety being clicked off echoed in the warehouse, and my head pounded as I hung sideways, my grip barely holding on. Any movement and I would surely catch their attention.

"You do understand this isn't merely a threat?" the man asked.

Frank nodded.

Three of the five men turned around, and I caught a glimpse of TRAC printed on the back of their jackets as they took a few steps away from Frank.

Afraid to make any noise, I slowly let out my breath through my mouth and squeezed my fingers as tightly as possible.

"Alright, boys," the man said and that was it.

The gun went off and Frank crumpled into a lifeless pile on the concrete floor. My body began shaking, and my mouth fell open as I watched the pool of blood seep into the concrete floor.

CHAPTER NINE

Every muscle in my body burned like it was on fire. I was still shaking and my hair was drenched in sweat. As long as I didn't look down at Frank, I felt like I might be able to regain some sort of control to get myself out of here. Grief wanted to push its way in and take over, but I couldn't allow it. I wouldn't allow it. I was so confused. Why would they have killed him? Why were they after me? Who were they? Why didn't Frank just point to where I was perched.

Unless he knew he'd die either way.

After the group did a quick search of the gym, they'd left, but I'd remained clinging up in the air, near the ceiling. I was too afraid to come down, and I figured if they knew my truck was outside, they'd just wait until I showed up.

I'd been hanging for what felt like hours, but I think it was only around ten minutes. I needed to get out of here. I needed to get help. I remained still for a few more moments as I collected my thoughts and to ensure that no one else was lurking inside the gym.

I took slow and controlled breaths through my nose as I steadied my nerves and began to focus on how to descend from here. I was getting weaker from hanging on. I squeezed my eyes closed and let go of the metal rings. My body fell underneath the trapeze, as my knees stayed securely wrapped around the bar.

So far so good.

I opened my eyes as I hung upside down and began swinging my body back and forth toward the chain-link. On about the tenth attempt, my fingers locked onto the large crisscrossed wire. My ears pounded as the blood settled in my head and thoughts of Frank drifted into my mind. It was too late for him, but it wasn't too late for me. I slid my fingers around the wire and hooked each one as if my life depended on it because it did. I was now completely stretched like a crescent moon with my knees locked on the trapeze bar and my fingers latched onto the fence. I had no idea my body could bend like this, but I was grateful.

Now for the scary part.

I slowly straightened out my legs and felt the trapeze bar roll away from my legs, and before I had the chance to control anything else, the weight of my body fell from above and crashed into the fence. The wire jammed into my jaw as I scrambled to lock my feet into the small holes. As the fence stopped vibrating and clanking from the thrust of my body, I climbed down the fence and hopped onto the mat.

Being this close to the ground, to Frank's body, made my entire body tremble. I felt like jelly as I tried to move forward. I heard a large vehicle outside and instantly wanted to climb back up into the safety of the swings above. I was now far too exposed standing in the middle of the gym, but I certainly couldn't go out front. I opened the cage door and quietly closed it. I ran to the locker to grab my bag and phone. There was a storage room in the back where I could call for help. But who would I call? If it was TRAC members who were involved, the authorities would believe their story before mine, and I didn't want to chance exposing myself to whoever was looking for me.

I opened the door to the storage room and closed it behind me. I slid my body between the back wall and some cardboard boxes and caught my breath as I dialed the one person in the world who wouldn't call me crazy—Preston. The phone rang one, two, three, four times when he finally picked up.

"I'm on my way," Preston said. I could almost feel the smile over the phone.

"Preston," I whispered. "I need help."

"What's going on? Where are you at?" he questioned, his voice low and urgent.

"Someone's been murdered and I saw some of the—"

"No more," Preston said. I heard the rumble of his truck as he started the engine. "Don't say anything else over the phone. Just tell me where you are."

"The gym on 45th and Larkspur."

"I think they're outside still. They were after me, and they know my truck is parked outside."

"Is there a back entrance?" Preston asked.

"There is, but I don't know if anyone is watching it. I'd assume so. There aren't any windows where I can check."

"Don't worry about that. I'll be there in five

minutes. If there's anything I need to take care of, I will. Wait until you hear three short knocks and then open the backdoor. Got it?"

"Got it," I breathed into the phone, glancing at the EXIT sign. At least the back entrance was in the storage room.

Preston ended the call, and I pressed my head up against the wall. I had no idea what had changed so suddenly in my world, but I had a feeling it was the same thing that had in Gavin's as well.

I waited quietly, my eyes closed, as I leaned against the wall. The rumbling of a truck outside broke my trance. The engine remained running, and I heard a quiet popping sound and began to slowly make my way to the exit.

Had there been someone out back waiting for me? Three quick knocks banged on the backdoor, and I opened it to reveal Preston's worried expression as he grabbed me.

"We've gotta get outta here," he said, hauling me out the door.

My eyes fell to the parking lot where a TRAC member was lying down face-first. So there was someone waiting back here for me. I ran to the passenger side of Preston's truck and jumped in. He was already in the driver's seat and reversed out of the parking lot, leaving my nightmare far behind.

"Tell me what happened," Preston said, giving me a sideways glance.

"I decided to go to the gym after a straggler was at my house. I needed to blow off steam and—" I stopped myself as the image of Frank lying on the concrete floor smashed into my mind. How did this happen?

"Keep going," Preston urged.

For some reason, I wanted to try some cage and climbing work. I'd never really concentrated on that before. It was just me and two other fighters in the gym, besides Frank," my voice caught. "I climbed up the cage and began working with the rings and that's when it happened. A group barged into the gym, asking for Frank."

"Who's Frank?" he asked.

"He is…was the owner of the gym," I tried to steady my voice. "They asked where the girl was, and I wondered who they were talking about. I knew at one point I'd been the only female who had a membership there…He wouldn't answer. They demanded that Frank tell them where the girl with the truck was. That's when I knew it really was me they were after. I was absolutely paralyzed. I held onto the rings near the ceiling for all I was worth. Frank could have told them where I was, that I was strung above their heads. But he didn't…even when they pointed the pistol directly at him." My hands trembled as I relived the moment.

"He knew they'd kill him regardless," Preston said, placing his hand on my knee. "You're okay now."

"I don't feel very okay." I glanced outside the window and watched the city go by. "What do we do? Should we call the police? Did you kill that guy?"

"No. Just stunned him with a tranquilizer. Normally I would say yes about calling the police, but because of who you saw there, I don't think that would be a very good idea."

As tears filled my eyes, I stayed focused on the buildings outside. Frank was dead and it was because of me. An overwhelming amount of guilt spread through me, along with a constant stream of hopelessness.

"Do I take a right up here?" Preston asked.

"Yeah. Just take a right and stay on the road for two blocks and turn left into the subdivision. Thank you," I whispered.

"It might not be safe for you to stay here any longer," Preston said, pulling into my driveway.

"I can't live in hiding," I protested.

He turned off the engine and let out a deep breath. "You may have no choice. The idea of you working at the bar is out, obviously. I think my time there has run its course as well."

"I'm not leaving my house."

Preston's jaw clenched and he stared straight ahead.

"Where would I even go? If they can track down what gym I belong to, they already know where I live. My guess is that whatever it is that they plan on doing to me will happen in a public space. I don't think they'll do anything that'll tie them to my residence."

"That's a pretty big risk you're willing to take."

"Maybe, but I think going out for coffee is probably riskier than staying at home," I said, as I opened the front door cautiously.

He knew he wasn't going to get anywhere with me.

He craned his neck to make sure that there was no one waiting inside for us. I flipped on the lights and closed the door.

"There's nothing to be worried about," I told him. "No one's been here."

"How can you be so certain?" he asked, his brow arched.

"I have the place booby-trapped."

Preston started laughing. "Of course you do."

"So where did the straggler get into the yard?" Preston asked, attempting to change the subject.

"It busted through the fence out back."

He walked over to the sliding glass door, which was covered in oily smudges from the zombie continually running into it. "Have some Windex?"

I turned and smiled at him. "You don't have to do that."

"Might as well while you get packed up," he said.

"I'm not going anywhere." I reached into the cabinet under the sink and grabbed the Windex wipes and handed them to him.

"We'll see about that," he said, opening the slider and wiping away the evidence of the straggler's lack of intelligence.

"After seeing the straggler this morning, it verifies what I know I saw with Gavin," I said, standing next to Preston as he wiped the glass clean. "Stragglers are the kinds of zombies I'm used to dealing with, the unthinking kind. The ones that stole Gavin, and even the fighters, have something more guiding them."

"I still think they're unthinking," Preston said. "But maybe amped up a bit."

"Maybe."

He finished with the window and glanced at the hole in the fence. "You have any wood or anything I could use to patch the fence up?" he asked.

"You really don't need to worry about it. I was going to call someone out."

He shrugged. "It's not a big deal. Might as well get it done right now. We still have about an hour before we have to meet your friend."

I groaned. I had completely forgotten about

meeting Abby. "I'm gonna cancel."

"I wouldn't do that if I were you," he said, placing the Windex wipes on the counter. "The wood in the garage?"

I nodded.

"I know you've been through a lot today, but you can't forget that you're already walking on thin ice with her. Any excuse you give her will make you look flaky. And remember, we're trying to keep you safe and…"

"I know. I'm sorry," I interrupted, realizing he was right. Now wasn't the time to blow off Abby. "Everything you need should be in the garage. I'm gonna go upstairs and try to start the day over again."

I reached the top of the stairs and my muscles finally gave up. Every single movement either caused my joints to ache or my muscles to burn. I didn't even want to imagine what tomorrow was going to be like. I grabbed a pair of jeans and a baggy sweatshirt and dumped them on the bathroom counter. As the water warmed and the steam began rolling through the bathroom, I stripped and stood under the hot water. My mind drifted back to Frank, and his willingness to sacrifice his life for me. I was hoping the water from the shower would wash away everything from today, but all it did was make me feel worse about leaving Frank in the gym. He deserved better than that, and I had to figure out a way to make his death mean something. I just wasn't sure how—maybe finding answers? I rinsed the soap out of my hair and turned the water off. I dried off, dressed, and made my way downstairs.

I walked outside, my hair still wet, and watched Preston attaching a piece of plywood. He was hammering in the last nail as I stood next to him. The breeze had picked up, making me wish I'd dried my hair more.

"It didn't work," I said flatly.

"Wanted to wash it all away, huh?" he asked, his voice kind.

"That was the hope."

"Doesn't look as good as the original, but it should keep any other stragglers out," he said, pointing at the repair job.

"Thank you. I really appreciate it," I said, almost whispering. I felt the tears roll down my cheek and quickly wiped them away.

"Hey, you okay?" Preston asked.

"Yeah. I'm sorry," I said, sniffing.

"There's nothing to be sorry about."

"Gavin built this fence. Seeing it get damaged this morning really messed with me. What confuses me most is that I've let myself cry more over the fence being destroyed than him." I pressed my lips together as I mulled over what I'd actually said. It was true, and yet I confessed it to an almost stranger.

"Grief manifests itself in countless ways," Preston said, stepping away from the fence. He picked up some spare nails and shoved them in his pocket. "But if you keep holding it in—"

"I know," I said, cutting him off. "I know. Abby tells me that all the time."

We walked inside and he dumped the nails out of his pocket onto the sofa table.

"I'd like to show you Gavin's notebook. Maybe you can make some sense of it."

He followed me over to the door leading to the basement. I unlocked it and flipped on the light. The moment I stepped inside, I felt calmer. There was no way I was going to leave my house. That was ridiculous.

Preston gave a low whistle when we hit the bottom of the staircase. "This is impressive."

He looked around the room, his eyes stopping only to take in the various maps I'd hung on the wall, outlining different hotspots of underground activities. "I had no idea you were so far along with everything."

"It's all I do. Mind turning around?" I asked.

"Sure."

I crawled under my desk and pulled on the baseboard of the wall, revealing Gavin's notebook that I'd stuffed behind the drywall. I secured the trim back and stood up, plopping the folder on the desk.

"Okay. You can turn around now."

Preston spun around, his eyes falling on the notebook and then at me. "You're sure you don't mind me taking a look?"

I shook my head. "If we're going to be partners, I have to give you a little something to work off of too."

He flipped open the cover and glanced down at the first page and let out a sigh.

"What?" I asked.

"I think we might just be on to something," he whispered, flipping through the pages.

"It isn't the same as what your sister had in hers?"

"It's not the same, but his work certainly compliments hers nicely." He turned to look at me. "I'm pretty certain your husband and my sister were working on something together. Now we just have to investigate what it was that would have gotten them killed."

CHAPTER TEN

"Look at some of these notes," Preston said, his fingers tracing down the first page.

I didn't even need to look at the pages. I had them memorized.

"It looks like he was focusing on the proton-proton chain during fusion. A helium-3 atom…" his voice trailed off.

"I don't exactly know what to make of it. I thought he was studying genetics, but what would that have to do with nuclear fission?"

Preston nodded and flipped the pages. "Yeah. He's got the entire process detailed. The reactions, which produce the high energy particles and…" He flipped the page. "Regardless of what you thought he was studying, this notebook is completely filled with theory on nuclear fusion."

"I thought it was nuclear fission?" I asked.

He shook his head. "No. It's fusion. Nuclear reactors use fission to generate power by splitting one atom into two atoms. With fusion, two atoms are joined together to create only one atom. It's the same type of reaction that powers the sun."

"Really," I stated. "I'm not sure how that has anything to do with gene therapy."

"Maybe he wasn't honest with you about what he was studying."

"He would have told me if he switched concentrations. He wouldn't hide something like that from me."

Preston was quiet as he continued to flip through the book.

"I'm sure of it," I whispered more to myself than to him. "He would never lie to me, even if it were only by omission. He would never lie to me."

Preston didn't attempt to correct me. Instead, he steered the conversation back to the notebook. "He really goes into the conditions needed and the elements for production..."

"How does this relate to what your sister was studying? What you found in her notebook?" I asked.

"She was focusing on the source of ignition, the heat source to ignite the—"

"Source of ignition?" I interrupted.

"It's almost like a spark. From what I gathered, they only need to capture enough power for a millionth of a second to create the energy. It looked like she was focusing on using a laser to heat or "ignite" the pea-sized plasma, theoretically creating the heat and pressure needed for production."

"I still feel like we're missing the real purpose of his studies," I said, staring at Preston.

"It wouldn't surprise me," Preston said. "Neither of us are scientists."

"Well, whatever they were onto was important to someone so hopefully we can figure it out or find someone who can."

"Which brings me back to my earlier statement. You shouldn't be staying here."

I smiled at him and crossed my arms. "Not only is this place booby-trapped, but this room you're standing in? It's a safe room. Nothing and no one will get in here, until I say so. My house is the safest place to be."

"You're telling me that you think that measly door up there will stop people from coming down here?"

"Not at all. But the blast door that drops down behind it certainly will. This room is built to withstand just about anything, and Gavin even put in a air filtration system that will keep out nuclear, biological, and chemical threats." As the words rolled off my tongue, I couldn't believe I hadn't put two and two together.

Preston pressed his lips together as he watched my reaction.

"Nuclear threats," I said quietly. "That certainly aligns with his studies, doesn't it?"

I couldn't believe I didn't see it before. What did he know?

Preston nodded. "Whatever threat he was concerned about had him worried enough to secure his home."

"I guess our relationship wasn't as transparent as I thought," I said, grabbing the notebook.

"He was probably only trying to protect you."

"Do I look like the type of girl who needs protecting?"

"No. But that's what we do. We're wired that way.

At least, the good ones are," he said, smiling.

"It's really hard for me to think he was keeping things from me, and my guess is that whoever was after me this morning thinks I know more about what Gavin was up to than I do."

Preston pressed his fingers on his neck and began squeezing the tension out of his muscles as he looked at the maps.

"Someone died because of me. Do you know what that feels like?" I asked. My throat felt like it was closing up at the thought of what I'd admitted.

"No I don't, but I can imagine."

"Whatever you're imagining, make it a hundred times more paralyzing," I muttered, letting out a deep sigh. "I need answers. I need to feel like I'm doing something. Do you know where they keep the zombies before bringing them to the pit?"

"It's not a safe place."

"I don't expect it to be. Let's go there after we meet with Abby."

Preston let out a deep breath and shook his head.

"Turn around. I'm gonna put the notebook back where it came from, and then we can take off. I don't want to keep Abby waiting."

I looked around the room at everything as I had many times before, but this time I was left feeling empty and deceived. My eyes glossed over at the maps and printouts I'd pinned to the wall. Did those really matter? Was I barking up the wrong tree? Did it matter if Gavin never felt the need to tell me what he was studying? I didn't want to believe that the last few months we'd shared were full of lies and omissions about whatever it was that killed him. That wasn't who I remembered, who I wanted to remember. He'd never lied to me in all the years we were together. Ever.

Or maybe he had been all along and I just never knew it.

As I was crawling on the floor, placing the notebook back behind the wall, I thought of Frank again and the guilt flooded through me.

***

The coffee shop was pretty busy for the afternoon. Stacks of cookies and brownies lined the bakery shelves, and the strong aroma of coffee immediately made me feel better. There was something comforting about it, normal. There was a small line of customers waiting to place their orders, and Preston and I managed to scoot by them. He hadn't said anything more about Gavin on the ride over. I think he sensed the confusion I felt surrounding everything.

I spotted Abby, already sprawled out on two tables that were shoved together. She was sitting in the far corner of the coffee shop, sipping a latte when she spotted me, but her eyes immediately fell to Preston who was directly behind me.

"I come bearing gifts," I told Abby.

I gave Abby a quick kiss and pulled out a chair. Preston placed the bags next to me and leaned over, asking what type of drink I'd like. His mouth was closer than I expected, and when I turned to give him my drink order, our lips almost touched. I knew I had to play the part, but I felt like such a traitor to Gavin even though this minor gesture meant nothing. It was all an act.

"An iced latte," I said, feeling Abby's gaze on me.

Preston took off toward the counter and Abby leaned in. "What was that?" she asked, her eyes wide.

I glanced at the tall ficus plant behind Abby, not wanting to look directly at her as I lied, but I knew I needed to.

I shrugged and brought my gaze back to her. "He's just a friend."

"That didn't look like just a friend to me," Abby said.

"Well, that's all it is," I insisted.

"Is that why you've been avoiding us lately? You didn't think we'd understand?" Abby's voice softened. "Because we would. We do."

I glanced behind me and watched Preston giving our order to the cashier. It was working exactly as he said it would.

I nodded slowly and returned my gaze back to Abby.

"Where did you meet him?" she asked.

"Shackles."

"When were you at Shackles?" Abby laughed. "That's a hardcore place."

I grinned and sat back in the chair, realizing the worst of the lying was over. Now I could just skip over some stuff and gloss over the rest.

"He's the bartender there."

Abby grinned and took a sip of her drink, glancing at Preston. "He is pretty gorgeous."

"I guess he is, yeah."

"You guess?" she teased.

"He's very protective and I appreciate that." I tried to shift the topic away from thinking of him in a romantic way. "I had a straggler in my backyard this morning. Busted in through the fence. He patched it up so that was nice."

Preston sat down and handed me the drink.

"I wanted to give you a little something for putting up with me," I told Abby, gesturing toward the bags.

"You didn't have to do that," Abby said, her eyes flicking to Preston's and then back to me.

I slid the first bag over to her, and she reached right in and found the photo album. It was a collection of all of her and Caleb's favorite places. Gavin and I actually started making it for them after the outbreak. It was fun for us to go out finding the places and taking pictures. Plus it kept us busy and distracted, and we knew they'd appreciate it.

"Gavin and I started it for you," I said, not even thinking about the act I was playing with Preston.

Abby glanced up at Preston who didn't seem fazed by it and then at me. "It's so thoughtful," she said, flipping through the pages.

"Open the second gift."

Gabby grabbed the second bag and opened it up. She brought her hands up to her mouth and blinked back tears.

"You don't have to do this," she whispered.

"It's okay. I know Gavin would want Caleb to have it. I have plenty of things that remind me of him, and this seems fitting."

She pulled the leather baseball mitt out of the bag and held it tightly. Caleb and Gavin played baseball together in high school. After the outbreak had ended, it was the little things like playing catch while we barbequed that let us dream of living a normal life again. Now I wasn't so sure that was even possible.

"Thank you, hun. I know Caleb will treasure this forever." She kissed it and placed it back in the bag.

"Thanks again for not giving up on me," I said to Abby, wishing that was how I actually felt.

She leaned and placed her hand on mine. "That's what friends are for."

I felt a scowl attempt to take over my expression, and Preston started to chuckle as he wrapped his arm around my shoulder, distracting me enough to shake the scowl free.

"You have a really strange eye color," Abby said, looking at Preston. Her eyes narrowed as she analyzed them. "They aren't really blue or green, but a cross of the two colors. I don't think I've ever seen that before."

I turned to look at Preston's eyes and noticed what she was talking about. I hadn't really paid much attention. They were unique, pretty actually.

"Yeah, they're really pretty," I said.

"Thanks." His eyes locked on mine. "And so are yours."

I felt slightly uncomfortable at this mention by Preston. Not because he said it, but because I didn't quite mind hearing him say it.

"Yeah. I've always loved Becky's eye color," Abby gushed. "They're brown, but when they catch the sunlight, they're almost golden."

"So what are you up to the rest of the day?" I asked, changing the subject.

"I have to finish an article for school. I volunteered to head up the newsletter for the art department. Little did I know that really meant babysitting and writing most of the articles myself."

"You know you love it," I teased.

"Possibly," she laughed.

Abby always loved being in charge and she loved writing. She also enjoyed the role of the martyr and pulled it off flawlessly. I loved her for it. She'd always made me laugh with her depiction of the events surrounding her.

As Abby and Preston talked, my mind drifted to Frank. Had anyone found him yet and were the TRAC members still surrounding the gym? The only connection I could come up with was the zombie fights. I'd never even heard of TRAC until that night at the fight, and now they were after me. But why?

"It sounds like you two should get on the road soon," Abby said, interrupting my thoughts. "That's gonna be a long drive."

I had no idea what she was talking about so I just looked at Preston and nodded.

"It was so good to see you, girl," Abby said, giving me a hug. "And thank you again for the gifts. They mean so much."

I smiled and watched her march through the coffee shop completely oblivious, and I had to push down a small pang of jealousy.

"That wasn't so bad, was it?" Preston teased.

I laughed and took another sip of my latte when a flicker of light bounced off the glass in front of me. I tensed and slowly turned to look behind me.

"Oh no," I whispered.

A loud crack sounded and Preston grabbed me, pulling me to the tile floor. I felt the coldness of the tile against my body as Preston laid on top of me. Glass shattered around us as metal canisters clanked to the ground.

"Stay low," he whispered.

"I have no choice. You're on top of me."

I watched as a canister rolled by on the floor, stopping right by my head. Preston shoved it away as another canister fell to the ground.

"I told you going out for coffee would be more dangerous than staying at the house," I half-mumbled as my cheek was squished between the tile and the weight of his shoulder.

Customers were screaming as the hissing of the canisters released the white fog into the air. I looked around seeing huddled customers along the floor, and the sounds of men being given instructions outside. It looked like all of the windows had been blown out.

"It's a TRAC team," Preston whispered.

The smoke continued to fill the room. Everything was a haze. I clenched my eyes to remove the sting, but it only made it worse. Preston's body relaxed on mine, and his breathing changed. I attempted to roll out from under him, but instead, I was met with a pair of black boots standing in front of me. A spray hit my face and that was the last thing I remembered.

CHAPTER ELEVEN

I was weak, and my body felt as if it weren't my own. I rolled my head to the side and slowly opened my eyes. I had been tied to a chair, my wrists and ankles anchored to the frame with rope that dug deeply into my skin. I tugged my wrists, but the movement only tightened the ropes. I took a deep breath in, but the ache in my lungs started a coughing fit that I tried to muffle. It looked like I was in a warehouse, and I didn't see anyone else around.

But then I heard voices. My cough alerted them that I was awake.

Damn it.

The concrete floor directly around me was dry, but I noticed dark marks, smudges, and splatters leading away from me. The lights were dim so it was hard for me to focus or make sense of what I saw until my eyes stopped following the trail.

It was blood and there was a pool of it. I looked up and saw Preston hanging from the ceiling. His hands were tied above his head with ropes wrapped around his wrists. His body hung lifeless by chains attached to the beams near the ceiling. He had no shirt and his jeans were tattered in shreds. His head lolled to the side, and I saw whip marks all along his flesh from his shoulders down his chest to his abdomen. The wounds were still fresh but the blood had dried. His skin glistened with sweat around the slash marks. He was unconscious but in enough pain that his body responded. At least he was alive.

I wanted to call out to him.

Footsteps scurried toward our room and the large fluorescent lights flashed on overhead. My pulse raced at the thought of who or what I'd encounter. I glanced back at Preston who still hung motionless, eyes closed, and prayed he'd make it through—that we'd both make it through.

"Alright, boys," a female voice called. I tried to place it. It sounded familiar, but I wasn't sure who...

Brenda! It was Brenda.

"Give her some water. Don't untie her. We can't trust her to sit still."

I brought my head up to watch Brenda as she walked into the room. My dry lips cracked and split as I opened my mouth to say something. The tiny cuts burned as I ran my tongue over my lips. I snapped my mouth shut as the taste of metal— blood—coated my mouth. Whatever I had to say wasn't important.

Two men dressed in TRAC uniforms walked over to me, one of them held a water bottle, the other held a stun gun.

The man with the stun gun grabbed my hair and wrenched my head backward, opening my mouth. My lips split more as I stared at him, waiting for the other man to pour water into my mouth. The moment the liquid reached my lips and tongue, I began slurping and swallowing, fighting against the man who was pulling my hair so hard. The moisture seeped into my skin as I gulped the water down.

"Enough," Brenda yelled, and the two men stepped away from me. The one man tossed the mostly full water bottle to the ground. My thirst came back immediately.

I saw Preston's left foot twitch out of the corner of my eye, but I stared directly at Brenda.

"It seems your prying has gotten you into trouble, silly girl," she began. "If you'd only left well enough alone."

Brenda began pacing in front of me, taking only a few steps at a time, her arms fastened behind her.

"I don't know what you're talking about," I spit out.

"There's no point in being coy with me."

"I'm not."

Brenda let out a deep breath. "I liked you so this makes it extra painful on me."

"I'm sure it does," I replied flatly.

"And Preston. I never would have guessed. Although my hunch tells me that he was just at the wrong place at the wrong time, but my boss didn't want to hear it."

I glanced over at Preston, his body swayed only slightly from the breeze, but his eyes remained closed.

"Whatever you think I'm involved with—"

"Quiet," she yelled, taking two steps toward me. She leaned over, and her face was only inches from mine. "You have made some people—my bosses—very angry, and it is my job to make them happy again. You understand?"

I narrowed my eyes at her and gathered as much liquid as I could inside my mouth.

"Well?" she asked again.

I smiled and then puckered, releasing a shot of spit on her face. Not very polite but what can I say?

Her expression fell as she wiped the spray off her face. She removed a syringe from her back pocket and I began to squirm.

"Maybe you should've thought things through before you spit on me," Brenda said, tapping the syringe. "But, nonetheless, this will get us the answers we need. And then we'll see where we're at."

She jabbed the needle into my neck, pushing the serum into my body. I sat calmly in the chair, my eyes not leaving Brenda as she tossed the syringe onto the concrete floor.

There were no windows in the building so I had no idea what time it was. It felt like it was night, but I had no idea if it was or not. I took a deep breath in and began to feel very relaxed. I slouched in the chair slightly as my shoulders released the tension that had built up. The room wasn't spinning, but I was as I looked around.

"Why did you come to Shackles?" she asked.

That was an easy question.

"To find a place full of creeps, and I lucked out," I replied, smiling.

"What do you mean by creeps?" she asked.

Wasn't it obvious?

"Scumbags. You know people who prey on—" I forgot what I was saying.

Brenda's face flushed with anger and I had no idea why. I thought she wanted me to be honest.

"What makes you think you're better than others, Rebekah?" she asked, glaring at me.

I glared back.

"I don't."

"What was your intention the night you went to the zombie pit?"

"I wanted to see what the zombies looked like, and I hoped to run into Preston again."

Oops! I did? I glanced at Preston. His eyes were still closed.

"What do you mean what they looked like?" Brenda took a step closer.

"To see if they were normal."

"And were they?"

"As normal as zombies can be," I said.

Did I just lie?

"What did you think about our collection?"

"I thought about how every single one of them used to have families that loved them."

"Did you think that about Payback?"

"You mean Peter?" I asked.

"Who is Peter?" she questioned, a sardonic smile spreading across her lips.

"My brother-in-law and he deserved better. That's what I thought about him."

"Tell me about your husband, Gavin," she continued.

At the mention of his name, a deadly mixture of anger and sadness began pumping through my veins. I wanted to hurt her. No. I wanted to kill her.

"There isn't much to tell," I hissed. "He apparently kept things from me, and I now question everything about him, about us."

"Like what?" she pressed.

"If I knew that, I wouldn't be so angry at him. I wouldn't be questioning things between us now, would I?" I hissed. I saw a twitch of a smile on Preston's lips and my pulse quickened.

"What did he do for a job?"

"He went to school. He was an assistant researcher. I wouldn't call it a job."

"What did he research?"

"Beats the hell out of me," I confessed.

Another shadow of a smile surfaced across Preston's face, and a new surge of adrenaline pumped through me. I had to get us out of here.

"Why wouldn't you know that?" she huffed, more to herself than me.

"Clearly, you weren't listening to my answers. He kept things from me."

Brenda was obviously agitated. She crossed her arms and scowled at me.

I scowled back.

"You wanted to see if our zombies were normal?" she asked, after a few moments of silence.

I nodded.

"Well, I think I'll give you the opportunity to find out for yourself," she laughed and signaled to the men to move me. Preston's eyes opened slightly as he watched them prepare me, and then he closed them.

They turned me around, and my heart sank when I saw a cage exactly like the one I saw at the pit. They wanted me to fight one of theirs.

"We wanted to arrange a bit of a family reunion. Actually, I didn't originally approve of this, but the bosses felt it necessary. I'll admit once you spit on me, I decided I supported the get-together."

As the two men dragged me to the cage, my entire

body felt like I was in a crushing tidal wave. The room spun around me, and I wasn't able to catch my breath. My arms and legs wouldn't function. Every bone in my body felt as if it had already been crushed.

"Boys, open it up," she hollered, glancing behind her at Preston. His eyes remained closed.

They hauled me up the steps, untied me, and opened the gate, tossing me inside. My body hit the mat with a painful thud. I slowly crawled to the opposite side and attempted to climb up the links to stand. That was when I saw all of the cuts on my hands and arms. What had they done to me? Why didn't I remember?

"I will not fight him," I said, staring at her as I leaned against the chain-link.

"Then you will die," she said.

"She'll die either way," the man muttered, who was still gripping the stun gun tightly.

"What do you think you'll prove by dying at the hands of your brother-in-law?" she asked, coming close to the cage. Her head was at about the height of my knees. I cursed the protection of the fence in between us. How I would love to knee her right in the nose.

"It's about standing for something," I whispered.

Brenda started laughing. "And what exactly is it that you stand for, my dear?"

"The truth," I said, my head lolling to the left. The stinging pain in my cheek was only getting worse as I continued to stand. If my hands and arms were this damaged, I couldn't imagine what my face looked like.

"I think it's about time we start the show."

The two men left the warehouse, while Brenda

grabbed a chair and positioned it far enough back from the ring so that she wouldn't get dirty. I slid down the fence and tucked my legs into me. Wrapping my arms around my knees, I noticed a lump under my skin. Pressing my thumb over the mound, I glanced down briefly and noticed a pale red glow just under my flesh. What was that?

"It's do or die," Brenda said, clapping.

My cheeks were hot with anger as I thought about what laid ahead. The people surrounding me were truly evil, and if they'd take this much time with someone as inconsequential as me, I didn't want to imagine what they were capable of on a larger scale.

I heard the clanking of chains against the concrete as the two men walked my brother-in-law toward the ring. My heart rate pumped rapidly, and my ears were ringing with terror. I watched Peter slowly shuffle toward the gate, being roughly pulled and tugged toward the opening. He looked different than the first time I saw him. His flesh was beaten up more, like maybe the other fights hadn't been as kind as the first one he won.

"This is going to be great," Brenda said, laughing.

The two men detached the chains and pushed Peter into the ring. I glanced briefly over Peter's shoulders and saw Preston. He was watching me closely. I also saw both men slowly walking backward from the ring, unaware of how closely they were standing to Preston. My eyes landed on the one with the stun gun. Preston followed my gaze to the man and nodded.

I turned my attention back to my brother-in-law, waiting for him to attack. I pressed my back against the chain-link and felt it digging into my skin.

Apparently, I wasn't any luckier than Preston. The tenderness of my skin made me cringe, but I didn't take my eyes off the zombie in front of me.

A red light flashed and Peter lunged at me. I dodged out of the way as Peter crashed into the side of the cage. He got up and immediately came for me, his mouth gaping and hands outstretched. I kicked him in the gut, pushing him back into the chain-link. Ridiculously, I hoped for a flicker of recognition as he bounced against the cage. None came.

I wrapped my fingers through the cage and rapidly began to climb. My hands worked at a speed I didn't know possible as I lifted my body quickly. Just as I was almost out of reach from Peter's clutching hands, my foot slipped. Peter grabbed my ankle and tugged me so hard my hands slipped from the cage, but I was able to grab onto another rung. As I frantically worked my foot away from him, he held on tighter and brought it to his mouth. In one swift motion, I whipped my knee up toward my chest, which released my foot from my shoe, leaving Peter clasping onto the empty shoe. It took him a moment to realize there was nothing in the shoe—no flesh—which gave me enough time to climb up the cage a couple more feet. He threw the shoe to the mat. I watched it bounce and knew how close I was to slipping into his grasp. He grunted and sprung up slightly on the balls of his feet. His hands alternated between clutching empty air and twisting onto the fence. Zombies weren't supposed to get frustrated, but I felt like that was what I saw. I scrambled up a few more slots, not taking my eyes off of Peter, when I noticed his birthmark was missing. He had a small strawberry birthmark on the back of his neck and it was gone.

Not a trace.

That didn't make any sense. My mind ran over various scenarios and none computed. He was my brother-in-law. It was Peter. It looked exactly like him. Exactly. But he was missing part of him. My eyes ran over his hair, Peter's hair! His eyes, nose, lips, they were all Peter's features. It had to be him. There was only one way to find out if it was really Peter or not, his tattoo. He had a raven inked into his skin on his eighteenth birthday.

Hanging above his head, I dangled my arm over his head, fastened to the cage by only my left hand. Circling my hand over him, I whispered, "Peter give me a sign it's really you." He continued grasping at my hand so I kicked out my free leg, attempting to distract him. He lunged at my shoeless foot just as I grabbed his tattered red shirt. I ripped the material right off his shoulder, revealing solid grey flesh and nothing more. There was no tattoo.

CHAPTER TWELVE

I had seen what these creatures could do to one another and to humans. I couldn't let myself fall into his clutches. I climbed up to the top of the cage, but the two men took a step forward away from Preston. I glanced at Preston and realized he wouldn't be able to do anything unless I relieved the men's fears. I descended a few feet down the chain-link and saw the two men relax and take a step back. Preston would be able to reach them. They were, no doubt, worried about getting dirty. I shivered at the thought and continued to stare down at the zombie. I would no longer refer to this stranger—or replica—as Peter. This wasn't my brother-in-law. I steadied my breath and considered my options for survival. If I jumped down, feet first and toppled him, I might have a chance of crushing his neck. Might have a chance. That wasn't certain enough.

I glanced at Brenda who looked to be getting very frustrated at the lack of action. I couldn't help myself and waved at her, catching Preston as he sprung to life. He hooked his feet over the head of the man with the stun gun and twisted his body so that the rope cracked the man's neck. Preston unhooked his feet, and the man dropped as the other man attempted to stop Preston, but it was too late. Preston had already lodged his feet into the man's head. He hit the floor, his head smacking against the concrete.

I scaled the cage and pitched my legs over the top, dropping feet at a time down the chain-link as my fingers barely held on. Brenda was already charging me by the time I hit the floor, but I managed to grab the chain that had been fastened around the zombie and whipped it toward her face.

The crushing sound as the metal connected with bone sent her flying toward the cage. I lashed the heavy chain toward her again just as her body crashed into the chain-link. The sudden movement and noise alerted the zombie to her presence. He dashed over to her and before she had a chance to realize what was happening, the zombie shoved his hands through the links, his rotting flesh falling to the floor. I turned away as her screams echoed into the air and he finished.

"Grab the chair," Preston yelled, snapping me out of my horror.

I hauled the chair over and placed it underneath Preston and climbed on.

"The guy over there's only knocked out. He might come to any second."

"Okay," I panted.

I wanted to give that guy a kick in the stomach, but the way my luck has been, I'd probably kick him awake.

"I'm going to use your shoulders to stand on as I work my way up the chain. I think I can throw myself onto the beam up there and unhook the chain."

"How are you going to get back down?"

Brenda's screams had turned to quiet moans, and I shoved the thought away. I couldn't afford to worry about it. After all, she was going to kill us.

Do or die, right?

"I'll figure it out once I'm up there," he said, as his hands began clamping on the chain, working his way up.

Preston placed his feet lightly on my shoulders and pressed off, hauling himself further up the chain. His body swayed with the weight of his movements, and my stomach was in my throat. The moment his feet left my shoulders, I hopped off the chair and grabbed the stun gun that was on the floor. I ran to the hallway where Brenda and the two men had come from and cautiously walked down toward the other room. I slid slowly toward the opening with my back pressed against the wall and rounded the bend, stun gun at the ready. But the room was empty and it was small. There was a small cage in the corner like the ones from the zombie pit where they kept the undead pre-fight.

I ran back to the main warehouse, forcing myself not to look at the cage, looking up toward the metal ceiling instead. Preston had already reached the top and unhooked the chain from the beam.

"I think I can saw this rope off so stand back. It'll drop the chain with it."

"Okay."

The groaning had completely subsided, leaving only the shuffling of the zombie. I refused to look. I watched as Preston quickly slid his wrists back and forth against the rough edge of the beam until they were finally freed. The chain crashed to the floor with a thud as Preston turned himself around and began untying the rope around his ankles, freeing them after several seconds. He glanced down at me, a smile spreading across his lips.

"I wasn't sure we were going to make it out of here," he said, inching his way to the wall.

"We haven't yet," I warned, raising a brow as I watched him swiftly climb down the metal wall, his feet moving from one horizontal support to another.

The moment his feet touched the ground, I ran over to him and threw myself on him.

He groaned from the pain, and I stepped back, horrified, covering my mouth. "I'm so sorry. I forgot. I don't know what came over me. I just—"

He grinned and wrapped his arms around me. "It's nice to know I might have been missed."

"More than you know," I whispered, my cheek pressing onto his bare chest.

"This building looks clear, but I have no idea where we are or if there are other buildings on the grounds or…"

The man on the floor moved and Preston grabbed the stun gun out of my hand, zapping him. Preston searched the man for weapons and found a knife and a pistol. He shoved the knife in his back pocket and the pistol in between his waistband. He searched the other man and handed me a knife, pistol, and canister. I tucked the knife in my sock and the pistol in my waistband and held onto the canister. It reminded me of the one that had been tossed into the coffee shop.

"I need to finish the job," he whispered, looking

into my eyes.

My eyes fell to the man on the floor. It was true. He would be a threat once he woke up, and neither one of us knew what we faced on the other side of these walls. I took a deep breath in and nodded. I turned toward the exit and heard the gun go off. The zombie began shaking the cage violently from the blast. It would only be a matter of time before he broke through.

"I'm so sorry, Rebekah," he whispered, as he aimed the pistol at the zombie and pulled the trigger.

I watched the zombie fall to the ground and fisted my hands to stop the trembling.

That wasn't my brother-in-law.

It wasn't.

I needed a distraction.

"If there's anyone outside, they would've heard the shots so either we're lucky and there's no one outside or they're waiting for us."

"I'd like to go with the first option," he said.

"You and me both," I said, as pain slowly replaced the adrenaline. "Let's go out through the office." I pointed down the hall and Preston nodded.

"I'll take the lead," he said, walking in front of me.

"My pleasure."

My eyes followed along his shoulder blades, down the long length of his back, and a shudder went through me seeing the lash marks up close. I knew my wounds were nothing compared to his.

We reached the metal door, and he signaled for me to stand to the side. We both readied our pistols as he wrapped his fingers around the door handle. I took a deep breath in and watched as he slowly opened the door, revealing a bit of daylight and nothing more.

There was no one and nothing outside except for what looked like wheat fields and cattle fencing. There was a grey cargo van to the left but other than that, the place was barren.

"Keys?" I asked, glancing back at the desk behind us.

"There weren't any on the two guys. I would have felt them."

"Let's hope they're not on Brenda," I mumbled, opening the middle drawer of the desk. No keys. I opened the side drawer and was relieved to see a vehicle key.

"Let's hope." I dangled it briefly before sliding it into my pocket.

I opened up the other drawers and fumbled through mostly bills and paperwork. I decided to grab it all. Who knew what it might tell us? I followed Preston outside and glanced around the property. The only building appeared to be the one we'd been in. It felt like we were in the middle of nowhere and judging by the wheat fields, I'd say that was the case.

"Doesn't that soil look pretty roughed up?" I asked, pointing toward a corral.

"It does," Preston confirmed, walking to the van.

"I'm gonna go check it out." I ran to Preston and handed him the papers and took off toward the corral.

"We really shouldn't be hanging around here," Preston said, shoving the papers inside the van.

He was right, but I had to know. I made it to the fencing that wove throughout a large pasture, finally ending at a larger pen. It reminded me of a non-functioning cattle ranch, everything falling apart, rusty, and old. But judging by the ground, it was recently used. So where were the cows?

I ducked in between two railings and began walking along the enclosure.

"Come on," Preston hollered, leaning against the van.

Something glimmered in the mud and caught my attention. I ducked down and pulled a chain out of the dirt with a red thumb drive on the other end of it. A shot of satisfaction ran through my blood as I clasped my fingers around my souvenir. I walked a few more steps and saw something awful on one of the metal latches securing the fencing in place. My stomach turned queasy when I leaned in and saw the pieces of fabric and flesh stuck onto the metal. I began stumbling backward as I realized that this wasn't a pen for cattle.

I dipped under the fence railings and ran toward the van.

"Let's get the hell out of here," I yelled.

Preston jumped into the driver's side and turned the engine on. I hopped in and slammed my door, completely out of breath.

"What did you see?" he asked, stepping on the accelerator.

The dust billowed around the van as we peeled down the dirt road; the vehicle jumping over potholes and diving into ruts.

"Come on. What did you see?" he repeated.

I looked at Preston, his eyes focused on the road ahead of us, his grip squeezing the wheel. He was on the edge of the seat so his back wouldn't touch the seat.

"We have to find them before they find us," I muttered, ignoring his question. "Or they'll turn us into them."

My mind flashed back to Peter. He was an imposter. He had to have been.

"What are you talking about?"

"It was a pen for humans," I replied.

But the question remained, living or undead?

.

CHAPTER THIRTEEN

After a few wrong turns and unfamiliar street signs, we figured out we were on the other side of the mountains in Eastern Washington. Preston had been driving for several hours, and I could see that he was getting tired. I convinced him that I could drive the rest of the way home while he rested. I hadn't been in this region of the state since the outbreak when Gavin and I had been on the run. It was a lot less green over here. The country was also more rural, which made it more difficult to gauge the level of devastation. Some towns looked completely untouched, while others were left in shambles.

I pulled into one of the towns that looked to be slowly piecing itself back together. The town consisted of a main street with buildings on both sides of the road. The brick façade of the building to the right was crumbling in sections and shop signs either dangled or were completely missing. There was a drugstore on the corner that had the word 'open' spray painted in big red letters on the plywood where windows were once housed. Next to the pharmacy was a consignment store that looked untouched. Across the street there was a Laundromat and a café.

I parallel parked in front of the drugstore and turned off the engine.

"We should get something to fix you up a little," I said softly, attempting to wake up Preston. His head was pressed against the window, his arms crossed in front of him, and he was breathing heavily.

I touched his knee gently and he woke up like a shot, looking around quickly.

"Sorry," I whispered.

"What's up?" he asked, rubbing the sleep from his eyes.

"I thought we should get some medicine on your back before we get to the other side. I don't know what's going to be waiting for us…"

He nodded. "Probably a good idea."

"I'll run in and grab some bandages and whatever else I can think of," I said, opening the door.

"Rebekah?" Preston said, his eyes teasing. "You might want to put one of those on. Not only are you missing a shoe, you look like hell." He pointed to a stack of jackets behind the driver's seat and I started laughing. "And make sure to button it up."

I grabbed the coat and snapped it shut.

"Doubt it's going to make people not notice the busted up lip and swollen cheek, but I guess it's a start."

"We'll take what we can get," he laughed.

I walked into the drugstore and met the curious stare of the clerk behind the counter. "Rough day," I replied, scanning the aisles for first-aid.

Of course, the supplies were in the far corner. The fluorescent lights above flickered in sections as I made my way over. Many of the metal shelves were empty and missing the novelties that these types of places were once known for. I only hoped that the store had plenty of first aid supplies.

When I reached the section, I was relieved to see several boxes of salve, rolls of gauze, and bandages, along with some other first aid products. I grabbed them all and hauled them up to the cashier.

"Miss, are you alright?" the female clerk asked. She was in her fifties and wore a red vest.

"I am," I said, grinning. The pain as my lip cracked made me drop my smile. "Just these." I placed everything on the counter, and she began scanning the items and placing them in a plastic bag. I tossed a few candy bars into the pile and my stomach growled. "And these, please."

"It's not my place, but ma'am, anyone who did that to you doesn't deserve to live."

My gaze fell to the glass counter and I laughed. "I couldn't agree more."

I paid for the items and took off, glancing at her one last time. Her eyes connected with mine, and a flicker of familiarity flashed through me. I stopped and turned back around to face her.

"You helped us."

"Pardon me?" she asked, puzzled.

"During the outbreak."

"You must have me confused with someone else."

"You were in Spokane, right?" I pressed.

She shook her head, "No. This has always been my home."

"Huh," I said, turning back around. I waved at her

one last time and walked to the van.

I was sure she was the lady who gave Gavin and me a place to stay for a night. We had found an old farmhouse, which we thought was abandoned, and a woman who looked like the clerk greeted us with a shotgun but eventually let us stay.

"Get what you wanted?" Preston asked, as I slid into the seat.

"I did. Now turn around," I muttered, searching in the bag for the rubbing alcohol and cotton swabs.

Preston unbuckled his seatbelt and slowly turned to face the passenger window. I soaked a cotton swab and began pressing it along the cuts and gashes in his flesh. His body tensed as I gently cleaned the sores.

"Sorry," I whispered. "I just think it's best we clean it out."

Preston sucked in a breath through his teeth and nodded as I continued to clean his lacerations. When I finished the last of the wounds, I switched to dabbing the antibiotic ointment along his back.

"You're a real mess," I said.

"You're one to talk," he said, taking in a deep breath as my finger glided along the longest gash on his back. "Judging from what I saw on you, I should be doing the same."

He was probably right. I felt my shirt sticking to most of my back and every time the fabric moved, it felt like my skin was being ripped off. I twisted the cap back on the ointment and tossed it in the plastic bag.

"Your turn," he said, moving to face me.

"No way. I just dole out the charity."

"Charity?" His brow arched and a smirk appeared.

"You know what I mean."

"Turn around," his voice became gruffer, and I did what he said.

I removed the oversized jacket and tossed it in the back of the van where it had come from. I gingerly began to unbutton my shirt, afraid to cause too much movement between my flesh and the cotton. Once I hit the last button I took a deep breath and slipped the shirt from my shoulders. My skin prickled from the chill in the air, but I continued to remove my shirt until I couldn't tug it free.

"It's stuck," I said, quietly. It felt as if the material was glued to my back.

"I got it," Preston whispered.

I dropped my hands and closed my eyes as he carefully removed my shirt, only stopping to gently nudge the material away from the wounds. The pain shot through me, but I clenched my teeth and exhaled slowly.

"You're one tough woman," he muttered.

I didn't feel tough. Inside, I felt like I wanted to crumble or maybe I already had. I really didn't know any longer. I heard the rustle of the bag as he removed the rubbing alcohol and cotton balls. The swish of the liquid as he poured it onto the cotton made my body tense.

"I'm going to start by your neck," he said softly.

I nodded and felt the sting of the cold liquid as he gently applied the rubbing alcohol to my wounds.

"Is it as bad as it feels?" I asked.

"It's not great," he said, working his way down my back.

Every so often the burn made me gasp, but I tried to remain silent as he cleaned off my lacerations.

"Amazing what adrenaline will do," I whispered,

as he switched to patting the ointment onto my back. "I had no idea my injuries were so bad."

"Our bodies are far more resilient than we give them credit for," he agreed.

Resilient. Was it really resilience?

"At times," I agreed.

There was a moment of silence between us, and I stared out the window. I noticed a couple going into the café, and my stomach growled.

"Hungry?" Preston laughed.

"I like to eat."

"My kind of woman," Preston joked, smoothing the ointment into my skin.

He helped me slide my shirt back on and the pain was almost unbearable, but I ground my teeth into my bottom lip and sat forward in the seat.

"Shit," I muttered, as a red glow surfaced under the skin on my arm, reminding me of what I had seen earlier.

"What?" Preston asked.

I shoved my arm in front of him and his eyes steadied on the blinking light.

"Do you think it's a tracker?" I asked. "I saw it back at the warehouse and completely forgot about it."

"Man, I don't know. But we've gotta get it out. It doesn't look that deep."

"You probably have one too," I replied. "There are some small scissors in the first aid kit. I don't know how sharp they are."

He searched in the bag and found the kit, unzipping it and pulling out a tiny pair of scissors.

"I didn't see anything like it on your arms or back," I said, turning over my arm in front of him.

"Just cut it out."

He let out a deep breath and steadied his hand as he pressed the stainless steel point against my flesh. Preston opened the scissors and stuck the point in, clipping the skin once as the tiny device popped out of my arm.

"I don't think that's a tracker," he said, holding it in between his fingers.

"How can you be sure?" I asked, pressing gauze on the tiny wound. It wasn't as painful as the wounds on my back, which was surprising.

"I can't." He opened the door and flicked it out the door.

"You wanna slide your pants down and check?" I asked.

He laughed and unbuttoned his pants, slowly moving them down when I spotted the device embedded in his lower abdomen. It wasn't flashing.

"You want me to do it?" I asked, pouring the alcohol over the scissors.

He nodded, and without wasting any time, I poked the scissors into his flesh and snipped the skin, freeing the device.

"Odd that this one isn't on or flashing," he muttered as I quickly dabbed the area with alcohol.

"Just another piece to the puzzle." I sighed, as he tossed it outside.

A few moments of awkward silence passed between us as he pulled the waistband on his pants back up, and I tried not to glance at his body.

"Is there a reason why you didn't tell me that Payback was your brother-in-law?" Preston asked. His voice fell to a hushed tone.

I chewed on the inside of my cheek and glanced

over at him.

"I didn't trust you," I replied, turning on the ignition.

"Do you now?" he asked gently, his gaze probing.

"More than I trust myself," I whispered, feeling the lump in my throat surface out of nowhere.

And it was true. I had been reckless, and now an innocent person was dead. I didn't feel like I could trust my own gut reactions any longer.

Preston didn't say anything for several minutes as I followed the road to the highway.

"You can't stay at your house," Preston began.

"I know," I sighed. "But I want to get some things out of it, if I can."

He nodded. "If they haven't figured out that we escaped already, they will shortly. I'm not sure it'll be safe to go back."

"I want to get my truck back from the gym," I said.

"I don't think that's the best idea."

"I don't either, but it's something I need to do."

"We'll play it by ear," Preston mumbled, as he looked out the window.

I shrugged. A twinge of annoyance sprang up. I wasn't asking for permission. I'd already made up my mind. As long as there wasn't anyone around, I didn't see the problem with picking my truck up. I had so few possessions anymore the thought of losing one so meaningful made my heart ache.

Sparse landscape was traded for green fir trees and an abundance of blackberries as we drove over the western side of the mountain pass, and I began getting anxious. What would we find? Who would be looking for us?

"Do you mind if I turn on the radio?" I asked.

"No."

The radio reception was horrible, and I flipped it back off. I felt Preston's eyes on me, and wondered what he was thinking. I stayed focused on the road ahead of me.

"I hope that thumb drive has something useful on it," I muttered.

"We can hope." He was quiet for a moment. "I'm really sorry about your brother-in-law. I can't even imagine."

I took in a deep breath and thought about telling him what I noticed but something held me back.

"It just left me with more questions than answers," I replied quietly. "Seems to be the trend in my life right now."

Preston nodded and looked out the window. I glanced over at him and decided to say something.

"I'm not sure that was Peter. The real Peter."

"What do you mean?"

"My brother-in-law had a birthmark on the back of his neck, and he also had a tattoo. Both were missing." I pressed my lips together and waited for his response.

"Had there been any injuries surrounding the areas?" Preston asked.

I shook my head. "The flesh was intact in both places so the birthmark and ink should've showed up."

Admitting this out loud produced something inside of me, a desperation of sorts, as the lack of information festered in my mind. There were too many loose ends and incomplete observations. I was frantic for answers—knowledge—and that was beginning to wear me down.

"I need answers, Preston," I whispered. "Or I'm not sure how much longer I really care to continue. It's so hard to navigate in this new world."

Preston moved his hand to my knee. "I know," was all he replied.

We drove in silence until we made it back to town.

"I'm going to drive by the gym."

Preston nodded as I turned down the street. The parking lot was empty, except for my truck. I turned into the lot and parked the van. We both got out of the car, and I ran to the door of the building, searching for Frank. The lights were off, but I was able to see where he should have been. He was gone and so was any evidence that something had happened. The concrete looked as if it had been scrubbed clean of any evidence. If they were able to sweep things clean like this, I wasn't sure we'd ever be able to get ahead of them.

"Let's get a move on it," Preston said, coming behind me. His hand slid along my waist, and he ushered me over to the truck.

"Keys?" he asked

I turned around and grabbed the truck key out of my bra. I didn't trust pockets and so far my bra had served me well. I opened the door, slid in, and reached across the bench to unlock his door.

"The coffee shop is only a few blocks away, and it's on the way to the house," I suggested.

"I don't think they'd be able to clean up that mess like this one," he said. "But there's only one way to find out."

I turned onto the street and looked around for anything unusual, but everything seemed as it did before we were captured. I made a right into the parking lot, and we drove along the strip mall until we hit the coffee shop. Construction workers were already replacing the glass. There was police tape cordoning off the front entrance.

"So the police got involved in this one," I said, as we drove by.

"Pull over up there," Preston said, pointing at the grocery store.

"Do you think you should really go in there?" I asked.

"I'm not. Just gonna grab a newspaper out front."

He hopped out of the truck and jogged over to the newspaper stand. Tossing in the coins, he grabbed the paper and glanced at the front page. His expression changed as he got back in the truck and I pulled away.

"They got involved alright, but they're blaming local gangs," his voice grim.

"Serious?" I sighed.

"Yeah." He read through the article and shook his head. "They're pointing at a dispute between two rival gangs but no arrests have been made."

"With all the witnesses? Come on," I said, irritated. "The guys were in TRAC uniforms for shit's sake."

I turned down the street, slowing as we approached my home. So far it looked unscathed. "Does it mention any names in the article?" I asked.

"It does. There's an Albert Bense, who is the self-proclaimed leader of the South City Faction and Terrence Falino of the Western Port. Both claim no involvement."

I turned into the drive, and my nerves began getting the better of me.

"I'll make it as quick as possible," I promised.

Preston nodded and followed my gaze to the front door. "Let's do it."

We both walked to the entrance. The door was still locked and the wire was still in place. If someone had entered this way, the wire wouldn't be exposed.

"So far so good," I whispered, opening the door.

"They might not know we've escaped yet," Preston said.

Everything inside looked exactly like I'd left it. The basement door was still secure and all the lights were still off. It was getting dark outside, but I wasn't sure it would be a great idea to turn any lights on so I didn't.

I grabbed two duffle bags out of the hall closet and tossed one to Preston. "You can get some clothes from upstairs. The bedroom's all the way at the end of the hall." I told him. "You guys are the same size." I turned away after the words tumbled out.

He nodded and went up the stairs while I unlocked the door to the basement. I hastily removed all of the maps off the wall, rolling them up. I began emptying out the drawers and a wave of sadness hit me from nowhere. There were so many things I needed from here. I crawled under the desk and grabbed Gavin's notebook from behind the wall. I stuffed it in the duffle and began filling the bag with my notes, laptop, and anything else I could cram inside.

Preston walked down the stairs, startling me when I looked up. He was in a grey Henley and jeans, one of Gavin's standbys. I forced my gaze away and picked up the duffle.

"I took a quick shower. We should probably put some more ointment on," he said, reaching for my duffle.

I nodded and handed it to him. "Where are we going? Do you actually have a place in mind?"

"I do. There's a safe house that our family used off and on during the outbreak. It's underground and anyone who knew about it is dead."

I shivered at the harshness of his words. I knew he didn't mean it, but they still had an unintended effect. "Should we try to bring these?" I slid a section of the wall to reveal all the weapons I'd collected so far.

"Wow. You're certainly prepared for something, aren't you?"

I twisted my lips as I contemplated what it was I really wanted to accomplish any longer. "I'm gonna go take a shower. You wanna figure out how to get everything in the truck?"

He nodded and I jogged up the stairs, holding back the tears that so desperately wanted to escape. Weeks ago, my life had purpose. I wanted revenge. I was on the pursuit of truth and vindication. I wanted to find out what happened to Gavin, what really happened to Gavin. Now it felt like everything I'd worked for was being dismissed…everything was just about staying alive, and I wasn't sure that I really cared about that any longer

.

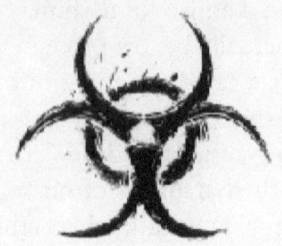

CHAPTER FOURTEEN

It was pitch black. We'd been driving a little over two hours when Preston turned off onto an old forestry road. The truck bounced and hopped down the dirt road with only the truck's parking lights leading the way. Tree branches hit the windshield and scraped the side of the truck.

"If I had known this was what we'd be doing, I wouldn't have had us switch out the vehicles," I said, holding onto the grab bar tightly.

"Then you really won't like what I'm about to do," he said, turning off into the woods.

"So I'm guessing we don't have wifi where we're going?"

"Actually, we do," he said. "But this isn't where we'll end up. We need to trade vehicles."

"What? We can't leave the truck here," I objected, panic setting in. It felt like pieces of Gavin were being littered along the way, and before I knew it, all traces of him would be gone.

"We have to," Preston replied. "I wouldn't be a bit surprised if they had a tracer on this truck."

"You think they could be tracking us right now?" I folded my arms as he put the truck in park.

"Pretty likely."

He flipped off the lights and the surrounding forest went dark. If he was right, the longer I put up a fight the more I put us in danger.

"Chances are the truck will be fine," I muttered, opening the door.

Preston turned on a flashlight and grabbed two bags. I grabbed my duffle and followed him only fifteen or so feet to another truck. He opened up the driver's side and checked the engine. It turned over quickly and he threw his bags in the front and so did I. We hauled everything from one truck to the other and took off the same way we came in.

"Now, we're headed up north," he said, turning on only the parking lights as we drove slowly back onto the forestry road. "It'll be a couple hours longer."

I leaned into the seat and relaxed my neck against the headrest as hollowness began spreading through me. The clash of emotions inside me made me leery of the choices I'd recently made.

"Do you even think we have a shot at this?" I asked, turning my neck to look at Preston.

"By this you mean…"

I smiled. "Motive, finding a motive."

"Depends how we go about it."

"My back is killing me." I cringed at what I sounded like. As if he wasn't hurting too.

My eyes focused on Preston as he continued to drive, and I felt some of the fear begin to dissipate. Being around him somehow made me feel safer, more secure, and it was a sensation I didn't know I'd missed until I had it again.

"Sorry for whining."

He started laughing. "Rebekah, believe me. That wasn't whining."

"Well, thank you."

My lids began to feel very heavy as I watched his expression change from surprise to satisfaction at my remark. He was a handsome man, kind. The only noise surrounding us was the sound of the highway and our steady breathing. It wasn't long before I couldn't fight sleep any more, and my mind drifted into another world far from the one we lived in where peace and calm resided.

***

The sound of a woman's voice blaring through a speaker woke me up. My eyes blinked open, and two large lights shined through the windshield. I glanced over at Preston and realized he was ordering us both cheeseburgers and those lights belonged to the fast food restaurant our truck idled at.

What a rude awakening.

"And two strawberry shakes."

I sat up straighter in the seat and flipped down the mirror. My brown hair was completely flattened against my head, and the swelling hadn't gone down in my face, not even a little bit. But my lips no longer looked as if they were going to fall off so that was a plus. I grabbed my lip balm and plastered it all over my mouth.

Preston pulled ahead and put the truck in park. There was only one other car in front of us.

"I'm starving," I said, running my fingers through my hair attempting to fluff it up a little. Not that it really mattered.

"Me too," he said.

He pulled us forward and handed over his cash in exchange for one bag of food and two milkshakes.

I took a sip of the shake and relished the taste as the cold, creamy liquid ran down my throat.

"We're almost there," he said, grabbing a French fry out of the bag. "I just thought we'd like something greasy and heavy before we buried ourselves in."

"Good call," I said, shoving a handful of fries into my mouth.

As we pulled onto the road, I looked around trying to place where we were. There were two other fast food restaurants across the street, a grocery store, and a bank.

"Where are we?" I asked, wishing I hadn't fallen asleep.

"On our way toward Diablo Lake," he said, smiling. "We used this spot off and on during the outbreak, but we never stayed in one place all that long for safety sake."

I nodded watching the town disappear as we began our climb up the mountain road.

"It's underground."

"You guys had a safe house that was underground?" I asked, bewildered. "That would've taken some time to construct."

Preston looked embarrassed as he thought about what to say.

"My father was a bit paranoid, to say the least. He had it built around the whole Y2K thing."

"The disaster that never came. I remember reading about that," I said, not wanting to make Preston any more uncomfortable than he already looked. "Wasn't it something about computers not being readied or something? People thought the world was going to fall apart, revolutions in the street?"

"Something like that," he laughed. "Who would've thought it wasn't machines that took us down but zombies."

"No kidding."

"Well, 2012 went by as peacefully as the year 2000 and my mom started getting annoyed about my dad's pastime."

"I can't imagine why," I laughed.

"Once my sister and I were born, my dad cooled his jets slightly. We still visited the place, but we stayed on top of the ground. And then the outbreak happened..." his voice trailed off.

"He wasn't so crazy after all," I said, as Preston turned off the mountain road, down a dirt road.

"There was so much conflicting information floating around that we didn't know what to do. We'd hide out here, and then we'd take off, and then we'd wind up back here."

"I know. It was a crazy time," I said, remembering back to my family. "One moment the government said to stay inside, then they'd announce to flee any well populated areas. Then it was stay on the run."

"Which turned into stay in one place and wait for help," Preston said, his voice tipped with anger. We turned off the dirt road and drove under sweeping fir trees.

"I never imagined our government would be so inept dealing with an outbreak. We're lucky the scientists figured it out," I said.

Preston nodded. "True. One of the biggest disappointments in my dad's life was that his son went to work for one the agencies. He thought I was just feeding into the system. You can imagine what he thought once the outbreak occurred. I guess he was right."

"Well, we can always look at our histories and make sense of the nonsensical after the fact, but that's no way to live. Look at all of the failed predictions over the last century. The one thing that nobody had accounted for was what almost demolished the world."

Preston parked under a large tree, and I reached over and grabbed his hand. "Your father would be very proud of you."

Preston smiled. "Ready to see our new abode for the time being? It's nothing fancy."

"I'll take hidden over luxury any day." I followed Preston to a large boulder and was completely enthralled with the setup as the rock began to move, revealing a staircase.

"Wow," I uttered in complete amazement, looking down into the ground. The metal stairwell was encased in dim lighting, leading the way under the very earth we stood on.

"Let's get everything hauled downstairs for the night," Preston said.

I grabbed my duffle and two other bags, carefully placing the straps along my shoulders. The weight of the bags thumped against my back every so often as I walked, making me wince as the pain erupted from my injuries. I didn't know how he was doing it all with a backpack strapped to him.

Following him down the metal stairs, I was astonished at what I saw. There was a living room and kitchenette directly in front of us and behind that, a half-wall separated the living space from the sleeping quarters. A control room was tucked under the stairs with a desk and several tablets hanging on the wall.

In a way, it felt like I was walking into a time capsule. Decades-old décor hinted of a simpler time, a happier time. The brown couch had two patchwork quilts draped over it, and there was a beige throw rug on the floor.

"Wow. I can't believe you guys ever left this place," I whispered, wishing I could take it back as soon as I said it.

"I wish we hadn't," he said, his eyes flicking to mine. "My family would probably still be intact. Let's go get the rest of the stuff. I'll show you where we can put the weapons and supplies."

"You mean there's more?" I asked, looking around the space.

"Yeah, behind the bedroom wall." He pointed across the room.

"Okay." I followed him up the stairs.

Once we reached the top, I was reminded how cold it was. The season was definitely turning. It was really surprising how warm it was below the earth. We walked to the truck and gathered the remaining bags and boxes, locking the truck behind us.

The soft glow of the living room was inviting and the couch was calling to me. I made myself comfortable, wrapping my arms around one of the pillows, and I felt the anxiety began to drip out of my extremities.

"I've been dying to look on that thumb drive," I said, once Preston locked the boulder back into place.

"So no taking tonight off?" he laughed.

I looked around the place. "And do what?" I

laughed.

He shrugged. "Point taken."

Preston ducked under the stairs and flipped on a tablet and a printer. A light hum as the electronics booted up reminded me how silent it was underground.

"I think we should lay low for a few days, let ourselves heal up…" his voice trailed off.

I wasn't so sure. I bit my lip and looked down at the coffee table. There was a People magazine, the cover plastered with people I didn't recognize. I picked it up and glanced at the date. "April 20, 2020. Impressive," I mumbled, flipping through the news of many years before.

"Have the thumb drive?" he asked, walking over to me.

The lighting softened the marks on his face and arms. His color had gotten better and he didn't seem as stiff. There was something relaxed behind his expression as well. I, on the other hand, still felt horrible. I snaked my fingers into my jeans and grabbed out the little device, handing it over to him. Our fingers touched slightly, and I felt something flash through me, which made me uneasy. I glanced away and he didn't say a word.

I watched him shove the thumb drive into the USB port on one of the tablets. He hooked it to the mini box and the images projected onto the wall.

"There are lots of files on this little guy," Preston said.

I shifted to see the wall better and squinted my eyes.

"Are you just gonna stay over there? I don't bite." His eyes connected with mine, and it felt like he could read the uncertainty I was feeling inside.

"Sorry," I mumbled and walked over quickly. He pulled out a chair and I sat down as we read through document names. "Look at that one." I pointed at a title that read, 'Genetic Development Foundation'. He clicked on it, opening up an Excel spreadsheet listing names, titles, and schools.

"What is this?" I asked, searching through the names.

"Looks like one big data dump. I'm not sure that we'll get anything out of this."

"There's always a method to someone's madness," I laughed.

I clicked on a new spreadsheet and began typing in formulas that would run a macro looking for shared characteristics and graph the findings.

"Where'd you learn that?" he asked.

"Before art school, I thought I wanted to be a data analyst, but I was very, very wrong."

"Well, you never know what will prove to be useful, huh?"

As the data continued churning, I watched as the graphical equations began grabbing some of the consistent data points.

"These people are genetic researchers," I said, taking a closer look.

"Really," he said, scooting in closer to get a better view.

"Yeah." I watched as another data point flashed onto the screen. "And they all seem to have one thing in common."

"What's that?" he asked, his eyes fastening onto mine.

"They're dead."

CHAPTER FIFTEEN

We both sat in stunned silence. Gavin's name appeared on that list and so did Preston's sister, Sophie. Who'd been keeping track and for what purpose? I stood up slowly and walked over to the couch as the heaviness of the revelation ruined me for discussion.

"Whoever the person was, probably no longer exists," I said, slouching onto the couch. The pain from my wounds as I pressed into the cushion awoke my senses. "At least in a capacity that would be helpful."

I looked up and stared at the metal ceiling and let my mind rewind through the events of the last several weeks. There had to be clues I was missing. Why a zombie pit? Why waste time on pinning the creatures against one another? I was sure they were making money from it, but enough to make it matter?

"I think we should meet with Albert or Terrence," I said, bringing my attention back to Preston.

"Who?" he asked, his eyes completely void of emotion.

"The gang members," I said. "I'm sure they're not thrilled about getting pinned with something they didn't do. That might make them willing to talk to us."

"What makes you think they'd know anything?" Preston walked over to where I was and took a seat on one of the chairs.

"All good criminals have a pulse on what's happening on their turf, especially if they're getting targeted. It's just a hunch, but I think we should talk to one of them before they get charged with anything in the coffee shop incident."

"I was really thinking that we should stay low for awhile, stay hidden here," Preston said, twisting his lips together.

"Every day that we let slip by, brings us closer to failure. We have to find out what's going on before it's too late."

Preston let out a groan, but a smile was right under the surface of his expression.

"I think this is the perfect base for us, but I never would've agreed to come up here, if I knew you planned on hanging out and hiding in it until everything reveals itself." I arched a brow.

"That's not what I intended at all. I only thought we could give our bodies a chance to—"

"Resilient," I interrupted. That was what Preston had said about humans, our bodies. I don't know why it didn't occur to me sooner.

"What about resilient?" he asked, sitting up straighter.

"Our bodies are resilient, but zombies aren't," I

paused for a few moments. "Imagine if they were. They'd be unstoppable. If zombies could regenerate…"

Preston let out a deep breath and said, "The zombie pits. Once we know how those incorporate into Marcus's bigger scheme, we might have a shot at stopping whatever it is he's planning."

"He has a team. There are only two of us. As much as I'd like to cower in the corner and never leave this refuge, I think we've got one night here and that's it. I want to find a way to talk to either Terrence or Albert," I told him.

Preston nodded and shoved his hands through his hair as he stared at the floor.

"I'm not tired after the nap, but something tells me I better enjoy tonight's sleep. We should get up as early as we can handle tomorrow and head out," I said.

Preston nodded and glanced at the bed. "You take the bed. I'll take the couch."

"Don't be ridiculous. We can share the bed. We're grownups. We both need a good night's sleep. I'm gonna go look some stuff up and then I'll be in."

Preston's gaze dropped away from mine.

"You can handle that, right?" I teased, as Preston walked slowly toward the bedroom.

He only laughed.

I made my way to the tablet and began swiping through news articles relating to Albert, hoping I'd find something that listed where he lived. Sliding my finger from one tidbit of information to another about this guy made me very uneasy. He wasn't a good guy, and I was beginning to doubt why I thought he'd be willing to give us any information whatsoever. I turned my search to Terrence and found more of the same. It was really a crapshoot between who to pick until I saw a picture of Terrence's house. I captured the image and dragged it to the search engine. I tapped on the screen, and a satellite image of the same house popped up, this one with a street address.

Guess we'd be visiting Terrence. I hoped he still lived there. I turned off the small light and turned around to see Preston gently working his shirt away from his wounds. He was probably right. Staying here and healing before we started it up again was the smart thing to do. But I didn't feel we had the time. In fact, I knew we didn't have it.

"Let me help," I said, walking through the living room and into the partially separated bedroom.

His lips twisted in pain as the shirt stuck to his skin. I felt a pulse of guilt as I thought about what I was asking of him, of us.

"Spin around," I instructed, placing my fingertips along the hem of the Henley. I slowly glided my other hand underneath the fabric, releasing the skin and cotton from each other. His breathing changed as I got closer to his shoulders. That was where the injuries were most severe.

"I'm so sorry," I whispered.

He nodded, and I used that as a distraction as I lifted the fabric from his skin.

"Thanks," he said.

"Believe it or not, it's looking better," I said, my eyes falling down the length of his back. The wounds were not as red, and the skin around the lacerations had calmed down and were now back to flesh color.

I felt air movement between my back and the shirt

I was wearing, which told me that my skin wasn't as attached to my shirt as his was.

"Let me do the honors," he said, moving his hands to my shirt before I had the chance to object. He worked the material away from my skin and raised it over my head.

I felt completely exposed at this simple gesture. It wasn't sexual, but it felt sensual. And my wounded mind and body shuddered at the thought. How twisted was it that two people damaged by a gruesome war were left peeling off layers of themselves?

"In other news," I said, trying to shake the unexpected feelings away. "I found Terrence's address. Hopefully, he's still there."

Preston removed sheets and a comforter out of a plastic box and made the bed.

"Here's to finding out what he knows tomorrow," Preston mumbled, and I wondered if he felt the same odd connection to one another as I did.

He slid under the covers and hugged the edge so tightly I thought he was going to fall off.

"I don't bite," I teased, slipping under the covers.

He laughed.

"I just don't want you accidentally flopping an arm on my back. I think that would be the last straw," he confessed. "My back feels like it's on fire again."

"Don't laugh, but I think I'm going to wear leather from now on."

Of course, he started laughing.

"From head to toe." I started laughing too.

Soon the laughter turned to silence as I heard Preston's breathing steady and signal that he had fallen asleep.

I laid on my side and moved the comforter over my shoulders. It smelled slightly musty, but for some reason that was reassuring as if to tell me that I was safe here, buried under the ground. The silence inside this box beneath the earth was actually deafening. As I closed my eyes, I attempted to make myself relax but that was impossible. Even the heavy sound of my heart beating made me feel uneasy, like it was the sound of a clock reminding me that I shouldn't be wasting time in a bed. The thought was ridiculous. I knew that, but sleep felt like a guilty pleasure.

Preston shifted slightly and his breathing changed. I wasn't alone any longer. At least for now. I'd been so used to being alone with my own thoughts that sharing them left me filling anxious, jittery.

Preston's hypnotic breaths tricked me into falling asleep, and before I knew it, I was dreaming again of a world untouched by war.

***

We drove in silence to the address that was listed on the satellite image. Preston was at the wheel, and I was determined to make sure we didn't make any wrong turns. Both of us were armed, but our weapons were concealed.

"Turn right at the next light," I said, stretching my body as much as I could while anchored in a seat belt. We'd been driving for almost two hours back toward the city, which was where Terrence theoretically lived.

"You ready?" he asked.

"As ready as I'll ever be," I said. "I feel less frightened about encountering him than Marcus, though. How crazy is that?"

"Not crazy at all."

"There it is." I pointed at an old house that

matched the images perfectly. It was a pre-centennial home that had seen better days. The siding was falling off in places and the shutters seemed to be held on by only a nail. The fence surrounding the yard was rusty, and the landscape was completely overgrown. My hope faded that he was still living here as I took in the condition of the property.

"I guess they haven't gotten around to updating the satellite images," I muttered.

Preston parked along the street and looked over at me. "You ready?"

I nodded and we both got out of the car and slowly walked over to the home. There was a kid's bicycle out in the front yard and two deflated soccer balls. Again, not promising.

The gate was wide open, which allowed us to walk right up the cement sidewalk leading to the front door. The sidewalk was covered with cracks and weeds as if this was a trail not often used. There were bars on the two front windows and a storm door covering the entrance.

Preston banged on the frame and waited. I heard a shuffling in the home and glanced at Preston.

"What do you want?" a man's voice boomed through the door.

"We want to talk to you about the coffee shop," I said, hoping my female voice would diminish the fears of whoever was on the other side of the door.

"Talk with my lawyer," his voice gruff.

It was him!

"We aren't with the authorities," I offered.

"The press can go to hell," he snarled.

"We aren't with the press either. I was hoping to ask you a few questions about TRAC."

The front door flew open, and he unlocked the storm door, pushing it forward. And there in front of us stood Terrence, holding a shotgun by his side. A known criminal, who looked utterly beat down by his own world. He was heavy-set, in his mid-thirties with black hair and pockmarked skin. He wore an oversized button-down shirt and sweat pants.

"If you try anything, I'm not promising I won't kill you," he threatened, gesturing us inside.

"I won't promise that either," I said, Preston following behind me.

We stepped into a small entry, which was painted red with the underlying white color beneath exposed in many places from chipped paint. There was a shelf hung on the far wall filled with trinkets. Not very gangsterish of him. He led us through the small space to a great room, exposing a cluttered living area. It bordered on filthy with leftover food cartons tipped over on the coffee table and stacks of newspapers, magazines and empty beer cans piled high. Regardless of the toys I saw in the front yard, I was pretty confident he lived alone.

"So what do you want to know about TRAC?" he asked, sitting in a recliner. I glanced at the couch nearest us and thought better of sitting down.

"We know you had nothing to do with the events at the coffee shop. We were both there and saw members of the TRAC team attack the customers," I began.

"Why should I believe you?" Terrence asked.

"Because they were after us, and we'd have no reason to lie to you," I paused. "At least about that."

Terrence seemed to appreciate my honesty and nodded. "So why do you feel it's important to come tell me this? I already know I'm innocent."

"Yeah, but the rest of the world doesn't." I folded my arms and waited.

He took a sip from one of the beer bottles he had lined up, and I wondered how he even knew that one was full.

"Do you know Marcus?" he asked, a cynical look coming across his face.

"I know of him," I said.

"And I know him, from a distance. I worked at Shackles for a few months," Preston said.

"Ah, one of his many enterprises," Terrence laughed.

"So what can you tell us about him and TRAC?" I asked. "He's obviously been able to wrangle some power within the private sector that others haven't."

"The best criminals are the ones who wrap themselves in the camouflage of the flaws around them. Marcus is an expert at that."

"Meaning?" I asked.

"He's got everything covered. First, he's got a private security company that exposes the imperfections of the government's own ability to protect its citizens. Second, he's got a network that's tapped into the underground gambling scene, allowing him to have direct access to various criminal organizations, and he even uses his own security forces to manage everything. Third, he understands how vital zombies are to the afterworld."

My blood chilled. I felt the pressure of his statement squeeze me from the outside in as if I might implode with the implications.

"The new economy depends on zombies in one form or another, and he's been able to exploit that,"

Terrence said. "He's an opportunist in the highest sense, and he won't stop until he gets what he wants."

His words worked into me, embedding another layer of desperation through me.

"Which is what?" Preston asked.

"If I knew that, do you think I'd be in this situation? As of now, I have no negotiating power with him or the people he controls. And to be honest, it's of no concern to me."

I realized that while he was willing to give us information, he had no intention of helping us beyond relaying the facts. Because he didn't care. The lives in jeopardy meant nothing to him. But someone had meant something to him at one point, or he wouldn't be in this stalemate with his own life. I noticed a doll's leg underneath the couch.

"How old was your daughter?" I asked.

Terrence stiffened and he took another swig of beer.

"What happened to her?" I tried again.

"They took her," he growled. "My bitch of a wife didn't know how to deal with her after the outbreak and reported my baby as—"

"Unfit to rejoin society," Preston said.

"I haven't seen her since," Terrence replied. "I know he's part of that too."

"Marcus?" I asked, bewildered.

Terrence nodded and I glanced at Preston. His expression didn't change at all.

"Those asylums are dangerous places. The entire public is so scared of 'em, they'd rather act like they don't exist. Let that agency run quietly and without disruption on its own. But I'm telling you, if there's danger, Marcus is somehow involved."

He was right. And I didn't understand why I didn't see it until now.

Camouflage. The best way to divert attention for whatever Marcus was doing was to seep into a system that no one wanted to be involved in or even acknowledge that it existed. He would be able to blend in and distort or replicate the problems of others while appearing to fix the problems that arise. Once we could find out what made him connected in the MHA, which oversaw the survivors' mental health administration, we might be able to pin down what his motive was. What his involvement with the zombies really was.

TRAC had to be the private security company monitoring the facilities. Had to!

Terrence narrowed his eyes at me. "There is no beating Marcus at whatever game he wants to play. There's no point even trying to figure out what it is because he will win. I owned these streets before the war and after," Terrence said, working his hands alongside the chair cushion.

He pulled out pictures and shoved them toward us. Preston grabbed them, and his body stiffened.

"Until Marcus arrived to play in my world, I had hope. I have none now," Terrence replied coldly.

I looked over at the pictures Preston was flipping through. A teenage girl stared back at the lens, lifeless. She had hung herself in whatever institution she was placed at. The last photo in the pile documented it and I felt a shiver pass through me.

"I'm so sorry," I whispered.

Preston handed the photos back to Terrence, and he pointed toward the front door. It was time for us to leave. As I followed Preston down the hallway, I thought about what kind of person would send pictures like that to another human being.

Preston opened the front door, and we walked outside, closing the door softly behind us.

"You were right about coming here to visit him," Preston whispered.

"Never miss a chance to get in close with the enemy because the opening might never reoccur," I said, shaking my head. I felt a shiver run up my spine and hugged myself as I glanced at Preston.

We took a step forward and heard the single gunshot.

Terrence joined his daughter.

CHAPTER SIXTEEN

"I worked for the MHA and didn't see what was right in front of me," he said, more to himself than to me.

"We can sit around beating ourselves up or we can be useful," I said, touching his cheek softly, bringing his eyes to mine. "Everything happens when it should as it should. For instance, those facilities are hidden. The locations aren't known by the general public, but I bet you know exactly where they're located because you worked there. And it's not the agency. Only the organization that protects the facilities. There's no reason why you would suspect a security firm in the disappearance of your sister."

Preston let out a sigh. "You're right. I'm just—"

"Human," I whispered. "You're just human. Unfortunately, I'm afraid Marcus might not be, which means we've got to change how we go about things. We need to think like a killer, like an evil dictator, like someone who doesn't know what it's like to love, to live, to care, to feel…"

We were sitting in the truck outside a café right off the highway. We had just grabbed a bite to eat, even though neither of us wanted food, and had made the decision to go check out one of the MHA facilities that was only an hour away.

"We're dealing with a psychopath." I pressed my head against the neck rest and let out a sigh.

"If we can shut down TRAC, I think the world has a shot at experiencing decency once again," he said, rubbing his fingers along his neck.

"The problem is that the majority of citizens think everything is fine or as fine as it can be after an outbreak. Somehow we've got to find like-minded people who we can trust," I said. "Take my friend, Abby. She's pinning her entire existence on normalcy and getting back into the groove at college. I don't think there's much of anything that would change her mind, and that's the popular way of thinking. I was like that when Gavin was around. I felt alive with the thought of making it through the outbreak. For the first time I'd felt hopeful again. It was a brilliant time. Unfortunately, it ended for me fairly quickly. Everyone else is still living in that high and they don't want to come out of it."

Preston had turned on the main highway, heading south toward the country, as he discussed a few places where he'd run across survivors with similar experiences. I mostly listened and tried to place the likelihood of experience with the stories that the survivors relayed to Preston.

"Do you worry some of the survivors you ran into are just crying wolf? There's always conspiracy theorists," I said, glancing out the window. The area we were driving through was completely rural with fir trees lining the narrow stretch of highway. Every so often a mailbox and an overgrown dirt driveway would appear, but that was seldom.

Preston began laughing and laughing.

"What?" I demanded.

He shook his head, laughing more.

"Seriously. What?" I drilled my eyes through him.

"We're getting close," he said, ignoring me.

I looked out the window and saw a large concrete block wall along the perimeter of some property just ahead of us.

"What was so funny?" I asked, snapping my attention back to Preston who was still grinning.

"I find it hilarious that a woman who is teetering on being reported to the MHA and who's been accused of conspiracy theories herself is so quick to judge others?" His brow arched and he waited patiently for a response.

"Point taken," I muttered. "I just like to be cautious."

"Right. That's definitely a trait you've exhibited thus far."

"Whatever." I felt my cheeks ignite.

He was completely right. I'd been accused of being a wacko conspiracy theorist myself, but the difference was I knew I wasn't.

I guess that was what we all thought. I started laughing and looked back out the window. The concrete wall looked endless. I couldn't see any structures on the other side because the wall was so high, but I assumed there had to be quite a few. I saw a stop sign up ahead and Preston came to a slow stop and turned the corner, following more of the concrete wall.

There was a gap up ahead in the wall, and as we drove closer, I spotted a large bronze plaque that read 'MHA FACILITY 21SWA'. There was a gate joining the two sections of concrete wall and a guard station. We drove right on by.

"What does 21SWA stand for?" I asked Preston.

"It's the twenty-first facility in the state of Washington located in the southern quadrant."

"Huh."

"And I don't know if you caught it, but the guard in the booth was most definitely armed and wearing a TRAC uniform," he said.

I didn't catch it.

"So are you going to start trusting me, or do I get to look forward to more of the same?" he asked.

"What do you mean?" I shot back.

"Well, your trust issues don't seem to be getting any better. I doubt you believe half the things I mention. I get the feeling the moment you could go at this alone, you would. And I'm really not sure this is what I had imagined as far as a partnership. I'd like to take you for a visit. I have some friends close by who've experienced similar situations and—"

"You're not really asking me are you?"

He shook his head. "Not really."

The sound of the engine rumbled as we continued down the road with the concrete wall on one side and a heavily timbered forest on the other.

"Do you think there's any hope for me?" I glanced at Preston. It didn't really occur to me how much I'd only thought of myself.

"Possibly," he joked. "The place we're going is a B&B."

"A B&B?"

"Yeah. My friends always wanted to own a farm and have a bed and breakfast on it. They finally got the resources to do it." He pressed his lips together.

"Amazing what opportunities the outbreak afforded us all," I said sarcastically. I thought back to the zombie pit and the countless people throwing their money away as if it was tainted, and in a way, it was. "I understand why the zombie pit is such an attraction. The government payouts seems stained and dirty, like holding onto it is a constant reminder of what we're all missing, who we're all missing."

"And Marcus and his group certainly tapped into that," Preston said.

"And more. It's the more I'm really interested in. So how far away is this place?"

"About thirty minutes."

I nodded and watched as we continued past the last of the concrete wall. There was absolutely nothing to see from the outside. We'd have to go in, if we wanted answers.

***

We pulled down a long, dirt driveway with pasture lining both sides. We were definitely deep into the country. I hadn't seen any sort of civilization from the moment we'd left the MHA facility. It had been a thirty-minute trip, but that was only because Preston was going about eighty miles-per-hour on a two-lane country road. After our trip, I wasn't sure who was the reckless one.

"Do they know we're coming?" I asked.

He shook his head. "They live off the grid."

"Probably smart. But how does that work with opening their home to visitors and B&B guests?"

He laughed. "It doesn't."

We rode along the bumpy drive for several minutes before we rounded a corner, and I was able to catch a glimpse of a building behind a burst of alder trees. It didn't look like a home, possibly a barn. As we wound along the side of the building, the home came into view. It was a beautiful brick building that looked completely untouched by the horrors we all experienced.

"Wow. This isn't what I'd call a farmhouse."

The architecture was stunning. It looked like a Victorian Villa plucked out of 1890. There were six bay windows that were equally spaced, stained glass atop the front entry and above the bay windows, the roof was made of slate, patterned brick designs were located in each quadrant of the rectangular building, and ironwork twisted along the windows and doors. Two of the chimneys released smoke into the air at opposite ends of the house.

Preston pulled in front of the home and turned off the ignition.

"They aren't very trusting, so I should go talk to them first," he said.

"Sound like my kind of people."

Preston gave me a huge smile and left the truck, swiftly walking to the front stoop. He knocked on the door and within seconds the front door opened wide. A woman about my age wrapped her arms around Preston's neck, kissing his cheek endlessly. A man stepped out from the door and gave Preston a hug just as the woman released Preston from her grasp.

She spotted me in the truck, and her expression completely slipped into one of suspicion and alarm. Preston turned to look at me and waved as he explained who I was. I actually wanted to hear what he said because I wasn't even sure about myself any longer. I watched as the woman's expression softened slightly and she waved me over.

I got out of the truck and slowly made my way to Preston and his friends. The woman had strawberry blonde hair that was tied in a loose bun. She was dressed in a pair of jeans and a sweatshirt. The man's expression turned distant as I approached. His black hair was disheveled and his clothes were dirty, probably from working on the property.

"This is Rebekah," Preston said. "Rebekah, this is Emily and her husband, Trick."

My head jolted toward the man. He didn't look like a Trick.

Preston started laughing. "Kidding. His name is Braden."

His joke loosened up Emily and Braden, and my apprehension began to dissolve.

"Your humor never gets old," Emily said, laughing. "Let's get inside. It's freezing out here."

I nodded and thought about what Emily said. Humor? Preston…funny? I suddenly wanted to get to know Preston, the real Preston. Not the one I imagined him to be.

"You can stay for as long as you need," Emily offered.

The entry hall was as grand as the exterior. The dark wood floors complimented the pale walls. A long pew was placed against the far wall for seating, and above us hung a beautiful crystal chandelier. Preston shut the door, and as he did so, I spotted a large wardrobe cabinet packed full of photo albums rather than coats.

"You're home is really beautiful," I said, admiring

everything around me.

"It's been a nice escape," she said, smiling.

"Although, we never really escape it, do we?" Braden said softly, as he began down the hall.

I shook my head and felt Preston's fingers gently touch my back, pushing me forward. Glancing back at him, I smiled as I reached around my back and grabbed his fingers, sliding my hand into his.

We walked into the kitchen where an oversized farm table was placed in the corner with enough seating for ten people. The industrial size stove was in the center island. A double fridge was on the wall closest to me, and the sink was centered in front of a greenhouse window. Fresh herbs stretched for the sunlight, and a Christmas cactus sprawled behind the sink.

"We'd love to hear what you've been up to," Braden said, noticing my fingers intertwined in Preston's. I hastily dropped my hand from his and Preston laughed.

"More than I wish to relay, really," Preston said, taking a seat at the table.

"I'll put a pot of coffee on," Emily said.

"Probably a good idea," Preston said.

I took a seat next to him and watched Emily glide through the kitchen seamlessly. Her movements were so graceful, and I got the feeling that this wasn't all that unusual, having two people pop up at the start of an evening.

"You look like hell," Braden said, a wide grin spreading across his lips.

"Yeah, she really does," Preston said, glancing at me.

I punched him in the shoulder. "He wasn't talking

about me."

"How do you put up with him?" Braden joked.

"I haven't seen this side of him until we arrived," I confessed, catching Preston's mischievous expression. "But I kind of like it."

Preston's eyes fastened onto mine, and his carefree demeanor vanished.

"Last we heard, you were working at some dive bar," Emily said, missing the entire interaction as she scooped the grounds into the filter.

"No longer there, but I found out enough to carry our theory forward," he said, glancing at me. "This one came snooping around for info and a way into the pits while I was at the bar."

"Oh, girl. Why on earth would you want to go sniffing out that mess?" she asked, giving me a sympathetic smile. She grabbed a plate of cookies and placed them on the table, taking a seat across from me.

"I saw it online and couldn't believe that it could possibly exist. Zombies fighting one another? I had never seen that during the outbreak. They were never organized, or thinking, and it sounded like both those qualities would be needed during a fight. At least partially." I shifted in my seat and felt Braden's gaze on me.

"What made you interested in zombie behavior? That seems like kind of an odd preoccupation for a college girl," Braden said, eyeing me. Emily tapped his arm and gave him a disapproving look.

"My husband was killed by thinking, organized zombies. A horde of them surrounded us. They had their sights set on him. There was nothing I could do…" my voice trailed off.

"I'm so sorry," Braden said, glaring at Preston. "You should've told us, man."

"I've learned not to speak for her," Preston said, shrugging. "Well, whatever the case, TRAC seems to think we've come across some information that they don't want us to have. They kidnapped us—"

"And almost killed us," I interrupted.

"What information did you find that they're willing to kill you for?" Emily asked, her eyes wide.

"We have no idea," I said.

"Well, that's not good," Braden said, shoving his fingers through his hair. "TRAC, you say?"

Preston nodded, and I watched Emily and Braden trade worried glances.

"What?" I asked.

"I think we have a lot to talk about," Emily said, her eyes misting over.

CHAPTER SEVENTEEN

The cold air ignited my senses as I followed Preston outside to grab our things from the truck. Emily also suggested we move it back behind the house to a garage. I couldn't imagine anyone ever finding this house out in the middle of nowhere, but she obviously knew something I didn't.

"Are your walls starting to come down around these two?" Preston asked, hauling the large duffels out of the truck bed.

I glared at him with a smile anchored on my face. He saw right through me. "My walls might even be crumbling around you...marginally." I tossed my backpack on the steps next to the duffels.

He laughed and shook his head. "I'll believe it when I see it."

"Believe it or not, I do value what you have to say. I just have an odd way of showing it."

Preston's eyes met mine, running his finger along his jawline. The look in his eyes was intense, sharpening his already chiseled features. He was good-looking in a rugged sort of way. A ping of guilt rattled inside of me for noticing, and I dropped my gaze to the ground.

"You can go back inside, and I'll move the truck," he offered, noticing my reaction.

"That's okay. I'll come with you." I walked around to the passenger door and climbed onto the truck bench.

"You suddenly shy to go in there by yourself?" he teased, but his expression was warm, kind.

"No."

Maybe I was.

"So are you going to tell me what this place really is?" I asked, as he drove the truck along the side of the large home, reaching the back garage.

"I'll let them explain it to you," he said, driving the truck inside the dark garage. There was another older model car. They obviously weren't believers in our new technology either, but I did notice an auto-driver under a carport.

We slowly walked to the front of the house to collect our bags. There were plots for several gardens that had already been covered over for the winter, and a few random sheds placed along the side of the property. The place felt lived in, like it had somehow missed the entire outbreak and nothing ever stopped moving forward. The rest of the world felt stagnant and so did some of the people in it. Whether I went to pick up a carton of milk at the grocery store or a piece of clothing at the mall, there was a certain expression some survivors wore. It was a mix between defeat and hopelessness, almost like they were experiencing the same lack of brain activity as the undead. Even though we were officially living in the afterworld, it didn't necessarily feel like anyone was living at all, myself included.

"Thanks for putting up with me," I said, glancing at Preston. "I kind of disconnected from the world and reality once Gavin was killed. I know I haven't been the most pleasant person at times, and I've gotten so used to working solo that I'm not always sure how to fit someone else in."

"Honestly, I understand." He stopped walking and turned to face me, gently grabbing my wrist. I unexpectedly took a step forward and looked up, his eyes focused on mine. I felt a wave of discomfort run through me and I didn't understand why. Was it the memory of Gavin?

"We've both seen things that very few people even believe exist. When I find others who have witnessed or experienced the same horrors, as twisted as this sounds, I find comfort in knowing I'm not alone. On some level, there's a connection that binds us all. That truth binds us all," he replied.

I looked over toward the woods and thought about how many months Gavin and I had been on the run, taking shelter wherever we could, running from the undead and then coming out of the outbreak alive and well. Yet months after the outbreak, here I stood alone and feeling dead inside. I understood what Preston was saying. I just wasn't sure I'd be able to be so willing to accept complete strangers into my life. I didn't see how that could make up for my losses, the heartache I pushed out of my mind every hour of every day.

Preston ran his finger along my chin to bring me back to him. "I've been so alone since I lost my mother and sister that these people, the believers, are like family. There's no judgment, they're accepting—supportive," he murmured. "Just like family."

I stayed silent as his words burrowed their way into me. Family. Something I no longer had. Something he no longer had. But somehow I was the one who felt completely alone. I was the one hardened, bitter and angry. He wasn't.

"Listen, I know it sounds odd, but having these relationships brings a strange sort of comfort," he said, bringing his hand away from my face. "Just something to think about."

The moment his touch left my skin, I felt an immediate emptiness. I craved the very comfort he was talking about, and I hadn't even realized it. I wanted to be held, touched. There was a reason humans built communities within communities. It was one of the many things that separated us from the zombies.

"Thanks," I said, moving away from him. The wind was picking up, blowing my hair all around. Anchoring a loose strand behind my ear, I glanced over at Preston. "I'm ready to hear what Braden and Emily have to say."

"Let's get on it," he replied, his stride twice as long as mine as he took off toward the front entrance.

I jogged to keep up with him, and Emily and Braden were already on the stairs, hauling our items inside. Emily had composed herself since we had moved the truck.

I picked up my stray backpack and trailed behind everyone as we moved inside. The hairs on the back of my neck stood up as if someone was watching me from behind. I glanced over my shoulder toward the driveway and wooded area and saw no one, not like I thought I would.

"Do you guys get lots of visitors?" I asked, closing the door behind me.

"Not unexpected ones," Braden said, punching Preston in the arm. "But we make an exception for this guy."

"Why's that?" I asked, placing my backpack on the floor.

"He's like family," Emily said, her eyes falling to the wood floor as if she'd suddenly revealed something she shouldn't have.

"So you're a B&B?" I asked. There wasn't any signage leading to the home, and it was as hidden as anything I'd ever encountered, besides maybe Preston's underground abode.

Braden laughed and shook his head. "That's what he told you?"

Perturbed, I glanced over at Preston, who was beaming. "Yeah. That's what he told me."

"I guess that's one way of looking at it. Follow me to the great room and we'll start from the beginning," Emily said, gesturing down the hall.

Preston rolled out his hands urging me to walk in front of him. As I stepped forward, he placed his hand on my shoulder, and rather than flinch, my body actually relaxed with his touch. He gave me a light squeeze as we began down the hall, and I caught a look of relief behind his expression.

Emily was pouring coffee into our mugs, and Braden grabbed the plate of cookies. I clutched two mugs of the steaming liquid for Preston and me, and I followed Braden down a long hallway, which led into the enormous great room.

"This house goes on forever," I said.

The room had a large sectional cornering the entire back of the room. One entire wall was lined with bookshelves, and a coffee table that looked like it was built out of computer boards was centered directly in front of the sectional. Soft snoring, from the corner of the room, alerted me to a tan-colored dog snoozing on an overstuffed pet bed.

Emily caught my gaze and started laughing. "How do you like our guard dog, Burt? He's a Shar Pei. Built of toughness."

I started laughing and watched Burt slowly wake up from the commotion and stretch his front paws before burying into the soft surrounds of his bed once more.

"Have a seat wherever you'd like," Braden said.

He sat at the end of the sectional, near a set of French doors that led onto a concrete patio. Emily sat next to him and tucked her feet underneath her. I took a spot directly in front of the coffee table and placed both of our mugs on top.

"That's an interesting piece of furniture," I said, looking at the coffee table more closely.

"Thanks. It's hooked into our main frame," Braden said. "Not what you're looking at... we just used those old motherboards and stuff to conceal the real jewel. We figured no one would actually think we'd make something so obvious. And it looks kind of cool."

Emily rolled her eyes and shook her head. "It only looks cool to a geek."

"Then I guess that's what I am," Braden laughed.

"Now about this B&B that isn't?" I asked.

"So what do you know about the BN?" Emily

asked, grinning.

I looked over at Preston and he just smiled.

"BN?" I asked. "Apparently nothing."

"Have you been hauling her around everywhere and not telling her anything?" Emily scolded Preston.

"I haven't been hauling her anywhere. I've just been trying to keep up with her." Preston held up his hand as if to dismiss his fault.

"It's the Believers Network. Kind of a lame thing to be called so we shortened it to BN," Emily said.

"Okay…" I raised a brow.

"What you experienced with your husband and Preston with his sister isn't as uncommon as one might think. It's actually quite widespread all through the states, and we don't know who is or isn't involved. We've been slowly creating an underground network and refuge where information is collected," Emily said.

"Almost every state has a safe house like this one, and some states even have two. It's a place where we can gather and help disseminate news and information about the occurrences that are continuing to pop up all over. Each home is equipped with enough food to survive three months for twenty people," Braden said. "We also are able to monitor potential recruits."

I didn't want to rain on their parade but twenty? Twenty people?

"It may not seem like much, but anything more, and we'd be noticed," Emily said, catching my expression. "But if you do the math, across the country we have the capability to feed and arm over seven-hundred people. A CTA at a moment's notice. As more safe houses are formed, obviously the numbers of fighters ready and willing will increase."

"I'm sorry. What's a CTA?" I questioned.

"Call to Action," Braden answered. "We also offer a place to stay for other members who are just passing through."

"So you're forming a network of people who will… what?" I asked.

"Who will be willing to stop at nothing to fight for the truth," Preston said, surprising me. "We take great precautions to search out people who've encountered similar situations."

"But first we have to find out what that whole truth is," I whispered.

"Exactly," Emily confirmed, trading a nervous glance with Preston.

And then it dawned on me. I didn't search out Shackles and the zombie pit. These three searched me out. That's why I was able to find the information so readily. They hacked into my wireless and ensured I found the information that would lead me directly to Shackles and into the hands of Preston. My heart started thumping inside my chest as I thought about what that really meant. I had been followed, hacked— spied on! One moment Preston was begging me to trust and the next violating everything I held dear. Furious was putting it mildly.

I stood up hurriedly, and my knee knocked the coffee table. "Excuse me," I said, attempting to get by Preston, but he didn't budge.

"You're not going anywhere," he said, his voice low, gravelly. He stood up and wrapped his hand around my elbow. "You need us as much as we need you." His eyes flashed a wildness I hadn't seen before.

And I knew I wasn't going anywhere.

CHAPTER EIGHTEEN

I paced back and forth in the bedroom that they forcibly brought me to, my shoes clacking against the hardwood floors. They had locked it from the outside. Not that I couldn't climb out the window or possibly even bust through the door...but then what?

I'd been so foolish to think I'd come up with the leads on my own. And worse, I was not only no closer to the truth but on the run for my life. Anger didn't even begin to cover my sentiment toward the people downstairs. And Preston...I shook my head and glanced at my backpack.

It had been unzipped partially.

Great. When did that happen?

I grabbed the pack and opened it the rest of the way. Gavin's notebook wasn't inside.

Of course.

I walked to the window that overlooked the back of the property and thought about my choices. Did I actually have any or was I only fooling myself once more?

What did they want with me? I turned back to the room and leaned against the window ledge. The room was quite spacious with a four-poster bed, a mirrored dresser, and two large chests of drawers. There was a light blue goose down comforter spread across the bed, and the walls were a complimentary grey. How soothing of them.

I took in a deep breath right when I heard a light tap on the door.

"Yeah?" I called.

"Can I come in?" Preston asked.

"I'm not the one who locked it, so go for it." I crossed my arms and waited for him to open it.

I watched as the wooden door slowly opened, and he entered, balancing a saucer containing a cup of tea and a cookie in his left hand.

"You shouldn't have," I said, half snarling.

"I thought you might like something a little less anxiety causing than—"

I laughed, interrupting him. "You think I'm going to drink something that any of you bring me?"

He placed the saucer on the dresser and picked up the cookie, taking a bite. "See, I'm not dying. I can take a sip of the tea, too, if you'd like."

"Is that supposed to reassure me? Because I distinctly remember our conversation outside about trust," I said, glaring at him.

He had changed from Gavin's clothes into a faded pair of jeans and a black wool sweater. His hair was damp from a shower, and he looked relaxed but concerned.

"Let me ask you this." He walked over to the bed and took a seat directly across from me, his eyes not leaving mine for a second. "How else would you have liked us to go about reaching you? Do you really think you would've given us the time of day if we showed up on your doorstep?"

I didn't respond, but I kept my gaze fastened to his.

"Everything I've told you has been true," he said softly.

"You haven't told me much," I said.

"You're right," he confessed. "But I had to ensure you really did believe that your husband was targeted and that you had the research he was working on."

I was so angry all I heard was my blood pounding in my ears. I saw his lips moving, but I didn't care what else he had to say. I had been played.

"You used me," I mumbled, interrupting his excuse-laden speech.

"Don't you think you were using me just as much?" his brow furrowed.

I guess I was.

"But I didn't have a network of seven-hundred people on my side while doing it. It was only me attempting to find answers about what happened to my husband."

Preston stood in front of me with a stone-faced expression, his arms folded in front of him.

"Was the story of your sister and your mother true?" I asked.

"Everything I told you was the truth. I just didn't tell you everything," he said, his voice carrying the strength I craved. "Listen, you can go at this alone. Walk away. I'll never contact you again. Or you can join us as we try to ascertain what's going on. And in all honesty, I haven't seen anyone with the kind of inner strength that you have. Our organization needs that. Needs you."

"Yeah. It seems like it," I scoffed. "Do you plan on giving me my notebook back?"

"Sorry about that," he replied. "They're taking copies."

"Of course they are. I'm guessing they snatched it while we were moving the truck?"

He nodded. "I gather so."

"Do they or you have more answers than me?" I asked, feeling my anger begin to diminish only slightly.

He was silent for a beat and stood up, taking a step toward me. "Answers? No. Access? Yes."

"What do you mean access?" I asked.

"We've been able to infiltrate certain agencies and organizations, sometimes with only one or two members, but it's better than nothing."

"So TRAC?" I asked.

He nodded, and heat ran up my cheeks. "You knew TRAC was involved in some way?" My voice rose with every syllable.

Preston shook his head and reached for my arm. I didn't move away as his fingers clasped around my forearm, anchoring me in place.

"No. We didn't know that until our incident."

"If that's what you want to call it." A shudder ran through me as I remembered back to the warehouse and Preston hanging from the ceiling.

"We still don't know who all is involved. We have two informants with TRAC, and we also have one stationed with Barrell's Security, TRAC's main competitor. They are one of the other main security contractors the government hires, but they have a primary focus on private security. Neither informant had run across anything that had led us to suspect either company."

"So how does the MHA facility work into all of this?" I asked. "You obviously have something planned or we wouldn't be here."

He nodded, letting my arm slip from his grasp. "True. Would you come down for dinner and we can discuss it?"

"Alright," I muttered, grabbing a hoodie from one of the bags. Standing by the window had gotten me chilly, and my hands were trembling. But that might not have been because of the temperature, maybe the company.

"Rebekah, I'm sorry for misleading you," Preston's voice rumbled. His eyes set on mine.

I knew he was, but I shrugged and moved past him.

Walking down the hallway on my terms, as opposed to being dragged along the hardwoods, allowed me to take inventory. There were seven doors in front of me. I glanced behind me and saw another three doors.

"How many bedrooms?" I asked.

"There are eight bedrooms on this level, one closet and a bathroom for the three bedrooms that don't already have an attached ensuite," Preston answered. "So you have nine ways to escape from the top floor, if that's what you're wondering."

"I don't know what gave you that idea." I stepped down the stairs, leading into the hallway that was next to the dining room and kitchen. The wonderful smells of garlic and onion drifted through the air, and I got annoyed with myself for noticing. It wasn't like this was a warm and fuzzy homecoming I was entering into.

Walking into the kitchen, I spotted Braden grabbing a container out of the fridge, and Emily stirring something in a pot on the stove.

Preston cleared his throat, and Emily quickly spun around, wiping her hands on the nearest kitchen towel. She gave me a sympathetic smile and bit her lip as she waited for Braden to say something.

I took a seat at the far end of the table. I wanted to keep my distance.

"Rebekah, we never meant to cause you harm. We all apologize, but we all agreed that this was the best way...the only way to ensure our safety," Braden said. He glanced over to the counter, and I followed his gaze to Gavin's folder.

"Do you mind if I take that back?" I almost growled.

"Not at all. We've added it to the database," Braden said, completely unfazed.

"And what does that database do?" I questioned, getting up to grab the folder, but Preston brought it to me. "Thanks," I said, tucking the folder under my curled fingers.

"We've got database administrators working on finding leads from all of the oddities we collect."

I had the thumb drive in my pocket that showed all of the researchers. Had Preston already handed over those files somehow?

"We've got several teams working on the ambient computer data, where fragments of information often end up. Kind of like waking up information in the dead space of computers," Emily spoke up. "Our goal right now is to preserve, identify, and extract what information we can from families who have had loved ones killed by this new breed of zombies."

"Do those families know?" I asked, already knowing the answer.

"No. Most do not," Emily confirmed. "There's no reason for those people to trust us, and we can't jeopardize our operation."

"So you're already building this organization on secrets and lies," I said, realizing that my fingernails were digging into the dining table.

"Remember when you said that you hoped we'd be able to find someone who would be able to find the link between what Gavin and Sophie were researching?" Preston asked, his voice softening from earlier.

"The nuclear fusion stuff. Yeah. I remember."

"Well, these are those people. The network that has been established is the best shot we have at cracking the code," he replied.

"You hope," I said, raising my brow.

"Yeah. You're right, Rebekah. I hope that we can find out the connection before it's too late. Before more people are killed," Preston said flatly. "What's going on here takes more than just one mind."

"As much as I believe in technology, I also don't trust it. My gut tells me the answers we're looking for will only be found in person, somehow," I said. "Not just burying ourselves in data."

"We've got a map of that MHA facility that Preston drove you by. One of our TRAC members was stationed there a few weeks ago, and he mapped out the layout and got it to us. All of the security personnel are rotated every two weeks from whatever job they're stationed at. Marcus obviously doesn't want anyone getting too comfortable, seeing too much," Braden said.

"Then that confirms my suspicion. Why else would Marcus worry about keeping his teams on the move. He doesn't want any of them staying around long enough to stumble upon anything. That's my guess," I said.

"We think you're possibly right about that," Preston confirmed, glancing at Braden.

"Our hope is that nothing more than getting help to the folks who need it within those walls is what's being focused on at MHA," Emily said. "But our informant couldn't confirm or deny anything inside of those walls. Every hallway was as silent as a ghost town. The patients' rooms were all secured and every window was blacked out. There was medical staff on each floor, but he never saw them attending to patients."

"Are you saying they're not treating patients?" I asked.

"We're saying we're not sure there are any patients," Emily said, her eyes dipping to her hands as she fought back tears. "But there is activity. Buses do go there. Shipments are received."

"Then what would they have done with all those people?" I asked, angry as I thought back to all of the people who needed help, counted on getting help, through the MHA. Family and friends thinking they're helping loved ones only to never hear from them again.

Emily walked over to the stove and turned off the burner. She grabbed the top plate and began scooping up a noodle dish of some sort.

"So we need to go in," I said, leaning back in the

chair. I pushed Gavin's files away, clearing a spot for the plate.

I caught a shadow of a smile on Preston's lips as he helped himself to the dinner.

"It sounds like you're coming around to our side," Braden said, laughing.

Emily placed a plate of steaming pasta in front of me, and it smelled delicious.

"Or you're coming around to mine," I said, twirling my fork in the noodles. "Now when can we get started on a preliminary run?

"We've got some reconnaissance we can share with you from images we took using a homemade drone. We thought it might be nice to get a bird's-eye view of the grounds, in addition to the map our guy managed to draw out, so you can familiarize yourselves with the buildings you want to stake out."

Emily sat down at the table with her plate of pasta and looked over at me. "I've been able to capture a vague timeline of their activities, which we can use to get you in and out as quickly and safely as possible."

"We'll do a run-through beforehand," Preston said.

"Alright. When do we want to start?" I asked.

"Tomorrow," Preston said, "before the next rotation of security is implemented. TRAC will change out the new security personnel two days from tomorrow."

"Better get on it," I mumbled. "We'll look at the footage after dinner?"

Emily nodded.

I looked around the table at Emily, Braden, and Preston and wondered if what we were planning was a death wish, or if we'd actually find any answers. And if we did, what would we do with them?

CHAPTER NINETEEN

Preston flipped on the lights to the basement, and I followed him down the stairs. A light flickered overhead, and I held onto the railing as I walked behind him, matching his quickened pace. It was damp feeling and hard to see much in front of Preston. It was only a little after six o'clock in the morning, but I was wired.

"You have a nice little arsenal at your home," Preston said. "But this is an entirely different level."

We reached the bottom of the stairs where we both stood in a little four-by-six room with a metal door directly in front of us. Preston pressed a code into the keypad and the door clicked open.

"Shouldn't I be privy to that information?" I asked.

"Not until I'm sure you don't want to shoot me," he laughed.

"Very funny," I said wryly. "After a good night's sleep of nearly four hours, I actually understand why you did what you did. I don't approve of it, but I understand."

Preston pushed the door open the rest of the way, and an overhead light switched on, revealing a weapons room that looked as if it belonged to a SWAT team or, maybe more fitting, a TRAC team.

"You already have your Glock 17 with you so I think you should take that too," he pointed at a compact pistol hanging on the wall among many larger handguns. It was like Toys-R-Us for gun enthusiasts. I grabbed it off the wall and ensured it wasn't loaded, showing Preston the empty chamber.

"It's a CZ 75 Compact SDP. Good backup gun for you," he said, as he grabbed himself a pistol and examined it before placing it on the counter in front of us. "Let's just hope none of us will need to use it today, considering we're only scouting out the place."

"No kidding," I said, grabbing a case of ammunition. "What do you think we'll find?" I began sliding the bullets into the magazine and watched Preston as he did the same. He was wearing all black, including a knit cap, and his stance was assured as he handled the weapon. The way his hands worked along the metal caught my attention, and I didn't want to look away.

"At this point, I'm not even sure. It's not like I think we'll go into this facility and have an epiphany about what TRAC's up to, but I'm hoping there'll be some sort of clue that might point us in the right direction." He caught my gaze as I continued to watch him and I blushed. A slight twitch of his lip as he fought a smile only made it worse. "You?"

"Same. I guess I'm making it more personal. I'm hoping I'll see something that will relate to what

Gavin was researching or…" I stopped and shrugged. "I don't know."

He nodded and slid two clips of ammo into his back pocket and I did the same. "If everything goes well today, we'll be in there tomorrow, and maybe, we'll start to get some answers."

I bit my lip and tried to round up my courage. It wasn't necessarily my business, but I had a concern. I wasn't sure how to bring it up so I decided to be direct.

"Is there a chance your mom's in this facility, Preston?" I asked.

His gaze darkened and he shook his head. "I honestly have no idea. I guess there's always a possibility of that, no matter how slim. There are hundreds of facilities across the country, and they don't always keep the patient in-state."

"Sorry for asking. I just wasn't sure what the odds were."

He shrugged and began walking toward the exit. "I don't really even know."

We closed the door and marched up the stairs.

"How about that code now?" I teased.

"99275," Preston muttered. "And then asterisk after you enter the number."

I was completely shocked he gave the code to me. I wasn't expecting it at all. Maybe I caught him off-guard.

"Thanks."

Braden and Emily were already in the hallway waiting, holding a cup of coffee for each of us.

"Appreciate it," Preston said, grabbing the cup and taking a sip.

"Yeah. Thanks," I said, taking the cup from Emily.

"Everything all sorted?" Emily asked.

"I think as much as it can be. I have everything memorized based on what you showed us last night, but we won't know until we actually get past the fence tomorrow," I confessed. "I hope it's all still accurate."

According to the map, the compound didn't just have the guard towers in the corners. The structures were also centered in the middle of the property so they weren't as easily spotted from the road. Why an MHA facility would need so much security was also cause for alarm. Our plan was to park within three miles on the backside of the facility and hike in the remaining distance. The walls were far too high to scale, and their informant was fairly certain that the top had some sort of invisible electrical fencing as well. He mentioned he had seen several crows perish instantly whenever one was brave enough to land on top of the wall. That was enough evidence for me.

"There's one other thing," Braden said, turning toward me outside.

"What's that?" I asked, an uneasy feeling spreading through me.

"We need to take the self-driver," Braden said, pressing his lips together. "It's quiet and can glide over surface streets that might be destroyed and last we checked that road was horrible," he finished before I could object.

"If there was another way…" Emily's voice trailed off.

"I understand," I muttered. I would have to face my fears eventually. Why not today?

Braden placed his thumbprint on the key and spoke softly. "Engage."

My stomach began twisting in knots as I watched

the black car turn the corner from the side of the house and pull up in front of us. They were right. Silence was even louder than these vehicles. They were a great invention. As long as they didn't fail. As long as humans could override them.

Preston opened the back door and motioned for me to climb in. My stomach was to my knees as I slid across the backseat and watched him climb in. Emily was in the front passenger seat and Braden fell into the driver's seat.

I watched as his fingers hastily programmed the vehicle and the dashboard lit up. I looked away and clenched my eyes shut as the images of Gavin and me came crashing down. The terror, blood, desperation—all the memories pummeling into me at once were almost more than I could bear.

Preston reached over and grabbed my hand, lightly squeezing it. I looked over at him and gave him a grateful smile. Regardless of what I found out last night about how he got me here, I still appreciated him and these small gestures. The car began gliding down the driveway, and I watched the scenery go by at a rapid pace. At this rate we'd be there in no time. That was another feature these self-drivers offered, speed.

"Everything we need is in the trunk," Emily said. "Braden put it in last night. I know none of us want to stick around this place longer than we have to, but I just wanted to mention it again. As for tomorrow, we'll be on the outside waiting for you to emerge so we have to ensure the pick-up place is decided upon today. We can't veer from it."

"The acreage around the property is far too vast and wild," Braden confirmed. "That could be one of our downfalls, no doubt."

"Sounds good to me," I said, happy to have a distraction. "Maybe we should make the extraction point the same as the entrance?"

"That might be risky," Braden said. "If anything goes wrong on the way in or you leave a trace that you didn't know about…"

"Yeah. You're right," I agreed, as the car turned off the main road. "We're not almost there, are we?"

"Pretty close," Emily said, glancing at the screen on the dashboard showing approximate mileage to destination.

"Wow. It took us like thirty minutes from the MHA facility to your house in the old truck," I said.

"This car could've easily shaved off ten minutes," Emily agreed, nodding as Braden pulled over on the side of the road.

"This is it," he said, pressing the button that put the car to sleep.

The towering conifers dwarfed our vehicle. The early morning light was barely trickling though the trees, not to mention the overcast skies blocked out most of the rays. The large boulders, sprays of sword ferns, and slippery moss were part of the landscape that made the Cascade forests absolutely beautiful, but it also made them absolutely treacherous. I got out of the car and stretched briefly, feeling the soreness along my back. The skin had been healing fairly well, but it was still quite painful at times and with certain movements. I wasn't really sure how that was going to work with what we were facing in the days ahead, but I didn't have the luxury of time on my side.

"It looks like there's an incline on this side?" I

asked.

Braden was handing cables and bags to us from the trunk when he nodded. "Yeah. This is the more hidden side from the towers, but it's also far more dangerous to scale."

"Of course," I laughed.

"You're not afraid of heights, are you?" Preston asked, a smirk appearing.

"You're asking me that now?" I laughed, looping the rope over my shoulder.

"There's a small bridge across a deep ravine with a creek at the bottom that we need to get over," Preston said.

The more Preston spoke, the more I realized that if we needed to get out of any situation quickly tomorrow, our chances weren't very good for surviving.

"We've got everything," Braden said, as the trunk closed softly by itself. "We don't want to slow ourselves down too much, but we also don't want to be reckless. If you need more time, let us know."

I nodded as we began entering the forest. The pine needles created a slick surface for our feet, and the deeper we plunged into the woods, the darker it became. The temperature dropped and the terrain became steeper. Before long I found myself grabbing onto limbs to steady myself and holding onto the ferns' fronds so I didn't slide back down the hill. Every so often my palm would scrape along a Douglas fir's bark as I tried to balance myself, and I'd curse myself for not wearing gloves. Definitely not making that mistake tomorrow.

Everyone's breathing was becoming labored as we climbed up the hill, but I began seeing sprays of light through the conifers. We had to be getting close to the top or to where we needed to cross over. Braden stopped and switched his gear from one side to the other, and I allowed myself a breather. I'd always considered myself to be in good shape, but this forest was kicking my ass.

"Not too much longer," Emily whispered.

I nodded and began my ascent again, following Preston. His stride was unmatchable and so was his speed. His breathing had shifted slightly but nothing like the rest of us.

"Apparently someone was a lumberjack in their former life," I whispered.

Preston's body shook as he held in his laughter, and I watched Braden come to a stop. I was hoping this was as far as we needed to go. Emily grabbed a spray can and marked a tree in hot pink.

"We'll take a look at things as we make our way across the bridge. We might do better spotting which tree would be the best for hanging the cable."

Just as he mentioned cable, my heart rate shot through the trees. The idea of sliding down a cable and over a possibly electrified fencing was horrifying, but it had to be done. It was doubtful we'd get this much support trying to sneak into any other MHA facility and the idea seemed plausible.

Successful? Not so sure.

I spotted the bridge ahead that looked more like a bandage than a safe place to cross and wondered when the last time someone stood on it might have been. It was probably best not to think about it.

Braden got to the bridge first and gingerly put one foot on the slick wood, tapping it lightly. When nothing fell off or creaked, he placed his other foot on it and it held his weight. He nodded and swiftly ran across, all of us holding our breath until he made it to the other side. Emily went next. Preston gently nudged me forward, and I took a deep breath before looking down. There would be no surviving a fall from this height, not to mention crashing against the boulders on the way down.

"You got it, Rebekah," Preston said, his voice low, encouraging.

I looked down at the dull wood strips and heard the gurgling of the water below. The thought of Frank crumpling to his death as I was perched from the same height, sprinted through my mind. When would these thoughts quit paralyzing me? My pulse was racing and as if sensing I wasn't going to budge, Preston gently pressed his hand on the small of my back and nudged me forward. I looked up to see Emily and Braden watching me on the other side and raced to meet them.

"Nice," Emily whispered, as Braden took stock of the conifers ahead.

I turned and watched Preston dash over the bridge. I got the sudden urge to hug him and did. I unlocked my arms from his neck as quickly as I had secured them and took a step back unsure of what just came over me.

"I think this one ought to work," Braden said, pointing at a large fir tree in front of us. "It lines up with that big tree across the fence."

It was difficult to see the entirety of the fence from our vantage point, but the trees did look to be perfectly lined up, and the distance not too far from the fence. My only question was how we were going to get out, considering we would be sliding down the cable once it was fastened across the way.

"I'm gonna scale the tree and secure the cable. When you guys come tomorrow, Preston is going to have to swing the other end over to that tree across the way, but I think it's manageable," Braden said, looking at Preston.

"Yeah, with a weighted end, it should be fine," Preston agreed.

"Just make sure the hook goes around and latches on the cable," Braden said, staring at Preston who nodded.

Braden grabbed the bag from Emily and the rope from me. He adjusted a quick loop around his waist as he walked over to the tree and began scaling the tree like he'd done it a million times before. Maybe he had. It didn't take long before I couldn't see him in between the branches, and the thought occurred to me that Preston would be up there tomorrow. I didn't like that idea. I wanted him on the ground with me.

"It'll take him a few more minutes, but you think you've got everything under control for tomorrow?" she asked, pointing in between the trees toward the compound.

"As much as we can," I said.

"Let's get back across the bridge. A group of us standing and staring, probably isn't the best idea," Preston said.

With the amount of brush surrounding the area, it would be surprising if anyone would be able to spot us from down below or up above, but he was right. Why risk it?

We made our way back across the bridge and this time, I had no near-death experience. We made our way down the hill, and Preston leaned up against one of the large conifers. Emily and I could still see Braden's tree but we were no longer exposed.

"I think he's coming down," Emily whispered.

I glanced up and saw a few of the branches bow and wiggle as he climbed back down the tree. Hopping off from about six feet up, he landed on his feet and made his way toward us. Emily waved and Braden smiled as he hit the bridge.

"Hey, this is protected federal property. You can't come hiking around here," a guard hollered out of the silence.

"Is it target practice time?" Another guard yelled.

"I don't know. Maybe if we're lucky," the first guard answered.

They broke into laughter.

"Drop your bag and put both hands up and slowly turn to face us," the first guard hollered.

Braden was armed just as the rest of us were. He could take them both out. Why wasn't he doing anything?

"I said, turn around," the man hollered again.

Preston stood deathly still against the tree as Emily and I saw Braden drop his bag over the bridge and slowly turn to face the guards.

"Now, what are you doing here?"

"Just wandering and getting in touch with nature," Braden said, flippantly.

They didn't respond.

"What about you? What makes two rent-a-cops feel the need to wander away from their post?" Braden asked and my heart stopped.

Why was he antagonizing them?

"A regular smart ass, huh?" the second guard laughed. "I don't think the world will miss him, do you?"

"Nah. I know I won't."

Emily's eyes were wide as we watched the TRAC security guard draw his gun and steady it on Braden. I reached for my pistol, but Emily wrapped her hand around my wrist, her nails digging into me. I glanced at her and she shook her head at me. She stopped me.

"Now I won't have to go to the range," the man laughed.

I took a deep breath in as the shot rang through the air, and we watched Braden's body tumble off the bridge into the ravine below. The guards laughed and turned back to where they came from as if their latest kill was a possum in a tree.

I heard barely a grunt from Emily as she held in her screams, and her body leaned into mine.

CHAPTER TWENTY

Preston caught Emily before she hit the ground. Her senses were on overload, and there was no way she'd make it back down to our car. Preston picked her up and carefully navigated down the slippery slope and I followed closely behind. Emily's eyes were shut, her head bouncing gently against Preston's chest, and only a stifled groan every so often would leave her otherwise expressionless face.

I didn't want to make the situation worse or sound like a cold, callous bitch, but I wondered if Braden had the only key for the car. If he did we'd be in a world of hurt.

When we emerged from the thick forest, our car was exactly where we left it, and Emily's eyes slowly peeled open. Even though tears hadn't fallen, her eyes were rimmed in pink and swollen.

"I'm going to put you down so we can get you in the car," Preston said quietly, and her eyes stared into nothingness as she nodded.

Her left hand moved into her front pocket and she slid a key out, handing it to Preston.

"I can't drive," she mumbled, leaning against the car. "I'll program you in as a driver."

I climbed in the back while the two of them worked on getting Preston loaded into the system. I leaned my head against the window and glanced toward the forest. If this happened during our run-through, I couldn't imagine what might go wrong tomorrow.

Preston spun the car in a U-turn and we were off. Emily looked out the side window, her lips white from pressing them together so tightly.

"I didn't see a bullet actually hit him," she whispered. "I think he jumped, spun to make it look like he was hit."

I hadn't actually seen the bullet hit him either, but I wouldn't expect him to just jump. That was certain death as much as the bullet.

Preston's gaze caught mine in the rearview, and I knew what he was thinking. He wanted to make sure Braden wasn't stuck on some boulder, injured. I gave him a slight nod in agreement. I wasn't sure how we'd manage, but it seemed like the right thing to do.

We pulled down the long driveway and Emily sniffed. I watched her wipe away the first of many tears. Preston stopped the car in front of the entry, and Emily and I both got out of the car.

I wrapped my arm around her shoulders and helped her to the door, her weight mostly positioned on me. She opened the door and handed me the keys.

"I won't be needing these," she mumbled.

"What do you mean?" I asked.

Tears began streaming down her face and I just

hugged her.

"I can't do this. I'm not strong. I only managed because Braden was in charge of everything," she sobbed into my shoulder.

"You are strong. The way you stood on that hill…"

She broke free from my embrace and shook her head. "I can't. I'll be leaving in the morning after I let everyone know. I'd only put you and the operation at risk."

What was she talking about? We needed her on the outside.

Preston came in through the front door and his gaze went from me to Emily. Their eyes connected and he nodded. "I'll let everyone know," he muttered.

She spun around and bolted out of the foyer.

"Why won't she stay?" I asked.

"Her heart was never in it like Braden's. To ask her to continue would be unfair," Preston said quietly.

I looked into his eyes and craved the comfort he offered. I never expected things to go so terribly wrong, obviously none of us did, but the thought of moving forward was terrifying.

"Do you think there's really a chance that he's…" I couldn't finish my sentence.

"Not really and the longer we wait, the less likely, but I think we need to make sure. Our entry was planned for dark, before sun-up. I think it won't add much time to do a quick sweep of the ravine…"

I didn't like this idea, but as I looked into his eyes I understood what he was saying before. This was his family, and now they were being plucked off too. I slid my arms around his waist, and he took a step forward, bringing our bodies together. His hand slowly slipped along my waist and he let out a sigh, as his head lowered, and he pressed his forehead against mine. He closed his eyes and so did I as his arms completely encircled my waist. I hadn't been held in so long, not like this, that the sensations that pulsed through me were unfamiliar but comforting.

"I should go start sending the emails," he whispered, the warmth of his breath running along my face as he spoke.

I slowly nodded as he broke free. The moment our bodies unhinged themselves, I felt alone—utterly alone. I used to desire that feeling of loneliness to remind me of what I was fighting for, who I was fighting for. I positioned myself in life to ensure that the sensation of loss would never leave so I could use it as fuel to accomplish what I wanted. But as I stood here, yearning to be held, I realized I had been situating myself to become stagnant in life, unable to grow and respond to the continually changing afterworld. I needed to participate in life again, whatever that incorporated at this point, because I honestly didn't know.

"Is there anything I can help with? Should I let her know that we're going to check on—" I began.

"No," he interrupted, shaking his head. "There's no point."

He just wanted confirmation for himself.

I heard footsteps upstairs and a few doors opened and closed, followed by muffled sobs. My heart ached for her as I thought about the moments, days, and weeks after Gavin's death. I cried that moment he was taken from me. But then the tears stopped. They wouldn't come no matter how hard I tried to pull them out. Instead, I shut down and focused on one thing.

Revenge.

"Maybe it would be better for Emily if she focused on seeking revenge. Channel her sorrow toward something productive," I offered.

Preston's gaze held mine. "Do you think that's the best way to go? Push away the grief? Fool yourself into thinking you've dealt with it?" he asked softly.

"It worked for me."

"Did it?" his brow arched.

"I'm functional. I'm not sure by tomorrow she will be. She doesn't understand that she needs something to throw herself into."

Preston grabbed my hand, and I felt a flutter of warmth run up my arm from his touch. "You don't understand your own strength. Not everyone can do what you do. I'm telling you, you're stronger than you give yourself credit for. It isn't just rage and anger fueling you. Emily isn't the anomaly. You are." He let go of my hand, and I dropped my gaze from his.

The meaning of his words slowly dug into me. Maybe he was right.

"Does she have anywhere to go? Anyone to go to?" I asked.

"Her sister, Isabelle, is alive…lives in Idaho somewhere. She'll be happy to have her. I know there was some sort of disagreement between them when Emily joined Braden on this hunt. Isabelle didn't understand why she was throwing herself into the mess, as she put it."

"How will she manage living there if her sister thinks she was crazy for leaving in the first place?"

Preston shrugged. "Hopefully, Isabelle will respect Emily's loss and keep her mouth shut."

I thought back to what it was like when my family was alive and found it unlikely.

"Okay. Well, I'm going to go check on her. See if there's anything I can help with."

"I'll be down in the basement if you need anything. Just remember, you two are very different. What might be right for you might not be for her," he said.

I nodded and watched him walk away. My heart ached at the thought of him being the one stuck on the bridge. I didn't think I could handle it twice.

***

We were already halfway up the hill, and I wasn't as out of breath as yesterday. Or would it still be today since we were back here in the middle of the night? Regardless, I was always amazed at how speedily the body adapted. Preston had rope looped over his shoulder, which he was going to use to rappel down to see if he could spot any sign of Braden. I wasn't happy with the idea, but I understood.

The quiet of the woods at this time of night, lent itself perfectly to the task at hand. Hearing only the softened hoot of a Great Horned owl or the squeak of a brown bat gave me a misguided sense of security. Every so often, I'd witness a bat darting from Douglas fir to Douglas fir or swooping in front of us in the pursuit of moths or other unsuspecting winged insects.

There was resilience within the woods and wildlife that surrounded most of the urban cities in the northwest. I only hoped that resilience would apply itself to the humans as well. What worried me was that the purely evil intent that drove many humans to make choices wasn't a part of the natural order. The only repeated cycle in nature was based on survival. There weren't evil instincts in the wild that shifted that balance like there was among humans and that worried me.

I spotted the tree that we were standing at when we witnessed Braden's fall, and my heart started pounding. Following Preston toward the bridge, I became very unsettled and agitated as I watched him attach the harness and loop the rope around the trunk of the nearest tree.

"I'm not going to flip my headlamp on until I get down deep enough," he whispered, crouching near the bridge.

I wanted to speak, but I couldn't. Instead, I only nodded and kneeled down, touching his cheek lightly. He looked up at me and the moonlight caught his blue eyes, making them appear more vivid than usual.

"I'll be right back," he whispered and pushed himself down the rugged terrain.

I slowly crawled over to the edge and saw nothing but darkness below. Finally a tiny light flipped on. I watched it flicker through the rocks and then no longer saw it. I had no idea how far down he was. I heard the water sloshing below, but I couldn't gauge the distance. My pulse raced while I remained stranded at the top, unsure of how long Preston would be down there investigating. The sounds of something plopping into the water heightened my senses, and my hands got clammy. It sounded like a large piece of rock or...

Without warning, I saw the flash of his light as he worked his way back up the crevice and then it extinguished. The sound of his boots grinding into the stone was hurried as he climbed back up. When he reached the top, he was completely breathless.

"He's alive," he whispered, grabbing the second length of rope we'd brought.

"Seriously."

"It's bad and I'm not sure what I'm going to have to do to haul him up…"

"It's all we can do. Just get him up here and we'll figure it out," I muttered, as Preston placed the other harness around his shoulder.

"Exactly my thoughts," Preston replied, as he rappelled down the boulder into the crevice.

"Let's just hope Emily's still at the house," I whispered to myself.

Preston's headlamp clicked on again, and I kept my eyes on that light until he vanished beneath the boulders once more. With every heartbeat, I patiently waited and counted for his return. After several minutes the patience I was holding onto was traded for exasperation at the situation. We were so exposed. I had no idea how we'd get him down the hill to the car, but I couldn't become paralyzed by getting ahead of myself. One step at a time.

I heard the sound of rustling and a few muffled groans before relief spread through me as I watched the tiny light grow as Preston worked his way back up the crevice. He flipped it off about ten feet below me, and he worked his way back up the last bit as Braden's body hung almost lifeless, only the bouncing shadows giving me the information I so desperately wanted.

"I've got him," Preston said, his voice almost inaudible. "He's harnessed to me from behind at the waist and shoulders. I can crawl up, but I've got to have a big space to heave my body over the rock."

I moved back about twenty paces and watched as Preston's head and shoulders came into view. The rope was pulled taunt, and my concern was that it wouldn't hold the weight of both of them. Preston's fingers worked quickly as he pressed himself against the rock, throwing himself over the last berm and wiggling both of them to safety. Preston crawled slowly away from the edge to ensure neither of them slipped backward and I ran over to him.

"I think I might as well keep him tied on my back while we make it down the hill."

I nodded and held out my hands in case Preston needed something else to grab onto. He stood on his knees and then threw one foot in front of him and lunged into a standing position.

"Ready?" he asked.

"I am," I said, and walked behind Preston as we carefully made our way down the slippery terrain. Every now and then my breath would catch as Preston slipped down a portion of the hill, or when he got caught up on a root. But we made it down, safely.

Preston opened the backdoor of the car and began hastily untying the rope around his body that anchored Braden to him. Braden's arms were plopped over Preston's shoulders, but I doubted they held any strength. When Preston finished untying the ropes, he slowly turned around as if he was planning on getting into the car.

"Go around to the other side and try to work him in carefully, lying him across the seat."

"Right," I said, running around to the other side.

Braden's back came toward me as Preston

carefully sat backward into the car. I grabbed under his arms and hauled him toward me as Preston began pushing on him.

We got him secured, and I hopped in the front passenger seat. I turned to look at Braden. His eyes remained closed, and his cheek was swollen but other than that his external injuries weren't horrible looking. Unfortunately, it was the internal ones that had Preston and me concerned.

The ride back home felt far longer than it ever had. When we turned down the drive, I felt Preston step on the accelerator just to close the gap even faster. Once the home came into view, my nerves finally began to calm. The front door opened slowly, allowing light to escape onto the porch. Emily stepped outside and glanced in our direction. Preston pulled the car to an abrupt stop and Braden groaned, which I took as a good sign. I opened the car door and ran to Emily with Preston right behind me.

"What are you doing back so quickly?" she asked, dropping her bags on the porch.

"He's alive," Preston said, hugging her.

Emily began crying and pounding Preston's chest. "You're lying. You're lying."

"We're not, hun. Can you go inside and call the doc?" he asked. "We'll bring him right in."

Emily's eyes were completely glazed as the shock of what Preston said settled over her. Rather than running to the car, she did as she was instructed, and I realized Preston was right. We were very different. She took commands. I gave them.

I followed Preston to the car.

"You guys have a doctor you trust?" I asked.

He nodded, slowly opening the door, as he

positioned his hands to catch Braden before he fell out.

Preston anchored his hands underneath Braden's armpits and began pulling.

"Grab his ankles and we'll get him inside and up the stairs."

I caught his ankles right before they dropped to the ground from the seat and followed Preston as he walked backward toward the house.

"We aren't planning to go back tonight, right?" I asked, unsure how many more adrenaline surges I could take.

"We have no choice," Preston muttered, climbing the front stairs carefully since he was unable to see where he was going.

"Doorway," I said, as he made his way through.

"The doctor will take care of him as best he can. There's no point in us delaying what needs to be done," Preston said, as he continued walking backward down the hall until we hit the staircase.

"No rest for the weary," I muttered, climbing the stairs slowly as the weight of Braden's body made my arm muscles ache.

"I don't buy for a second that you're weary. Wicked, maybe. But not weary," Preston said, smiling.

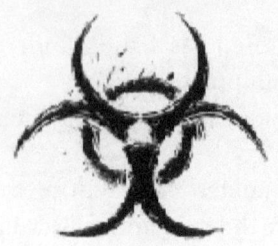

CHAPTER TWENTY-ONE

The air howled around me as my legs pounded against the solid ground. Grateful I was no longer on the rickety bridge or hanging from a spindly cable, I quickened my pace to catch up to Preston. Being on this side of the wall was the first battle we'd won and after the last week, I'd take any victory—small as it might be.

Even inside the fence, the compound was heavily treed, providing ample places to hide. The largest building was centered in the middle of the grounds with several outlying buildings that served many purposes. One was the barracks for TRAC members, another was for the medical staff, another building was the quarantine area, and the last building in the far corner was unidentified. All of the outlying buildings were made of concrete block, which was quite unusual for this region of the country, and all had red metal roofs. The only exception was the largest building, which acted as the main hospital. It was an old brick building from the twentieth century. Its exterior matched its age.

Preston stopped ahead, leaning against a cedar tree, and I quickly caught up to him.

"What do you say we check out the building we know nothing about first..." he stated more than asked. My heart was thumping inside my chest from the running, and I wasn't sure how well controlled my voice would be so I just nodded.

We snaked around the back of the buildings, the floodlights on the guard towers barely illuminating the ground underneath as the fog rolled in. Things were looking up. Preston slowed as he came to the end of the last building before our target. He held up his finger to his lip as I inched toward him. A girl's whimpering chilled my blood as I glanced at Preston. That must have been what slowed him to a standstill. He pointed in the direction where the eerie voice carried in the cool, damp air. It sounded like a young child but what would one be doing outside at this time of night in a place like this?

The sound of male laughter erupted next, and my fingers tingled with a desire to make something wrong right again. Preston slid along the wall, careful to step only on solid, clear ground, and I did the same. The whimpering continued steadily, but the laugher only erupted every so often. When Preston reached the corner of the building, he drew his knife out of his pocket, and I screwed my silencer on my pistol. It sounded like the group was only steps away from us. The girl's whimpering changed to a low hum, a chant possibly, as the men's laughter died down.

Preston curled his body around the building and I followed right on his heels. What I saw horrified me.

We were dealing with pure evil, and once more it was tied to TRAC.

In the shadows, I saw two men taunting a young girl who was tied to the trunk of a tree. Her blonde, gnarled hair hung in her face, and she was dressed in a hospital gown many sizes too large for her.

"You gonna try to sneak out again?" The man closest to Preston asked the girl.

She shook her head, her eyes meeting mine. And that was when Preston swiftly came up behind the guard, grabbed the man's head and sliced his neck, dropping him to his knees. The other guard spun around at the sound of the commotion and raised his pistol, pointing it directly at Preston. Without a moment's hesitation, I aimed squarely at the center of the guard's forehead and pulled the trigger, watching him collapse immediately.

"We have our way out of here," I whispered, as Preston ran to the little girl and began cutting through the ropes that tied her body to the tree.

I began peeling off the clothes from the guard directly in front of me before the material was completely blood-soaked.

Preston held the little girl as she stared at me quietly while I continued working on the next guard, stripping him almost bare.

"How old are you?" Preston asked the girl.

She turned to face him and raised her hands up, too frightened to speak. She flashed both hands in the air; all five fingers fully extended and then held up an additional finger immediately after. She was eleven. Attempting to hold my temper at bay, I began pulling the man back behind the building. The guards were dead but they deserved far worse. I heard Preston speaking something softly to the little girl, and then he appeared next to me behind the building, dragging the other guard.

"We can't make her go back in there," he said quietly. The girl was standing behind him, peering up at me.

I began tugging on the pants from the smallest guard and zipped them up, which left me in pants about three sizes too big. I hurriedly slipped his bulletproof vest and TRAC jacket over my arms and buttoned up. I grabbed the guard's helmet and buckled it just as Preston did the same.

"What do you expect us to do with her then?" I asked. It wasn't like we'd be able to let her tag along as we wandered around the grounds.

"I can stay here," she whispered. "Until you come back for me."

My eyes moved between the girl and Preston, and I let out a sigh. He took off his coat and handed it to the girl before slipping on the TRAC vest and jacket.

"Fine. But don't move, no matter what you hear," I told her. She looked relieved but did exactly as I said and took a seat on the ground, her back pressed against the concrete wall.

I glanced over at Preston and saw the softness in his eyes as he looked at the girl. She probably reminded him of his own sister when they were young. I got annoyed with myself, more specifically at my apparent lack of emotion. I was the female. Wasn't I supposed to be the one with the maternal instincts and warm and fuzzies inside?

"Let's get going," I said, nodding in the direction we needed to go.

"Good luck," the girl whispered.

I looked over my shoulder and saw her eyes fasten on us as we took off toward the concrete block building in the corner. With our luck, it was nothing more than a janitor supply closet or something. I glanced up toward the sky and saw the familiar inky shade begin to emerge. We were getting closer to sunrise and needed to hurry it up, whatever it was.

Just as I caught up to Preston, I heard a twig snap behind me and spun around, my pistol locked in front of me.

It was a bunny.

Preston picked the lock in front of us and pushed the door open slowly. The room was almost completely empty. White tile covered the floor, and two stainless steel tables were pushed along the wall to our right, but that was it. I closed the door behind us as Preston moved carefully and quietly to the grey metal door at the end of the room. His hand rested on the door handle until I got right behind him.

"It's unlocked," he whispered. "Ready?"

"I am."

He opened the door and it led into another sterile room, but this one had computer equipment lined up against the wall to our left on the floor, and there were monitors plastered on the wall. None of them were turned on. There was yet another door at the far end of the room, and I was beginning to feel that it would reveal just as little as the other two. I walked by Preston and placed my hand on the handle. It was unlocked. He came up behind me as I opened it. This time we weren't met with another room but with metal stairs leading underground.

There was a narrow tunnel that I could barely make out at the bottom of the stairs. I looked back at

Preston who pushed me to move forward, to the unknown. I took a deep breath and began the descent. The air immediately changed once I reached the bottom. Cold air surrounded me as I looked into the tunnel that had been carved out of the earth. Neither of us would be turning on lights for the simple fact that we didn't know what was down at the other end of the tunnel. We didn't want to risk showing ourselves or alerting anyone to our presence.

My heart hammered with every step forward. I had never felt claustrophobic before and had always thought that would be a terrible fate to encounter. But with each step deeper into the darkness, it felt as if the walls were closing in on me from all sides—top, bottom, left, and right. I imagined my world shrinking, threatening to crush me. My palms moistened as I tried to steady my breaths. Preston's footsteps were right behind me, but it didn't help.

I just wanted out.

I wanted out.

I needed out.

My breathing changed, and I flipped around, running smack into Preston.

I had probably only made it ten feet into the tunnel and it was ten feet too far. I wanted to get back to the girl and the fresh air.

"Whoa," his voice low, rumbly. "You're okay."

He slipped his hands over my shoulders, slowly turning me back to face my fears. The fears I never knew I had.

"I don't think I can do this," I whispered.

"You can, Rebekah. You must. There's no turning back."

There was something about the way he directed

me that gave me the assurance I needed, the confidence that we were in this together. Whatever we found at the other end of this passageway was our problem to face.

The tunnel remained the same in diameter all the way through, but it felt as if it were shrinking with every foot we delved deeper into the abyss. There was absolute silence as we continued the trek down the tunnel, only our muffled steps sounded as we moved forward, deeper into unfamiliar territory. I concentrated on how the silence reminded me of when the snow would first fall, coating and insulating all the surfaces, deadening noise immediately.

Something grazed the top of my head and I stopped abruptly, looking up into the shadows. The squeaking of metal echoed into the cavern. Preston reached up and stopped the object from swinging back and forth. It was a lantern.

We both remained still to ensure that we didn't alert anyone to our presence. Only silence greeted us. When I felt safe, I slowly walked forward, more alert to any dangling lanterns that might be ahead.

Preston's hand tapped my shoulder slowly and I stopped. Something caught his eye in front of us and now I needed to find out what. I slowly ducked to see if I could catch what it was he noticed. A faint flicker caught my eye about ten feet ahead. It was on the ground, tucked where the dirt wall met the dirt floor.

"Think it might be a sensor," he whispered, his lips against my ear. "Step over it."

I nodded and began moving forward again, this time my heart pounded more with each step. Was there finally someone to alert at the other end of the tunnel? I moved slowly and stopped just short of the flickering light, the size of a pencil eraser. Raising my leg I hopped over the mini beam of light and took a few steps forward to steady myself. Preston jumped, landing right next to me.

The tunnel turned slightly to the right. There were three equally spaced lanterns with green bulbs fastened to the dirt wall, slightly glowing, and directly ahead of us, another metal door.

I looked over my shoulder at Preston who glanced up at the lanterns and then over at the door. He took a deep breath in and placed his hand on my shoulder, gesturing that he wanted to go ahead of me.

I stepped toward the side of the tunnel, pressing my body against the wall to allow Preston to move by me. His body brushed against mine, and I squeezed closer to the dirt wall, feeling pieces of the earth tumble along my body.

We were only ten feet away from the door, but it felt like so much more. We were pinning so much on what might be on the other side of it. Preston looked over his shoulder at me and grinned, removing his knife from the holster. We slowly walked over to the metal door, his hand moving to the silver handle. He moved it slowly. It was unlocked.

My pulse pounded in my ears, deadening my world even more as he slowly opened the door in front of us. A gasp escaped as I saw row after row of adult-sized incubators containing the undead. There was no one living inside the walls in front of us, but for once I wasn't frightened by the undead, only by the living who put them here.

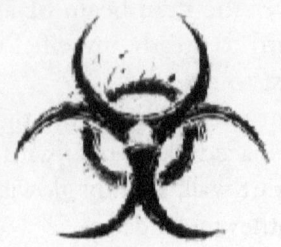

CHAPTER TWENTY-TWO

This was sick. The hair on the back of my neck stood up as I slowly walked down the rows where the undead resided in glass cases with solution surrounding their bodies, grey eyes wide open. Each being was housed in their own container, lying flat and nude. Their flesh was unmarked, carrying no signs of ever being outside this manipulated world. I maneuvered between the incubators, careful not to disrupt anything. I bent down to follow the tubing that was leading away from each of the glass containers. The tubing went down into grates in the flooring. I looked across the room and saw hundreds of clear tubes leading up from the floor roped along the wall going into a large, clear vessel. Bubbles continually pumped through the clear liquid, stirring the content before it was exchanged and rerouted back to the undead. I stood up and looked over at Preston. He was peering down at one container in particular several rows over from me.

"You okay?" I asked.

He glanced over at me and sucked on his lip as he thought about what to say. I watched his eyes wander from vessel to vessel as he became flooded with the same questions as me. How many? What for? Were they new? Why? They were all plastered on his face.

"My mind has been working on scenarios for months. Ever since Sophie was taken from me, my life has been dedicated to finding out why and how. I imagined all kinds of things but never this—never this…" his voice trailed off, and he began walking in the other direction, his fingers tabulating how many rows and how many vessels per row.

"These zombies are clean, new, just like the ones that attacked Gavin," I said quietly.

I wove through the rows toward a counter that wrapped along the wall, containing microscopes, slides, and papers. Whatever this place was, there had been recent activity. Glancing down at the piece of paper closest to me, I noticed some handwritten scribbles. There was a slide placed on the microscope so I stood on my toes and pressed my eyes against the eyepiece as I adjusted the magnification. I had no idea what I was looking at, possibly flesh, but why would they have left it here? I shuddered and took a step back. My movement shifted a couple of the papers and I saw something familiar, a set of the same equations and elements listed that Gavin had in his notes.

"Preston," I said softly. "Can you please come here?"

I watched him make his way over to me, his eyes scanning mine as he got closer.

"What's up?" he asked. I turned my attention to

the paper with the notes, and he followed my gaze. His fingers underlined the equations as he read aloud some of the notes. "These are almost verbatim to—"

"I know," I interrupted, turning around to watch the solution being pumped on the back wall. "What's the connection?"

"There definitely has to be one," he muttered, sifting through the other pages.

"Whenever researchers begin their research, they always know what it is that they are hoping to prove or disprove, even if it's subconscious. They don't go in blind. Gavin didn't go in blind. Someone had to be leading him down a certain trail."

"And this is just more of the same," Preston said shoving the rest of the papers aside. "But yeah. I think you're right. There's a reason there are so many researchers on the same path. We just have to come up with what it is."

"Whether these researchers know it or not, there is something inside of them guiding them to the answers they want to see—to the proof—that they want to believe exists… whether it does or not. But as we've seen there's always two sides to every discovery; two stories to tell with every new piece of information gathered." I sighed and shook my head.

Spotting an empty container, my eyes moved from Preston to one of the tubes. "I say we gather some of the fluid and get out of here before it's light out. Not to mention the extra baggage you have waiting for us outside."

"She's a girl, not baggage," he said, the tension in his jaw outlining his anger.

"Whatever," I said, reaching for the container. "A girl who will undoubtedly slow us down greatly as we try to leave this place."

Grabbing the container, I walked over to one of the incubators and bent down to see where the tube attached to the glass. I slid a lever over, which was located next to the tubing. I watched as the opening to the container was plugged, and I unclamped the fitting and allowed several inches of fluid to drain into my empty container. I put the container on the ground and clamped the tube back to its fitting and slid the lever into place, allowing the solution to continue flowing around the vessel once more. The finger of the undead creature twitched, and I flinched, falling back onto the tile floor.

"Did you see that?" I asked.

"The finger? Yeah. Hard to miss," Preston said, helping me up.

I grabbed the container and screwed the lid on tightly. There was a pile of bright white towels on the end of the counter and Preston tossed me one, which I used to wipe off the outside of the container in case anything was spilled. Since I had no idea what the solution was, it probably wasn't a good idea to touch it.

"Let's get out of here," I whispered.

"Gladly."

As we walked out of the room and back into the tunnel, exhilaration pumped through me as I thought about being one step closer to understanding what was happening—proving to myself I wasn't crazy. I knew what I saw that day, and now I had the proof. But that wouldn't be enough, not in the afterworld. This place could be shut down in a matter of hours and the bodies burned. In fact, the process could have already been started since it looked like everything was left in a hurry. My stomach clenched at the last thought, but I pushed through it. We definitely needed to pursue this more before going anywhere with the information.

I ran up the metal stairs, careful as I approached the door and wrapped my fingers around the metal handle, but my hand flew off it as soon as it touched the metal. It was hot!

"Shit," I said, flicking the pain away. "It's hot.

"What?" Preston said, but he heard me, pushing me aside as he tapped the handle. "Do you smell that?"

I took a deep breath in through my nose and realized it wasn't only the earthy, damp scent I had grown accustomed to—there was smoke.

"They knew we were here," I whispered, sliding down the dirt wall as the realization settled over me that flames now stood between us and our way out.

"Get up," Preston commanded, his voice harsh.

He was right.

"We can't stay down here. We'll suffocate…" I started coughing and raised the crook of my elbow to my nose to breath through my shirt.

"Well, we can't just run through the flames," Preston said.

"I've got an idea," I said, handing him the container and running back down the stairs. "Wait right there."

I ran through the tunnel at lightning speed. Funny how all the fears like claustrophobia magically vanish when one's life was actually on the line. Reaching the end of the tunnel, I threw open the door and beelined toward the stack of towels. There was no sink or any water source that I could find, but there was plenty of whatever that clear liquid was. I wrapped my arms around the huge pile of towels and ran toward the wall where all of the tubing ran into and out of the large glass container. I dumped the towels onto the floor and turned toward the tubing. Up close, the liquid that was running through the system didn't look so clear. There were tiny pieces of things floating around, flesh possibly. A small amount of bile rose up my throat, but I managed to force it down. We had two options burn to death peacefully or die fighting.

I reached up toward the first tube and yanked on it forcibly. The end flew out of the glass container, spraying the liquid onto the floor. Unsure of how toxic the substance was I clasped my fingers around the plastic and aimed the tube toward the pile of towels. I took a deep breath and tried to ignore that my hands were trembling as I placed my index finger under the clear liquid. It didn't burn. I brought my finger toward my nose and sniffed. It smelled like nothing. I tugged on one clear tube after another until the towels became completely saturated. I had no idea what the substance was that I was about to touch, but as I bent over and picked up the heavy load of towels, I no longer cared. This was possibly our only way out of the building. I ran as fast as I could back down the tunnel and started up the stairs when Preston met me halfway. I was exhausted and my arms burned, but I made it.

"Wrap these around your body, layer yourself as much as you can," I said, catching my breath as I picked up a wet towel and wrapped it around my waist.

Preston began around his leg. Wrapping a towel on each and then working his way up. We both looked like mummies and still had several wet towels lying on the floor.

"Now or never," he said, picking up the remaining towels and dividing them between us. We wrapped our heads, leaving only slits for eyes, and we ran up the stairs. His left hand had the index and thumb exposed so he could hold the container that held the solution—the same solution that was wrapped around our bodies.

This was it.

He placed one of the towels on the handle.

"Three, two, one," he said, tossing the door open.

The smoke was thick, but I didn't spot any flames. My eyes immediately began watering. As we both got on our hands and knees and began crawling, I knew this was too easy. If the flames weren't in this room, that meant they were in the next one. I followed him in a straight line and when we reached the door, I only felt more trepidation, knowing what had to be on the other side.

Preston stood on his knees and began coughing. He reworked and secured one of the towels over his mouth, but he still kept coughing.

"This is going to be bad," he yelled, but his voice was muffled.

I nodded as the stinging in my eyes became unbearable. I clenched them shut and fought the tickle that was deep within my lungs as I stood on all fours like a dog.

"Wait," I hollered, feeling coolness spread along my palms. "Do you feel that?"

He looked down at the same time I did and saw the water slowly leaking under the door.

"You can open the door," a small voice spoke

through the door.

"Slow us down, huh?" Preston laughed, standing up rapidly.

"I'm never afraid to admit when I'm wrong," I said, feeling the smile on my face shift the layers of wet cotton as he opened the door to reveal the little girl standing with a hose.

"I know you said to stay put, but I'm not stupid. I heard them evacuating the compound. There were buses everywhere, and then I saw the smoke coming from this building."

"For that I'm grateful," I said, unwrapping the towels from my head.

"Did you see anyone left?" I asked.

"There were two men standing in front of the building for awhile, but they took off in a black Escalade. One of the old ones," she replied.

"Marcus," Preston said, unwrapping the towels around his hands and arms.

The girl held out her hand to Preston, and he grabbed it as she led him through the front room and to the outside with me trailing right behind. I gulped the fresh air, but my lungs continued to burn and so did my eyes.

But we were out. We were alive. Two things I didn't think were going to happen, and I had an eleven-year old to thank.

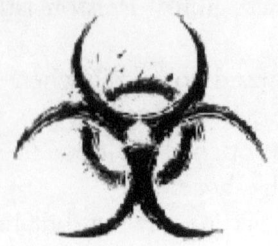

CHAPTER TWENTY-THREE

"Do we want to chance it?" I asked, glancing at the main building. "There could still be some TRAC left behind."

"When will we have the chance again?" he asked.

I glanced at the girl who was gripping Preston's hand as tight as she could and then returned my gaze back to Preston's.

"I don't know that hauling her through the halls up there is the best thing," I said.

"My name's Izzy," she said. "And I'm fine."

She reminded me of myself at that age and I smiled.

"I doubt there's anyone left in there anyway. The busses were packed," she continued. I saw her body tremble slightly. "I'm just glad I wasn't on the bus."

"That settles it then," Preston said. "We'll take a look at the building. And Izzy, will you hold this? Protect it?"

Her eyes fell to the container of clear liquid that he

held out to her.

"Like my life depends on it," she said.

"Izzy can point us in the right direction," I said, and her expression intensified with the new task that was given to her.

"I know all of the hideouts," she offered, slipping her hand from Preston's.

We slowly walked along the back fence. My eyes scanned for anything that might indicate there were still people here.

"Izzy, how did you end up here?" I asked.

She was more centered than most adults I knew who came through the outbreak.

"My sister, Beth, sent me here," she said, twisting her lips. "My parents died during the outbreak, and once we were vaccinated and no longer on the run, she didn't want anything to do with me so she turned me over."

"I'm so sorry," I muttered, catching Preston's expression harden. "I thought MHA's protocol was more in-depth than that."

She shrugged and pointed ahead to a door at the back of the main building. "We can enter that way; just in case there's anyone left inside. The patients were mostly shackled inside the rooms."

"Is that what they did to you?" I asked.

Izzy nodded and then stopped, spinning around to face me. She held out her wrists, exposing raw marks along the skin. "But I knew how to escape them."

My heart ached for this little girl.

"What can you tell us about the doctors and nurses? Were there any?" Preston questioned.

"There was one doctor and three nurses for eighty patients, but I'm not sure they were even real," she said, scrunching her nose.

"What do you mean?" I asked.

"I don't know. It's hard to explain. All they did was shove pills down our throats that made us sleepy. I always tried hide mine along my gum line and would spit them out when they left because I would fall asleep for what felt like days. And sometimes I saw the nurses taking the pills too," she said.

"What about the doctor?" I asked.

"I didn't see her take any pills. But she wasn't here that often. When she showed up, she just sat at the nurses' station and signed papers." She grabbed my hand and pulled me toward the building. Her fingers were cold, and I felt horrible for dragging this little girl back into the place that had treated her this way.

"There are stairs to the left that will take us all the way to the top floor," she said, standing in front of the door. I gently tugged on her hand and stepped to the side so Preston could go in front of us. Something told me this girl would run right in.

"We'll start at the top and work our way down," Preston said, opening the door.

The stairs were right where she said. We bolted over to them and began climbing as rapidly as we could manage, sometimes taking them two at a time. We hit a platform with the number two painted on the wall and then the next platform with three painted on the wall. Only two more floors.

We reached the fifth floor, and the door was already open. Preston held up his hand as he slowly moved along the wall. He craned his neck to the left and then to the right.

"Clear," he whispered, slowly walking through the door with Izzy and me following closely behind.

"This is where they took people who misbehaved," she whispered. I felt her little hand trembling in mine. She was obviously one of them. How many others could really be misbehaving if they were drugged though?

"They brought me here when they found the pills I'd spit out. After that, I got better at hiding them," she said quietly, looking up at me. I liked what I saw behind her expression, relentless determination.

The hallway was lined in white linoleum, and the walls were painted a stark white. I could see down the entire length of the building, with what looked like a nurses' station at the very end. But with only three nurses to cover five floors, I doubted any of them got much use. Did the MHA know about this? Were they involved or did Marcus have his TRAC team cover everything so well that MHA never had a clue?

We began walking down the corridor where the glass was blacked out just as our TRAC informant had described. All of the doors were open, however, so they must have hurriedly evacuated all of the patients. I had no idea why they bothered, really.

I popped my head into the first room and my stomach twisted in knots when I saw a reclining medical chair with restraints positioned in the center of the room. The tan leather seats were stained, and the restraints were worn down from use. I spotted a stainless steel instrument tray tucked in the corner. I started toward it, but Izzy wouldn't let go of my hand. I glanced at Preston over my shoulder and motioned for him to grab her other hand. I walked into the small room and glanced out the window, which overlooked the front of the building. It still looked vacant. I moved over to the tray, and a shiver marched up my spine as I saw two used scalpels, etched with a rust color and a pick.

I turned around slowly and my gaze caught something in the polished metal mirror—a person. My heart spiked and my hands tensed up as I watched the figure behind me, standing in a supply closet. Not wanting to make any sudden movements, I waited for Preston's gaze to meet mine. When he saw the expression on my face, he hastily moved Izzy down the hall. I heard him muttering something to her before he entered the room, pistol extended.

My heart was pounding with every step that Preston took. I had no idea who the person in the closet was or if he was armed. Preston was still out of the person's sightline as his eyes locked on mine and then shifted to the right.

I lunged to the left and rolled quickly, positioning myself so that I was now pointed at the closet. The figure didn't move and once Preston stepped aside, I saw why. The person was dangling from IV tubing wrapped around his neck. My gaze fell away as I stood up slowly.

Knowing I had been closer than I realized to being admitted to a place like this made my stomach turn.

"Let's move through this floor and get down to the next one," I muttered.

Preston nodded and waited for me to take the first step so he could shield me from continuing to want to look at the man who'd had enough.

The rest of the floor was, thankfully, uneventful. Floor four was a similar layout, but the rooms contained patient beds, equipped with restraints just as Izzy had told us. The rooms were bare and the smell just about more than I could handle. It was a stale, sour smell, and I didn't want to know why. We reached the nurses' station and I spotted two stacks of papers. I bet these were the ones Izzy was referring to. I glanced at the top copy of the nearest pile, and sure enough, there was a doctor's signature. The other pile must've been what he had left to sign off on. I perused through the records, most of the same terminology was listed from patient to patient.

Unspecified Disassociated Disorder

Assertiveness Training attended

Brief Reactive Psychosis

Traumatic Transference

Conversion Disorder

Delayed Memory Response

Adjunctive Therapies administered

"I somehow doubt anyone attended any sort of training," I muttered to myself as my eyes continued scanning the documents.

And then it hit me.

Dr. Joyce Falino

"Preston, what was Terrence's last name? Didn't it begin with an F?" I asked. He was working his way through drawers and turned to look at me.

"Falino," he said. "Why?"

"Because the doctor signing off on all of the records is Joyce Falino," I whispered.

"Whoa," he whistled.

"She was really pretty," Izzy said. "She had spikey red hair and was super skinny."

I grabbed Izzy's hand and motioned for Preston. It was time to move down to the next floor.

"This was my floor," Izzy whispered. "Floor three. I hate this floor almost as much as five."

I let her lead the way back down the stairs, but Preston jumped in front of us before she had a chance to open the door.

Floor three looked like floor four. Izzy hauled me down the hall and stopped in front of an open door. There was a mattress and restraints that were still buckled from Izzy slipping out of them.

"Nobody deserves this," Izzy said.

"You're right, honey," I whispered. "And we're going to make sure whoever's in charge is going to pay."

Preston was already looking through the nurses' station when we reached him.

"More of the same," he muttered. "I say we get out of here."

I nodded and felt Izzy's body relax.

"Do we dare go out the front?" I asked.

"Better than trying to crank ourselves back over the fence on the cable," Preston said.

We had brought two gadgets that were theoretically supposed to be able to winch us back over the cable, but we'd be sitting ducks for anyone as we dangled. And now that we had Izzy, I wasn't sure we'd be able to do it.

We ran down the stairs, only the echoes of our

footsteps bouncing against the walls.

"I find it funny how there are absolutely no computers in this building. Everything's handwritten? We've had electronic medical records for decades," I said.

"There are a lot of things that don't sit right about this place," Preston said, reaching the bottom of the steps.

He opened the door and the daylight sprayed inside. I squinted slightly as Izzy and I walked outside.

"We'll go along the backside of the buildings and cut over by the gate. I'll have you wait until I signal that it's clear. I don't know if they left two TRAC guards stationed at the entrance or not," Preston directed.

"My guess is no," I said, and Preston nodded.

We took off, darting behind trees and large laurels that had been planted between the administration buildings. Izzy was running as fast as her little legs could carry her, but I could tell she was slowing down. We made it to the last building, and Preston stopped, catching his breath.

"You should be able to see me from this spot. When I wave you over, that's when you and Izzy run as fast as you can but not a moment sooner," he said.

I nodded and looked over to the guard station. It looked empty, but the windows were so heavily tinted I couldn't be sure.

"Keep her safe," Preston told Izzy before his eyes connected with mine. A small smile surfaced on her otherwise expressionless face.

"She will," I said, grinning and he took off.

I watched him dart along the concrete wall and then toward a large cedar tree. He turned around and looked back at us before setting off for the guardhouse. My heart was in my throat as I watched him approach the guardhouse. He was running in a crouched position, pistol in hand. He snuck up to the back wall of the building and slid along the small structure. I saw him throw open the side door and held my breath as I waited for something—anything to confirm that we were alone.

A few seconds passed and then Preston stepped outside of the structure, waving us over. We didn't bother taking the route he did. We ran directly toward him, and when Izzy couldn't keep up, I scooped her up and kept going until I landed in Preston's arms.

"Now we just have to figure out how to get to the car," he said, laughing. His voice muffled by my hair as I held him tight.

CHAPTER TWENTY-FOUR

Emily was in the kitchen, rinsing out a mug when we walked in. The house was quiet except for the sound of the running water.

"Hey," I said softly. "What's the word?"

Emily spun around, her eyes ringed in red. She looked exhausted and still wore the same clothes from when we left.

"The doctor said he didn't believe in a higher power until he saw Braden's case." She crossed her arms. "I'm sure he was trying to make me feel better, but he failed."

Her eyes dipped to Izzy who was standing next to Preston.

"This is Izzy," I said, holding out my arm. Izzy walked over to me, and I placed my hand on her shoulder.

"Nice to meet you," she said extending her hand toward Emily.

The gesture managed to bring a smile to Emily's

lips, and she returned the handshake. "Nice to meet you. Would you like some cookies?"

Izzy nodded and found a seat at the table. She placed the container full of the solution on the table and waited quietly, analyzing her new surroundings.

"About Braden?" I continued.

"The doctor has him on morphine. He's upstairs sleeping. Apparently all of his Parkour training paid off," she attempted to smile. "Since he was the one who threw himself off the bridge, he had complete control over how and where he landed. He just misjudged how much his body could handle. The doctor says he won't be able to walk for a very long time."

The kitchen fell silent. Izzy glanced over at Preston and then down at the floor.

I walked over to Emily and gave her hug. "At least he's alive," she whispered, sniffing in. "I'm just so happy he's here."

"I know, and we'll all help in anyway we can," I said.

"Let's get you settled in a room," Preston told Izzy. I heard the chair slide against the wood floors, and their footsteps head toward the stairs.

"You smell like smoke," Emily said, wiping away her tears as she took a step back.

I laughed and shook my head. "Long story."

She grabbed a tissue and rubbed her nose before sitting down at the table. "So did you make it inside the compound?"

"We did." I quickly explained everything from the zombies in solution to the fire.

Her eyes were wide as she sat and listened.

Preston came into the kitchen and took a seat next

to me, sliding his hand to my knee. I placed mine on top and squeezed it.

"She's sleeping," he said.

"I forgot to get her cookies," Emily said, slapping her forehead.

"I think she'll forgive you. She needed sleep more anyway," I said.

"So you're telling me there was a basement full of undead?" she asked, rubbing her temples with her index fingers.

"Yeah. An underground tunnel led to a room with a very sophisticated setup. Even so, Marcus and his men didn't seem to mind if it was destroyed when they set the place on fire."

"True," Preston confirmed. "Which tells me they have others just like it."

"What did they look like?" Emily asked.

"They looked like brand-spanking new zombies," I said, nodding. "Like newly infected before activity takes a toll on their inability to regenerate."

"That's creepy." She shuddered.

"Do you think you'd be able to look up someone for us?" I asked. "I'd like to get out of these filthy clothes."

"Sure. Anything to keep me busy," she muttered.

"Joyce Falino is a doctor at the MHA Facility. Her last name matches someone who offed himself after we visited him."

"Falino? The gang member?" she asked, her brow arched. "I'll find out what I can." She got up from the chair and walked toward the family room, leaving Preston and I alone in the kitchen.

"What should we do about Izzy?" I asked, as Preston wrapped his arm around my shoulder. I leaned into him and enjoyed the security I felt being in his embrace.

"I was thinking about that," Preston said softly. I felt his breath skitter across my scalp and chills blasted through me. "Emily's sister in Idaho might be a good option. It's far enough away and she lives on a farm."

"But it didn't sound like Emily's sister thought much about everything, and this little girl has experienced more than—"

"Maybe it's Izzy's turn to be a young girl again," he interrupted. "Maybe getting to be with horses on a ranch and being far enough away from everything might help her."

"Yeah, maybe. We'll ask Emily about it. She certainly can't stay here," I replied, tapping his leg. I stretched and moved away from him. "Gotta go shower and then I'm gonna go crawl into bed before I fall over."

"Do you need any help?" Preston asked, his eyes glinting with mischief.

I laughed and shook my head even though my body was signaling something different.

"If I'm not up in a few hours wake me," I called, as I marched up the stairs.

"There's no saying I'll be up either," he laughed.

***

I had slept for over four hours and woke up feeling better than I had in a long time. It took a few moments before I oriented myself in the bedroom and shoved off the covers. I was only in a t-shirt and the cold got to me. I hopped out of bed and dressed in a pair of jeans and a sweatshirt. I quietly walked down the hall to check on Izzy. She was still asleep.

Preston's door was wide open and his bed was empty. Preston wasn't very good at following directions.

My mind drifted to everything we'd seen at the MHA facility. And then my thoughts drifted to Preston's mom. I couldn't imagine how he was coping with everything he saw. I walked down the stairs and heard Preston and Emily talking. It was a lighthearted conversation and one that I didn't feel like I was interrupting when I came into the kitchen.

Preston was leaning against the counter, freshly showered and his days of missed shaves a thing of the past. His lean body looked nice in the low hanging, faded jeans he wore and the fitted grey t-shirt that stretched across his chest. He looked pretty incredible for just going through everything we had. His eyes caught mine and I looked away, smiling. I'd been caught. Out of the corner of my eye, I saw him smirking as he watched me move toward the cabinet to grab a glass for some water.

"Emily called her sister, and she was more than willing to help out," Preston said.

"She even promised not to ask questions, which for her is a big thing," Emily said, stepping aside so I could grab a paper towel.

Preston and Emily exchanged glances.

"What?" I asked, before taking a sip of water.

"I've decided that Braden and I will be going to Idaho as well, with Izzy. He may not agree with me once he wakes up, but he needs to concentrate on healing," she said.

"And he can do a lot of the techie stuff from there just as well as here," Preston said, nodding.

"That seems reasonable…" my voice trailed off as I looked at Emily.

I had only known these people for a few days, and already I was missing them. Preston was right about family. When you're allowed to choose your own, it seemed to run deeper, quicker. But this would be best for Emily, Braden, and Izzy, and that was what I had to concentrate on.

I felt Preston's gaze on me and glanced at him. He extended his arm out, and I walked over and leaned into him. My body pressed into his, and I could feel the firmness of his chest and abdomen as he wrapped his hands loosely around my waist.

Emily smiled. "You look cute."

I rolled my eyes but didn't budge. I liked being wrapped in his embrace.

"Back to business," she teased. "Joyce Falino was married to Terrence. She divorced him right after the vaccines were administered. She oversees thirty seven MHA facilities as the attending physician."

"One physician for thirty seven facilities?" I repeated. "That's horrible."

"It gets more interesting," she continued. "Marcus changed his last name from Falino to Lordan."

"They were brothers?" I asked.

She nodded. "Yeah, and to top it off, Dr. Falino began seeing Marcus right after she got appointed to her attending physician duties. But I looked into it deeper, it's not unusual for there to be only one physician who oversees facilities like this because they're classified as rehabilitation centers versus a hospital. The rules are completely different when it comes to dispensing care. And Marcus gets paid per patient, which is why he evacuated everyone before attempting to set the building on fire where you two were. I still haven't figured out how he knew you two were there though."

"I think it had to do with the two guards who found Braden," Preston said.

"It's crazy how everything always links back to Marcus." I shook my head and cupped my hands over Preston's in front of me as I leaned back into him more.

"We have her address. What's suspicious about it is that it's in one of the cities that was completely destroyed during the outbreak. One of the few places declared uninhabitable."

"You don't think it could just be an old address for her?" I asked.

Emily shook her head. "No. She's definitely been there recently. But the satellite images don't show any functional structures in a five mile radius of where she could be hiding out."

"How far is it from here?" Preston asked.

"It's about five hours," she said. "Across the mountains."

"Of course." I sighed.

"We also have tests running on the liquid you brought back," Emily said, her eyes moving between Preston's and mine.

"We detected deuterium oxide or D2O as it is more commonly known," she said.

"Which is what?" I asked.

"It's heavy water," she paused, shifting her weight from one leg to the other. "It's a pretty common component in nuclear energy research. Have you ever heard about heavy water reactors?"

I nodded as my mind drifted back to Gavin's notebook, and all of the information pertaining to nuclear fusion and fission.

"Well, that was a common use back in the day," she said.

"So why would zombies be floating in vats of heavy water?" I asked. "Is it harmful?"

"Yeah. It's nothing you want to drink, and it wasn't great that you wrapped yourselves up in it, but we can't worry about that now," Emily continued. "But there are a few characteristics that make heavy water an interesting substance to study, especially when a test subject can be something as innate as the undead."

"You've lost me," I said.

"Heavy water behaves differently than say regular old H2O. It can actually affect the circadian oscillations."

I stared at her blankly and sighed.

"You know, like the circadian rhythm, the twenty-four clock that most biological life adheres to…" She was getting frustrated and so was I. "Whether it's humans, plants, or fungi there's this built-in clock that's pretty constant. Granted, there can be external cues depending on the local environment, but generally the rhythm still exists. If you keep a poinsettia in the dark it still responds to a twenty-four hour clock, the hormones are still released—everything still goes according to this plan. There are very few things that can disrupt that or stall it out, but heavy water is one of those things."

"Huh," I said.

"No one knows why cellular structures react with heavy water like that, but depending on the concentration anything from sterility to death can be a result of ingesting too much."

"But if you're already dead, what does it matter?" I

muttered. "Maybe it will keep the bodies from deteriorating. The zombies could be held indefinitely."

Emily nodded. "But this is the kicker. It's also known to slow down the aging process. But the problem is that the levels needed for every individual is based on that particular person's body composition. What might increase one person's life by twenty-five percent could kill another."

"Remember how I said Peter didn't have any of his tattoos?" I asked, turning to look at Preston. He loosened his arms and I stepped away to take a seat.

"Yeah." He nodded, placing his hands behind him, against the counter.

"What if that was a clone of my brother-in-law?"

Preston's blue eyes narrowed as I continued my theory.

"What if they're making clones and turning them into zombies, turning them into weapons?" It sounded crazy, but what I saw *was* crazy.

"That could be," Emily seconded. "I mean cloning nowadays can be done in a blink of an eye. They could get the clones to the physical age they want, turn them, and then keep them going with the heavy water until they're ready to use."

"But how are they training them?" I asked, thinking back to the zombie pits, the hordes that come and go on command.

Preston shook his head. "That's something we have to uncover or…"

"Yeah," I said, feeling the familiar rush of excitement pound through my veins at the latest revelations.

"And the zombie pits are the perfect cover.

Marcus is raking in the cash from all over. His company is contracted by the government to protect and serve, but what he's really up to is taking over the facilities, developing zombies. Then he manages to create a circuit where the creatures fight each other," Preston said, shaking his head.

"All the while, he's just testing out his creations in the ring, testing them, training them," I said.

"When Brenda said he was their top trainer, I doubt she even knew what he was really capable of," Preston said, his blue eyes darkening a shade.

"We need to go meet the doctor. Find out what she knows," I said.

A cough from upstairs startled us all. It was Braden. He was waking up.

CHAPTER TWENTY-FIVE

We didn't get on the road until early evening after Braden had woken up. He was groggy, confused, and puzzled to be alive—grateful, but puzzled. The news went about as well as it could, but in typical Braden style he was far more interested in what we'd found out and almost kicked us out of the house to get us on our way to the doctor's. Preston and I made it over the mountains but pulled off to get a good night's sleep before hitting the last two hours of the drive. Now here we were, driving into this area void of civilization.

The road leading into the city deemed uninhabitable was lined with downed power lines and gnarled trees. An occasional burst of green sprayed from the cracks in the street and sidewalks. It felt as if we were being watched—but by who? There was no one left.

"I hope this sheds some light on Peter," I said, looking at Preston, his hands tightly gripping the wheel. "And Gavin."

Without warning, Preston stopped the truck in the middle of the road. There was no point in pulling over in a place like this.

"What?" I asked, shifting in my seat, the harness limiting my movements.

"There was something else that Emily found in Gavin's notebook," Preston said, his eyes darkening a shade.

"That doesn't surprise me," I said. "There were all sorts of things listed inside."

He unbuckled his seatbelt and turned to face me. He grabbed my hands and placed them inside his.

This didn't seem good.

"There was a long chain of numbers," he began.

"Yeah?" I arched my brow, unsure of where this was headed.

"It led to a foreign bank account containing a very large sum of money. The deposit was made one week before Gavin was killed."

Getting large chunks of money wasn't that uncommon at the moment, considering all of the different agencies handing out subsidies. And tracking down relatives to transfer assets to was commonplace.

"So?" I asked.

"Emily dug a bit because the amount was so unsettling."

"How unsettling?" I asked, mentally calculating some of the most recent notifications I had received about funds being deposited. There was one recent deposit for seven hundred and eighty thousand, and another for three hundred thousand.

"Ten million," he said flatly.

"And the source?" I asked, as a chill settled over me.

"A subsidiary of ML Holdings, which—"

Marcus Lordan. I held up my hand, interrupting what Preston was about to say. My world would never be the same. How I looked at my own life, my own perceptions of people would never be the same. As the realization settled over me, I slowly turned away from Preston and removed my hands. Gavin was involved with Marcus. Was he researching for him? Did he develop what killed him?

"Sophie received a similar payout," Preston said softly.

"So what are you saying? The company paid them and then killed them?" I asked, perplexed. "Why wouldn't they get their money back first?"

"You are legally entitled to Gavin's money just as I am to Sophie's. But if either of us dies, and we have no offspring, the amount rolls back to ML Holdings."

It felt like I had been kicked in the gut, like attempting that next breath would be too much effort.

"That's why we've been of such interest to Marcus as of late. I doubt they figured we'd ever piece together what Gavin or Sophie discovered. They weren't after us for the notebooks. They were after us for the money," he said. "They already had what they needed from Gavin and Sophie."

The man I thought I knew was slowly disintegrating into nothing with every passing second. I tried reaching and pulling out certain things I loved about him, but the memories would slip away before I could catch them, feel them. This act of betrayal took away everything we shared. He had lived a lie and forced me to be part of it. I shivered as the hollowness spread out from the pit of my stomach.

"I'm sorry," he whispered.

I unbuckled my seatbelt and turned to face Preston. I raised my right hand up to his cheek and guided my fingers along his jaw line, feeling the prick of whiskers as I glided my fingers over his skin. My eyes focused on his beautiful eyes, full lips, and kind expression.

"Don't be," I whispered, feeling the sting of tears touch my cheeks.

A charge ran between us. Just as he said before, some revelations unexpectedly unite people while others tear them apart. Preston leaned toward me, the sunlight capturing the green in his normally blue eyes, as he softly cupped his hand behind my neck. He pressed his forehead against mine and let out a deep sigh—our souls so close to one another as we both mourned the people we thought we knew.

I felt at peace as Preston held me. I think on some level I knew there was a missing piece to the puzzle, a reason why Gavin was targeted. I just never thought it would be this ugly, this tainted.

"When did you find out?" I asked.

"While you were asleep." He slowly pulled away, and I touched his leg not wanting the connection we shared to vanish.

"I think I've had enough personal fun for the moment," I said, buckling myself back in the seat. "Let's get this over with."

As Preston continued down the road, I found myself laughing. I had been on the pursuit of truth, the road to retribution for Gavin. I wanted to avenge my husband's death.

I no longer cared about that.

I wanted answers for myself. I wanted answers for Izzy and the people who couldn't find answers for themselves. Whatever we were on the brink of discovering was larger than me, or my personal vendetta. I had to make things right. I had to stop what Gavin started.

"Glad you're able to find something funny about the situation," Preston said, smiling.

"My maniacal laughter didn't scare you? I'll have to work on it," I said, looking out the window at the vacant city. Something more than the outbreak happened here. Collapsed buildings lined the city streets, and the cracks in the roadway were several inches wide.

There were piles of rubble, mixed with the remnants of personal belongings, that looked as if they'd been set on fire.

"It almost looks like tanks came through and flattened everything," Preston said, scanning the street ahead.

"Yeah. Kinda does, except for the piles of debris," I agreed.

We were completely vulnerable as we drove down the street, exposed to anyone who cared to take a shot. The saving grace was that I didn't think there was anyone around to take a shot, except for possibly the doctor. But by all accounts she was probably underground somewhere. My eyes danced from one dilapidated building to the next, searching for cameras or any sign of surveillance, but I saw none.

"Up ahead," Preston said, the truck continuing to crawl over the road.

"You think that's it?" I asked.

The building in front of us was a charred mess. There was only a basic shell of what 'used to be' at the end of the road. I let out a sigh as I thought about having to go underground again. And then I remembered how easily I had fought the feelings of claustrophobia once I realized there were bigger fears to worry about, like not dying.

Preston parked the car, and we grabbed our weapons and secured them

"I can't keep it in any longer," Preston said, a smirk appearing as his eyes glinted with playfulness.

"What's that?" I asked.

"You look so hot in that," he said, biting his lip.

Heat ran up my spine, and I glanced down at my outfit. I was sucked into a black leather body suit. It was quite the switch from jeans and an oversized top, but I had to admit I loved the feeling it gave me. I felt kind of like a badass.

"Thanks," I said, grinning. "You're not so bad yourself."

We closed the doors and carefully made our way to the skeletal remains of the building. Our feet crunching along the pavement was the only hint we were coming, but that was probably enough.

I circled around the left-hand side of the building while Preston took the right. Neither of us wanted to go under the structure until we were certain where the opening to the underground quarters were. My eyes scanned along the twisted metal and down to the puddles of shattered glass.

"Over here," Preston hollered. I ducked down and saw him across the way about ten feet. "Come around the outside."

I jogged around the back of the structure and saw

him standing with his leg propped on a rusty metal cellar door.

"You think that's it?" I asked.

"Washington isn't really known for having cellars, so yeah. I think this is it."

I laughed. "Good point."

He opened one side of the door and then the other, exposing a steep staircase that would carry us deep into the earth. I waited for him to climb down next to me after he closed the doors. There were tiny light bulbs wrapped in wire caging that dotted the pathway and faintly illuminated it. The fixtures looked like something off of an old submarine. The tunnel going down was just as narrow as the one I'd encountered at the MHA facility, but this time around I felt absolutely nothing in the way of fear. I listened carefully as I moved ahead, wondering at what point we'd run into the doctor, if we'd run into the doctor.

We had fewer than five steps left below us when I heard a woman clearing her throat down the hallway somewhere. I stopped and looked behind me at Preston. He motioned to keep going.

My hand rested on my pistol grip, but I prayed I wouldn't need to use it. At least not until after we'd found out the answers to our questions.

I stepped down from the last step, my foot landing on plywood flooring, and I moved slowly to the side as Preston walked around me. The hallway in front of us was carved out of the earth, but it had been partially covered with stones. I wasn't sure if it was the doctor's idea of decorating or if it served a purpose like that of a retention wall. The air was cool but it wasn't cold. There had to be some sort of heat source. I heard a female cough and stopped. I craned my neck to see past the corner and was beyond surprised. The rustic tunnel led to white walls and glossy floors. There was a glass door that separated where we were from the rest of the cavern, but it was wide open and then I heard his voice.

"We're looking forward to taking it to the next level."

It was Marcus.

CHAPTER TWENTY-SIX

"I never intended to start another war," a woman's voice said quietly. "You're on a different road than I am. I see that now."

I glanced at Preston who was listening intently. He placed his hand on my waist, bringing his lips to my lobe and whispered, "Phone."

I nodded, unable to hide my smile. I really didn't feel like seeing Marcus today.

"I knew you were worthless. Any woman my brother had the hots for would be," Marcus yelled, causing the speakerphone to buzz.

"I'm sorry you feel that way," the woman replied. "I think it's best we hang up now before you say anything more you'll regret."

It had to be Dr. Falino in the room. I heard the phone go dead and the woman sigh. What would a doctor be doing with someone who talked down to her like that? Although, it wouldn't be the first time a smart woman got fooled. I can thank Gavin for that revelation.

Footsteps traveled away from us and a door clicked shut. Preston walked down the hall to the room and I followed. The space was white and completely sterile. There was a desk tucked in the far corner and a phone sat on top near the edge. There was a stainless steel table with several clay models of the human form displayed. Odd. I looked toward the ceiling and spotted a video camera.

"Damn," I whispered, pointing up toward the camera.

We walked out of range and waited a few minutes. If someone was watching it, chances were that they'd be here in seconds. But no one came in. The door that Dr. Falino exited through was stainless steel with a glass insert on the top, allowing us to see into the next hallway, which was empty.

"Now?" I mouthed.

Preston nodded and we ran to the exit. I went through the door first and he was right behind me. On each side of the hallway, the top portions of the walls were glass, allowing us to see into the rooms. The first two were empty and set up similarly with a hospital bed and cabinets along the far wall. We moved swiftly down the hallway, reaching another set of rooms. These rooms housed technical equipment on one side and the surveillance on the other. Thankfully, the chair was empty in front of the security monitors.

We reached the end of the hallway where another door led to yet another hallway.

"I think we're getting somewhere," he whispered.

"Really? You could've fooled me." I smiled as we opened the door and walked through, landing in an almost identical hallway as the one before.

However, immediately to our right there was another door that looked different from the rest. The top portion of the door wasn't all glass like the others, instead there was a window the size of a ship portal with glass that was several inches thick to match the density of the metal, and there was a hazardous waste symbol displayed prominently on the door.

"Looks pressurized and it probably has a fail-safe on it," Preston said.

"What's that?" I asked.

"If one door is open, the other one stays locked. You can't open it until the one you've moved through is closed. It's an airlock system."

I placed my hand on the door and turned the handle. A strong sucking sound and breeze surrounded me the moment I entered the hallway. Preston stepped inside and the door clicked behind us, securing the vacuum-sealed area. A surge of worry ran through me at the thought of what was on the other side of the doors. What needed to have these fail-safe measures? Suits hung in front of us next to the door, probably best if we put them on.

There were windows on both sides of the hallway, but this time they looked to be one-way mirrors, and we were on the wrong side. My skin prickled as Preston brushed up against me as he walked forward. He grabbed a suit and stepped inside, pulling it over one leg and then the other.

The vacuum pressured hallway smelled like nothing...exactly like nothing would smell if our world actually had that capability. But we were humans built to use our senses like taste, touch, and smell. Coming into contact with a place that was void of smell struck me odd. There was no hint of disinfectant, no small trace of bleach in the air. Yet everything was white, spotless, and glistening.

"Suit up," Preston said.

I nodded and stepped into the white jumpsuit, zipping it up. He slid a mask over his face and adjusted it as I did the same. He probably sensed that I was about to lose it so he gave me a quick nod and opened up the door. A big gush of wind flew by as we broke the hallway's seal.

The room now surrounding us was dark, dreary and nothing like I expected. The dark concrete floors were dull, and metal worktables were spread sporadically throughout the space. There was a line of empty gurneys to our left, except for one, which was horizontal to another door.

I hugged myself as I tried to focus on the person strapped to the gurney, taking slow steps toward it. Preston placed his hand on my back as we moved closer. I took a deep breath through my mask and felt the warmth of my breath hover around my mouth.

"Oh, my god," Preston muttered, dropping his hand from my back.

My gaze dipped to the being in front of us. A female with grey eyes stared straight at the ceiling, but her chest was moving slightly up and down, regardless of her apparent undead status. Her skin was splotchy and missing in some places, but there were just as many places where it was stitched up, and the stitches were tight. That made no sense. If the undead of the outbreak were stitched, their flesh would just rip and the whole area would fall off. I looked behind me and saw Preston taking her in with the same bewilderment I felt. A flood of emotions surged through my veins at the sadness this creature epitomized. It was like she was caught between two worlds.

I took a step back and just as I did the woman began convulsing, her back arching toward the ceiling. The gurney began rattling as her wrists and ankles shook violently. She was having some sort of seizure. Her entire body thrashed continuously, and there was nothing that either of us did…or wanted to do. She was too close to the undead.

The creature's head lolled to the side, her grey eyes staring directly at me. But then I saw something even more unexpected as her body continued to seize. Beads of sweat rolled down her forehead and onto the pillow.

The door in front of us was thrown open, revealing a woman in a black suit, carrying a syringe. The woman jammed the tip directly through the undead's clothes, into her chest.

The creature's movements began to stabilize with every passing second. Zombies weren't known for responding to drugs either.

"I've been expecting you," the woman replied coolly, looking up at us. "I'm Dr. Falino."

***

The doctor led us to her office. It was pleasant enough or as pleasant as a place can be underground and without windows. I noticed several photographs she had hung on her wall, along with a painting, which depicted a girl twirling in the tulip fields. Seemed rather odd.

We sat down in front of her large, pine desk while she walked behind it and collapsed in her chair. She leaned over, and I heard her opening a drawer and rustling around. Twisting off the lid to a pill bottle, she sprinkled a few in her hand and tossed them into the back of her mouth. She grabbed a bottle of gin from the same magical drawer and took a swig, swallowing the pills down.

"That woman was my sister," she said, glancing at the photographs on the wall. "She was why I kept trying."

"Trying to do what?" I asked.

She looked at me, void of emotion, and leaned back in her chair as if just the thought exhausted her. "Trying to save her."

She laughed wickedly, and Preston slid his hand to mine under the lip of the desk.

"You've been trying to save your sister and that is your sister out there?" I pointed behind me.

Dr. Falino's eyes were wild as she steadied her gaze on me. "Yes. And what I've learned is that you can only trick nature for so long before she gets her retribution. I've tried to fool this disease, change this disease, mutate it—anything." She shook her head. "But you can only screw with Mother Nature's plan so much."

"But we were able to come up with a vaccine," I replied.

"Yes, my dear. I know. I was on the CDC team that found that little fluke of nature."

"You helped to find the cure?" I asked.

"It's not a cure. That's the problem. It's a vaccine, but that was enough for the government. So all the poor innocent souls who were already infected never had a chance," she said, shuffling through some papers on her desk as if she was looking for something. I doubt she was.

"Research was suspended, and the vaccines were

manufactured at record speeds and administered even faster. Still what about all those wandering zombies?" she asked, looking at Preston.

Like her sister...

"That's where Marcus came in," Preston stated and she nodded her head.

"He was my husband's brother, and as you know, my husband wasn't exactly right with the law. I had a tendency to look the other way. It was an awkward pairing, the two of us. Anyway, Marcus learned about my research with the CDC and offered me a position I couldn't refuse. A chance to help the infected, my sister. The funds were unlimited as I worked on my research. And the resources were unimaginable, too good to be true. Marcus managed to infiltrate the top researchers at all of the main universities. They were at my disposal. He'd already worked his way into the MHA and was able to convince them to let him run not only the security but the administration. It's the perfect cover."

I pressed my lips together and shifted in my chair. I didn't like where this was going.

"Needless to say, all I've done is help line his pockets and create the deadliest weapon ever known to man," she said, her voice hoarse. "Well, I don't need to tell either of you that, now do I? You've both seen it firsthand. The hordes."

"Thank you for that," I said, my voice tipped with controlled anger.

"Marcus has been getting requests nonstop for these beasts. That's why the cloning began. It has to be fresh zombies. I watched as the research shifted completely away from finding a cure to—"

"Creating weapons unlike any the world had ever

encountered. Relentless, inescapable, and in great numbers completely overwhelming," I said harshly.

"So you're cloning people who what, won't be missed or who are already missing?" Preston asked, his fists tightly clamped.

"We can create a clean clone from living or undead beings," she answered.

"That explains Peter's missing tattoos," I muttered.

"The supply will be endless until he is stopped," she said.

"Then why don't you turn him in? Expose what's really going on?" Preston said, his words almost at shouting level.

"We can't let this get in the government's hands. Once they find out this can be done, they won't destroy it. They'll use it. Maybe not today or tomorrow but mark my words, they'll claim it. You need to stop Marcus. I know you can," she said, looking directly at me.

I scoffed at her statement and shook my head.

"Listen to me, I've grown close to Marcus. The only thing that resonates with him is money. If you can find out how to take that away from him, his entire operation will crumble. We live in a capitalist world. There are always competitors," she said, her brow arching.

"Sorry, I haven't ever had an urge get into the zombie wrangling business," I replied.

How twisted was the afterworld? Instead of going to the government, she was suggesting the way to end a worldwide threat was to give Marcus a run for his money? Add a little competition to the game?

"Why are you telling us these things?" I

questioned.

"Over the last week, I finally came to the realization that I won't be able to help my sister. You saw what happened to her out there. I've just prolonged her nightmare. I'm done. I'm leaving and hoping to never come back. I've lost everything I ever cared for and the reason generally points back to me," she said. "So I want to make things right as best I can."

Pointing to a metal briefcase against the far wall, she said, "Take that on your way out. It has everything you will need when the time is right. I'm not expecting you to believe me or take my advice. I wouldn't either. But just give it some thought."

"What about your daughter?" I asked. "What happened to her?"

"How did you know about her?" she asked, her eyes drilling into me.

"Your husband mentioned her," Preston responded. "Said she was taken away to an MHA facility where she—"

"She's still alive. I doctored a photo once I realized what was really going on. I didn't want her used as a pawn. I wanted both my husband and Marcus to think she was dead. She's somewhere no one will ever find her, and I will make sure it stays that way."

Dr. Falino stood up and straightened her skirt. "I know you have a lot to think about, and I doubt I'll ever see you two again, but I do look forward to seeing how the afterworld turns around. Hopefully, you'll ensure that it does."

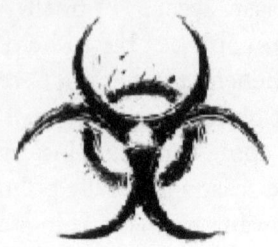

CHAPTER TWENTY-SEVEN

"So she screws shit up and wants us to fix it?" I asked, climbing out of the car.

"Out of everything, that's what pisses you off?" he laughed, closing the driver's door.

We arrived back at the house, and I saw a warm glow coming from Emily and Braden's bedroom. My heart weighed heavy with the thought of what they would be facing for months and years to come. And then Gavin flashed in my mind, and the anger that his image now conjured soared through my veins.

"We have an informant inside Barrell's Security as well, right?" I asked.

Preston nodded as we climbed the steps.

"I wonder if we should get him involved?" I questioned.

"Coming around to the doctor's suggestion, are we?" he teased.

"Meh," I said, shrugging my shoulder. "There's something else I wanted to run by you."

"Yeah?" Preston opened the door, and I walked through, setting the briefcase on the entry floor. My gaze hovered on the little RecruitZ decal on the briefcase. Clever.

"I want to take Abby to a zombie pit."

Preston was silent and I understood why. But as he spoke about the other believers as family, I considered Abby and Caleb as part of mine. It stung that they didn't believe what I did, and if I could show them even a tiny piece of the world I'd dug up maybe they wouldn't think I was crazy.

I watched the gears turn inside his mind as I waited for an answer. He let out a deep sigh and ran his fingers across his chin.

"You're not going to let up until you get your way, I'm assuming," he said, the corner of his mouth lifting slightly.

This time it was my turn to stay silent.

"Do you honestly think you'll be able to walk into the pit unnoticed?" His brow arched.

"I don't think he'll be expecting me or us."

"Us? I feel like there's something you're not telling me, and I thought we were over that hurdle."

"I know how much Abby and Caleb care about me and that kind of devotion can carry all of us a long way…if they could only see what I have seen."

"You're willing to put them at risk to prove your sanity?" he questioned.

"It's not only about that, but I would like them to wake up. Yes! Witness what's actually going on around them, and photos aren't going to cut it. They'd just tell me the images had been doctored or something," I said, following Preston to the family room.

"Why don't you cut to the chase and tell me what else you have in mind," he said, collapsing onto the couch.

I glanced at the chair across from him and then at the welcoming cushions surrounding him. I chose the chair.

"I was hoping we could introduce Barrell security to the zombie pits," I said, ready for him to shoot the idea down.

"Anything we do needs time to plan," Preston said, pressing his lips together.

"I don't agree. I don't think we have time. The longer Marcus has to spread the word about his RecruitZ, the worse off we'll be. If we can topple his little empire before it gets wings, our chances are better—not great—but better."

"And how do Abby and Caleb actually fit into this plan of yours? I'm not buying that you suddenly want them to know you're not insane."

"Believe it or not, that's actually important to me. But you're right. I do have ulterior motives..." my voice trailed off. I could hear footsteps above as Emily maneuvered around in their bedroom above us. I sat back in the chair. Preston's eyes were locked on mine, interested in whatever I had to say.

"From what I can tell the seven-hundred plus people our network has, are all involved in the cause because a love one died, or they witnessed something happen to a loved one. Correct?" I asked.

He nodded.

"A few weeks ago, I would've thought that would have created the perfect army—the perfect fighters—because they were fighting for what they believed was the truth. Revenge fueled them, fueled me. My guess is most of them would fight to their death if called upon to avenge their husbands, wives, sisters, and brothers…"

Preston nodded. "Absolutely." He clasped his hands in front of him and leaned forward. "That type of fury is explosive, powerful. It leads us all to do things we wouldn't normally do."

"Except when what you're fighting for isn't exactly what you thought. What if they're exposed to a truth that isn't something they can handle, something that cuts them off at the knees?" I asked. "Suddenly our army is weak, wounded from their previously unknown histories." I paused for a moment. "Finding out that Gavin wasn't who I thought he was, could have crippled me, ruined me. I'm just lucky it didn't or hasn't—yet."

"So you think if we can start bringing people in who haven't experienced that kind of loss and that's not what's driving their motives, our chances are better," he stated. "But the trust factor is—"

"Going to be difficult no matter how our network grows, but it needs to grow. Something tells me what we're facing right now with Marcus is only the tip of the iceberg and we need to be ready."

I tucked my foot underneath me and waited for Preston to respond.

"I know where the next fight is. They're not having it at the pit you went to." He smiled. "I was actually thinking the same thing about stopping by one to see how it has changed."

"Great minds think alike. When is the fight?"

"Tomorrow night," he said.

"Well, the contact information for the head of Barrell Security was conveniently placed in the

KARICE BOLTON

briefcase she gave us," I said. "And, yes, I know that could be a little too convenient. I'm hoping as much as you are that it's not a setup. Believe me. But one step at a time."

"Well, since you're going to do this with or without me, why don't you plan on meeting up with your friends, and I'll try to get ahold of the contact Dr. Falino has listed at Barrell.

***

I walked slowly toward Preston. My body felt achy with pain or maybe it was grief. I was too depressed to distinguish the slight nuance between the two. It was so hard to lose Gavin the way I did, but it was far more difficult to find out that the man I loved was hiding so many secrets. That was the most challenging thing I had to come to grips with, and I wasn't sure I could. I thought I was doing fine, but the thought that he was somehow involved in this, whatever this was, actually caused me pain, physical pain.

Preston was sitting on the bed, and he'd just removed his shirt. My eyes traced across the definition of his chest and then dipped lower following the trail over peaks and valleys down his abdomen. My eyes caught something I hadn't seen before. He had a tattoo on the left side of his torso. I sat down on the bed and smiled. My hand automatically traced the outline of his inked skin and I began to laugh.

"A haz-mat symbol?" I asked.

"That was pretty much how I felt right after things happened, after everything happened. Like I was a hazard to be around...until I met you," his voice low, vibrating a rush of emotions that had been hidden deep inside of me. His blue eyes locked on mine, igniting something I hadn't felt for a very, very long time. Human.

His words enclosed me, edging their way inside of me slowly as I dropped my gaze from his.

"I'm asking that you let me in," Preston said. "In the way that scares you."

I lifted my finger to the symbol etched into his skin and softly traced the image over and over again as I thought about what to say. Feeling the softness of his skin run under my finger was something I desperately missed. He caught my hand in his and brought it up to his lips. My breath caught as I felt the warmth, the softness of his lips against my knuckles.

A flash of heat bolted through me as his lips traced down my hand to my wrist. He slowly turned my hand over and began kissing the underside of my wrist. My skin was so sensitive to his touch that it was impossible to hide the goose bumps that ran over my skin in waves.

I slowly stood up and felt the tightness along my back where the skin had healed. The hurt had gone away from those wounds. The mending had begun, but as I thought about my past—my history with Gavin—I wasn't sure I'd be so lucky. I didn't know if the agony would ever go away, if those wounds could ever be healed.

Preston's eyes connected with mine and for the first time in a very long time, I no longer felt like a woman void of emotion.

"I'm no longer chasing a past that never existed," I whispered, looking into his eyes. I dropped my hands to his chest and felt the firmness underneath as my fingers traced along his pecs.

"I'll always be here for you," he replied. "No

matter what. No matter how long it takes."

He wrapped his arms around my waist, his fingers sliding up my spine as I dipped my head lower. His lips were so close to mine, I could feel the warmth of his breath skate across my skin. I wanted to feel his lips, taste his lips as I steadied my gaze on his mouth.

Without thinking, I crawled on his lap, straddling him as my lips crashed to his. The kisses began soft, as we explored one another, but the intention quickly changed as all the emotions we'd been afraid to let show collided with each other. The kisses deepened with every passing second as if we were hungry for more than just each other. My hands ran up his neck, grabbing his hair as I felt the heat of his mouth slowly trace along my jawline. But he slowly broke his mouth away, and I understood why.

I laid my head against the crook of his neck, catching my breath, feeling his heartbeat steady. The rawness that we both had bottled up for so long was unleashed with each kiss that we'd shared. And he knew I wasn't ready for it.

"I think the only way I'll get closure is to stop this, to stop them," I whispered, my eyes closed as I felt the comfort of his embrace. Our bodies as close to one another as they'd ever been, feeling the warmth rolling off his bare skin made the shirt I was wearing feel almost invisible.

He nodded and traced his finger along my collarbone, sending a shiver through me.

"I pray for the same closure," he said softly. "But I'm not sure it will ever come."

I took a deep breath in as I realized I was one step closer to becoming me again. I no longer believed that I was broken, that I wasn't whole without Gavin.

The idea brought peace along with it as I felt myself drift to sleep in Preston's arms.

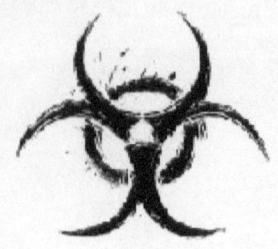

CHAPTER TWENTY-EIGHT

I fantasized about how I would do it. How I would end Marcus's life. What it would it would feel like, smell like, taste like—that kind of revenge. I wanted to watch his soul depart for his forever home in Hell. That was the dream I woke up with this morning. Some might call it a nightmare, but I wasn't one of them.

We parked the truck and walked into the coffee shop. I looked around to see ordinary life—the hustle and bustle of the commonplace—surround me. But it didn't call for me. Instead, I was left feeling anxious and worried. I didn't want that type of existence to swallow me whole, make me forget what's really going on in the afterworld.

We weren't too far from the fighting grounds we were going to check out later. Jeffrey Barrell was on his way over. The moment Preston mentioned Dr. Falino to Jeffrey, he was eager to hear what we had to tell him. Apparently, Jeffrey and Dr. Falino went way back, and he still believed in the woman even though he was quite aware of some of her mistakes. He lived in Vermont and somehow managed to secure a red-eye out here last night.

A black van pulled into the parking lot, and I felt uneasy as my mind flashed back to the TRAC attack last time.

"Think that's him?" I asked Preston.

He nodded. "He said he was going to swing by and gather some of his people in case we weren't to be trusted. He promised they'd wait in the van."

I laughed. "He's the one that needs to be worried?"

The driver's side door opened and a tall, well-built man stepped out. He had dark hair and looked to be well over six feet tall. He was dressed in light jeans and a green button down shirt. He ducked his head inside the van and then nodded before shutting the door.

He walked with a quickened pace and glanced around the parking lot, taking everything in.

I stood up once he came inside and motioned for him to join us. His eyes fell from mine to Preston's and he gave a quick nod.

He extended his hand to me. "Jeffrey Barrell."

"Rebekah Taylor."

"And you're Preston," he said, shaking Preston's hand before sitting down. "You've done a fairly good job of filling me in, and I had about six hours on the plane that I was able to read over some of the files you sent. In all honesty, some of the things I don't understand, but the images often spoke louder than the words."

"Yeah. They're pretty brutal," I agreed.

"So your brother-in-law was turned into a fighter?" he asked, gauging my reaction.

"A clone of my brother-in-law," I corrected.

"And there's one of these fights going on tonight near here?" he asked.

"Yeah. Less than thirty minutes away," Preston said.

"Well, I don't advise you going there tonight," Jeffrey said, looking at Preston. "They'll spot you within seconds, guaranteed. Now you mentioned payouts from Marcus's organization to your husband and your sister. What were these for, exactly?"

"They were some of the researchers that helped to develop the technology to get the undead to where they needed to be," Preston replied.

"I'll tell you what concerns me. I'm in security just as Marcus is. Granted, I'm doing it the legitimate way, but the money to be made still wouldn't allow for those kinds of distributions. I know Joyce doesn't think the government's involved and maybe they're not, but I do agree we can't get them involved—not yet anyway. We need to prolong the discovery stage for as long as possible."

"I agree. I feel like whatever's going on here isn't just so Marcus can arm the criminals of the world, although that's a start," I replied.

"Call off your friends too," Jeffrey said.

My skin prickled at Jeffrey's level of imperiousness.

"I already did," I said, glancing at Preston. Preston had already suggested the same this morning.

"Frankly, I think we need to lure Marcus away tonight, capture him, and find out if this thing he's got going can be stopped," Jeffrey said, looking at me.

"And I think you'll be the perfect bait."

"Absolutely not," Preston said, his voice sharp.

I glanced at Preston and smiled. "Jeffrey's right."

"That's far too dangerous," Preston objected.

"I'll have my team following her. She'll be fine. We'll swoop in before anything can go wrong," Jeffrey said.

Considering everything we had been through recently I couldn't help but laugh. Why not throw myself into the lion's den for the grand finale?

"We've got a lot of planning to do and not much time to do it so let's get going," Jeffrey said, standing up promptly.

I looked over at Preston. He was staring directly in front of us, his jaw clenched from being outvoted.

***

There he was—Marcus driving his Escalade. He pulled out of the parking lot heading east. I glanced in the rearview mirror and saw a quick flash of headlights from Jeffrey's van. I drove out of the parking lot, trailing Marcus. I needed to be noticed, but it had to look like it was because of my incompetence, not like I wanted to be noticed.

Unfortunately, allowing the distance to grow between our vehicles did nothing to calm the anxiety that was building. The old farm road that he turned onto seemed to lead to nowhere and everywhere at the same time.

Glancing in my rearview, I didn't notice another vehicle on the road yet, which had me slightly concerned. How would they swoop in if they weren't around? That was odd.

As I continued to focus on the rearview mirror, I let my guard down. Marcus's black Escalade swerved in front of me without warning, leaving nothing but a swirl of dust in the air, as he blocked the road in front of me.

Shit!

I slammed on my brakes, and before I realized what was really going down, he was out of his car, raising a machete high above his head with both arms stretched, taunting me. He sauntered towards me like there was some song playing in his head that I couldn't hear. He bounced his head over and over again to a beat that was only his own. Marcus was dressed in a sleeveless t-shirt, exposing all of his tattoos. He should have been intimidating, but he wasn't.

I'd seen more horror recently than he could produce with the swing of a machete.

The Escalade's passenger door swung open, allowing another productive member of society to exit the SUV. I didn't recognize him, but he was fully uniformed in TRAC gear. I let out a sigh and briefly scanned my mirror.

Nothing. Great!

"I should have known," Marcus hollered, his eyes tiny slits as he stared at me. "You just never leave well enough alone."

He was only a foot away from my vehicle and quickly swung the machete in the air, laughing. He looked completely maniacal. He probably was. He took another step closer and smiled wickedly once our gazes met.

"This will be so vindicating. You have been a thorn in my side from the beginning," he said, flashing a grin.

I watched the other man slowly walk behind his

boss and stand and wait. He was holding a pistol, but it was pointed at the ground.

Marcus banged the machete on the hood of my car, attempting to unnerve me. It didn't.

"Your time is almost up, Marcus," I hollered through the glass.

"I don't think so," he laughed. "But I think your friends Abby and Caleb might be on their way out."

My heart stopped at their mention. He was always one step ahead.

"Listen, I'll leave what few friends you have…alone, if you'll just let me end this once and for all. Lead me to your boyfriend, and I'll finish you both off quickly and painlessly."

I smiled and shook my head.

"I really don't want pieces of me used for your experiments, but thanks," I replied through the door.

"Your husband wasn't nearly as bullheaded as you are," Marcus shouted, now next to the driver's door.

I peered up at him, surprised at my non-reaction as he mentioned my husband. Had Gavin's truth set me free from his demons?

"He wasn't as smart as he thought he was," I replied.

"And you are?" Marcus laughed.

I placed my hand on the door handle. Marcus's gaze dipped to watch me open it.

"That's what I thought," he said, taking a step back.

As I stepped out of the car, I felt the metal of my pistol's barrel rub against my back, and an ache surfaced in my palm at the thought of getting to use it on Marcus.

"You're willing to destroy what's left of the

afterworld for profit," I said.

"That's a naïve statement," Marcus replied.

"Why don't you enlighten me then?" I asked, placing my hands on my waist, closer to my weapon.

"I'm simply trying to save the world from itself. It's only a matter of time before humans completely desecrate the planet. Mother Earth even tried to stop us by throwing a plague at us. That was her last cry for help. But once again we stepped in and found a cure," he said, his hand gripping the machete handle tight. His chest was puffed out and he looked absolutely sure of himself. I had to take him down a notch.

I tilted my head. "A vaccine, not a cure."

"Aah... So you've even been to see Joyce," he said, laughing. "You really do get around."

"I just have to tell you this. It's killing me inside," I replied, narrowing my eyes.

"What's that, doll?" he asked, taking a step forward.

"You look absolutely ridiculous waving that weed whacker around, especially in your sleeveless tee." His eyes flashed, and he sliced the machete through the air as it carved a piece of my calf.

My leg throbbed, and I dropped to my knees. The sound of an engine behind me brought little comfort as Marcus rammed me against my car, the blade etching a mark against my throat. Every movement, every swallow was painful as the blade worked its way into my flesh.

"You brought company," he whispered, his mouth was wretchedly close to mine as he leaned over me. "I hoped Preston wouldn't be too far behind. Looks like I was right."

My blood was pounding in my ears as I heard the sound of footsteps surrounding us, and saw guns drawn.

"Marcus, let her go. You're surrounded. Kill her and it's a certain death for you," Preston hollered.

"You bitch," he snarled, tossing the machete on the street before taking a step back.

I felt a warm trickle run down my throat. My fingers slid up my neck meeting a sticky substance when I realized I'd been cut a little worse than I thought. Marcus slowly began walking toward Jeffrey and Preston. I watched as Preston glanced toward me, giving Marcus the opening he needed.

Marcus dropped to his knees, grabbing a pistol out of his back holster. Without thinking, I reached for my pistol and took aim. The sound of the gunshot was a ringing celebration as I watched Marcus fall to the ground.

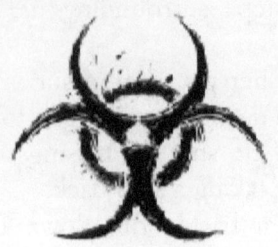

CHAPTER TWENTY-NINE

Jeffrey Barrell was a good man or as good of a man as could exist in the afterworld. He covered up Marcus's death in order to protect people he'd just met, which wasn't what I expected, but I appreciated it. Then again, we armed him with enough information to present to the government so that all of TRAC's contracts would roll over to his company. He was now going to be a very rich man.

I kept waiting for a release of some sort, like any moment that soul-crushing feeling would just disappear. Finding answers was supposed to have been my release. When that didn't happen, I assumed destroying the man who ruined Gavin would provide the relief. It didn't.

Don't get me wrong. That moment when I pulled the trigger was euphoric. When Marcus gave me an excuse to shoot him, and my finger quickly slipped onto the cold metal and simply pulled the trigger, it was an unexplainable rush. But the moment he dropped, I was left with that same emptiness that had been haunting me since the beginning.

I glanced up at the large stone building in front of us. Preston placed his hand on my shoulder as I took a deep breath in and stared at the entrance to the CCC.

"Controlled Cloning Center," I whispered.

I wasn't sure I would ever be ready to enter such a facility but in order to properly turn over everything to Barrell Security, we agreed to check out the facilities that were associated with ML Holdings. Dr. Falino included a list of locations across the country in the briefcase. We all wanted to keep things discreet, Jeffrey included, so we volunteered ourselves to begin with the facilities in this state. Once we found out what was typically at all of these different locations, then would come the hard part—figuring out what to do with what was inside of them.

"Ready?" Preston asked.

I turned to face him and looked into his blue eyes. "Abby was right. You're eyes really are an interesting color."

Preston's eyes locked on mine. "Are you beginning to warm up to me?" he asked, softly sweeping a kiss along my cheek.

I flashed a smile and turned around, climbing the steps of the CCC. I picked the lock and opened the door, noticing the reception desk was empty. Hopefully, the entire building would be vacant. Once word had spread that Marcus had been taken out, many of his supporters vanished. They didn't want to be connected in any way to the crimes that could be exposed if we were to take anything to the authorities.

The beige industrial carpeting and taupe chairs in

the lobby looked like any other type of waiting area with cheap art hung on the walls and a small sculpture stuck in the corner.

We walked past the reception area and down a hallway that led to the research area. I wasn't sure if we'd actually find various stages of cloning behind the doors or an empty space that had been cleared out. Nothing would compare to what we found underground at the MHA facility. That I was sure of.

Preston pushed open the double doors, and we walked into a large sterile room with microscopes lining one wall and file cabinets on another. Large metal desks were grouped together in the center of the room, and the strong smell of disinfectant stung my nostrils.

There was a large window overlooking another room. My heart began beating rapidly as I spotted incubators like the ones I saw underneath the MHA facility. My eyes briefly scanned the rest of the room, spotting cages and gurneys. But where were the subjects?

We made our way into the other room and the stench was hard to stomach. A mix of bleach and something sour, death maybe?—lingered in the air. I brought my shirt up to cover my mouth and nose while I breathed. I began examining the empty adult-sized incubators as well as the empty cages. They had been used recently so where did the experiments go?

"There's another door over there," Preston said, pointing behind me.

I would have missed it. It blended into the wall and a table had been shoved in front of it.

"I don't have a good feeling about what's behind there," I whispered.

Preston was already moving the table aside when I arrived, and I noticed the stench near the door was much worse. I listened carefully but didn't hear anything on the other side of the wall.

I stood next to Preston as he pushed on the door, and it moved in front of us, letting us slide by the narrow opening. The stale air suddenly hit me, and I began coughing as I looked around the dark space. Preston grabbed the flashlight I had attached to my belt and flipped it on as I tried to calm my lungs.

The narrow spray of light captured something I wasn't prepared for. He quickly turned around and used the flashlight to find a light switch. I spotted one and flipped it up.

What the light revealed was something I would try to flush from my mind for years to come. Rows of gurneys with the undead in various stages of decomposition were scattered through the room. But beyond those bodies, I saw tables with fresh, newly created undead hooked up to some sort of life-support.

"Why would they need ventilators?" I asked.

He shook his head. "Maybe they're not infected yet."

"Just clones?" I asked.

"Maybe," he said, as we snaked along the undead.

I gasped when I saw the bodies strapped down to the gurneys with restraints. None of them looked strong enough to do much of anything. My eyes jumped from one new shell of a body to the next.

"These look like the ones who killed Gavin."

"But I don't think these have been turned yet," he said.

"Maybe that's what this is," I said, pointing at the

solution bags with the IVs going into their arms.

I continued looking at the faces of the cloned beings. Their eyes were closed, mouths pressed tightly together…most had the same expression. I wouldn't necessarily call it a peaceful expression—maybe unknowing.

Preston was a few steps ahead of me when I heard him let out an absolutely piercing, guttural sound. He collapsed to his knees, his head falling on the gurney next to him.

I ran up behind him, my eyes running up the body until I reached her face, her eyes.

Oh no…please no!

They were the same greenish-blue as Preston's. It was Sophie. We were staring at a clone of Sophie.

"We've got to save her," he said, his eyes fierce as he stood up.

"It's not her," I said, quietly.

"It's her and we have to save her before the disease hits." He grabbed the IV and yanked it out of her arm tossing it onto the ground.

There was nothing I could do or say to stop him. He slid his arms under her back in an attempt to lift her off the gurney, but she shot up and snapped her neck toward Preston, her mouth gaping. She was infected. She lunged at him and he dodged her just in time. The restraints anchored her legs to the gurney, but that didn't stop the power behind this recreated body that was more like a machine.

Whatever this solution was, it made the undead look like the living, but gave them the power of the undead. The gurney fell on its side, the wheels spinning as the cloned Sophie's arms waved wildly, reaching for her brother to tear him apart.

Preston was out of her reach, and his eyes connected with mine, desperation and defeat hidden behind his cold exterior. He grabbed his pistol and pointed it toward the imposter writhing on the floor.

"I'm sorry," he whispered.

I clenched my eyes shut as the shot was fired into her body.

When the thrashing stopped, I looked down at the now still body. There was no blood. This body was not human. There was no soul in this body.

Preston fell to his knees and I ran over to him, pulling him into my arms.

"I'm so sorry, babe," I whispered.

He didn't shed tears. Instead, he shook free from my arms, stood up, and began walking back through the maze of undead. I followed him back to the lab and watched as he went over to the file cabinets and began opening all the drawers. I ran to his side and began looking through the files as well. I didn't know what either of us was looking for, but I hoped we'd know it when we saw it.

My hands ran along the files, mostly notes and status reports until a logo caught my eyes. I yanked the piece of paper out of the folder, unveiling the small blue rectangle with sprays of white and on top, three letters.

CDC

It was an email.

"Dr. Falino was wrong. At least one person in the government already knows," I whispered, handing the piece of paper to Preston. "Someone helped to fund Marcus's operation."

Our government was making weapons out of zombies with the help of TRAC.

Preston finished reading the email and shoved it back to me.

"We've got to warn Jeffrey," he muttered, pushing the file cabinet over.

He pushed another one down and another, the papers spilling out all over the floor. I watched his eyes dart around the room until he found what he was looking for—a way to ignite the papers on fire.

His pain guided his choices as I watched the events unfold around us. Small fires erupted around the room, and he shot out the glass separating the rooms. Preston's anger was directing how this would end, not logic, not intelligence. The very thing that separated us from the undead could be the very undoing of humanity—emotions and rage.

Preston grabbed my hand and pulled me out of the room. The shards of glass crunched under my feet, and the smell of smoke replaced the pungent smells of disinfectant. It wouldn't be long before the flames reached some of the more explosive elements in the building. I ran as fast I could, holding onto Preston until we pushed through the front door and reached the outside.

"I'm sorry," he said breathless. "I don't know what came over me."

"We're only human," I whispered, turning away to look at the building one last time.

Preston was already on the phone with Jeffrey, explaining to him what we'd just found out and it sounded like we were in time. He hadn't contacted the authorities yet.

I leaned against the car, listening to Preston calmly relay the latest information as I allowed myself to listen to my body. I was exhausted from pushing away the truth about Gavin. I didn't want to see it. I didn't want to believe it. But the reality—our reality—contained a type of existence that was built on fabrications and half-truths. I could no longer push aside the facts that surrounded me about my husband and our shared past—the strangers that we turned out to be.

But I could change my future and the way our history was shaped and that was what I intended to do.

This was why we needed a different kind of army to fight this war. We needed to fight fire with fire. No matter how much I detested these new creations, I needed them. I needed to use them to destroy them and that was what I intended to do.

AlibiZ
Afterworld Series (Book 2)

Coming Soon

Lonely Souls Excerpt

"Mom!" I hollered more for my benefit than hers.

I wasn't in earshot yet, but I loved the way my voice carried into the wind off the sea. The constant sloshing of the waves guided me to the rocky beach where my mom was collecting her thoughts and anything else that might catch her fancy. It was a pleasant night with only the moon's warm glow lighting my way on the very uneven path that weaved through the overgrown blackberries and tall beach grass. Doing my best to dodge the prick of the thorns, I carefully managed to stay on the trail. I didn't need to be all scarred up for my upcoming celebrations.

This little stretch of beach was hard to get to and rarely frequented by anyone, which was why we loved it. The beach wasn't what most people pictured when they thought of a beach. The beaches along Washington's coast, more often than not, had tiny rocks and pebbles in place of sand and many boulders and downed logs that made for awfully fine seating, not places to spread out on a beach towel and soak up the rays.

The makeshift trail finally ended, allowing me to spot my mom's pile of things. I hoped she was ready to leave. It was getting a little chilly, and I hadn't prepared to be here long. We had a crockpot full of chili waiting for us both, but she wanted me to meet her here at our special spot, so she could tell me something. I had no idea what it was that she wanted to tell me, but since so much was going on in my life right now it could be about anything. I just graduated from high school. My eighteenth birthday was almost here. Our huge summer solstice celebration, Litha was fast approaching, along with the big event, my acceptance into the Witch Avenue Coven on the same day.

"Mom?" I yelled, as I trudged my way over to her bag, looking around the empty beach.

Only the crashing of waves answered.

I didn't see her anywhere.

"Mom?" I tried again, batting down the worry that wanted to make its way into my consciousness.

Realizing my voice was no match for the roar of the waves, I started walking toward one of the larger boulders, in case she was sitting where I just couldn't see her. The pebbles were loose, creating an extra treacherous journey since I was only in flip-flops. Poor planning on my part, but I didn't think that I'd have to hunt her down. She could be sidetracked so easily.

Finally making it to the mammoth piece of black rock, I became annoyed when I saw she wasn't there. I wasn't in any way prepared to be marching up and down the beach looking for her. I grabbed my cellphone out of my pocket and dialed her number as I went back toward her pile of things to sit. Maybe I should stay put, and she'd return soon enough. As the phone rang on my end, I got closer to my mom's pile and heard her bag ringing. Darn! She didn't take it with her—odd. That was always a rule of hers when hiking or at the beach. We carried our phones with us at all times.

I squatted down to see what she brought with her, hoping an item might lead me in the right direction to find her. If she were gathering plants, then I'd know better where to go. I opened up her bag and panic set in immediately. The shirt she was wearing when she left our house was stuffed in her bag, wrapped around the shoes she was wearing. This made no sense. Her wallet and jewelry were in this bag. She wouldn't just leave all this stuff for a stranger to steal. Something was wrong. Jumping up, the insides of the bag dispersed onto the beach, but I didn't care.

"Mom!" I screamed, kicking off my flip-flops so that I could run up the hill closest to me.

Reaching the top of the hill, I scanned the grassy area quickly seeing nothing. Spinning around, I looked back toward the rocky beach. From this vantage point, I was able to see everything and nothing. My heart started pounding as I began dialing 9-1-1.

"911, what is your emergency?" The operator answered.

"My mom. She's missing," I cried into the phone, dread spreading everywhere.

"Calm down, ma'am. Where are you located?"

Calm down? I'm not hyper, just scared!

"I'm at the beach just off of Snoqualmie Avenue, down the trail," I replied

"Is your mother in the water? How long has she been missing?"

"I don't know!" I screamed into the phone. "Please just send help."

Okay, now I'm panicking! I can't calm down. My mom isn't where she's supposed to be.

"Ma'am, help is on the way. What is your name?"

"Triss," I replied, as I ran back down the hill to search the beach or the water, or anywhere but where I was.

Could my mom be in the water? I didn't even think of that. She wouldn't be in the water, would she?

"And what is your mother's name?" the operator asked blandly.

"Veronica Spires," my voice panted with the exertion.

"Where are they? When will they get here? She needs help!"

I reached the edge of the water. The waves were lapping against my bare feet. Looking out toward the sea, I saw nothing but water and rocks illuminated by the moon's light. There was no way she would be out there. She never went into the water without someone with her. Oh, my God, where could she be?

The police sirens, off in the distance, were becoming louder by the second. Help was on the way but not nearly soon enough.

"Veronica! Mom! Veronica!" I kept hollering. "Where are you?"

"Ma'am, help has arrived. They're making their way down the trail. I'm going to stay on the phone until they reach you."

My body crumpled. Falling on my knees, the tears began pouring down my face. This couldn't be happening. I turned off my phone. The police were almost to the beach, and I didn't need the operator to hear my cries. The police chatter of CB radios began rolling through the air mixed with the barks of the K-9 units.

This was a nightmare. There was no way this could be happening. My eyes darted back to the hilltop that I had just left. A man was standing on the hill, watching me, with the darkness working in his favor.

"Hey," I yelled, looking at him, trying to see any sort of distinguishing features. He froze in place.

I jumped back to my feet, with my jeans soaked from where I had been sitting. I started running up to the hill, and the stranger took off.

"Miss!" a policeman yelled.

"Someone was watching me!" I cried, not stopping my run. "They might have my mom!"

I reached the top of the hill in a flash, and there was no one to be seen.

A policeman came up right behind me.

"Are you, Triss?" His voice was gentle, probably used to dealing with lunatics, not sure which way they were headed in any given situation. "I'm Officer White."

"Yes, my mom. She's not here." The tears started again. "I was supposed to meet her and all that's here are her things. I can't find her. Clothes, wallet, jewelry are all that's here." I took a deep breath. "Then there was a guy, I think staring at me."

"Where at?" he asked immediately.

"Right here," I replied. "He was standing right here. I think it was a guy. That's why I came this way. It's so dark it's hard to tell. I was sitting on the beach right before you got here and noticed the person."

"Where are your mother's things, Triss?" he asked, scanning the area and coming up with the same thing as me, nothing. There was no one here.

I pointed over to the beach, completely defeated.

He nodded and looked briefly at the ground for any sign of tracks besides mine; he then turned to the officers at the base of the hill and signaled for them to wait.

We walked back down the hill, and Officer White explained to the others the situation. I had no idea how he got so much from my few sentences. He pointed at the two officers who were in control of the German shepherds, and he motioned for me to come with them to where my mom's belongings had been dumped by my carelessness.

"Triss, we are going to allow our K-9 members, Sunny and Brandy, to smell some of your mother's items, okay?" Officer White asked, looking intensely into my eyes. He had to be well over six feet tall and commanded the attention of anyone who looked in his direction.

All I could do was nod. It felt like if I even opened my mouth to breathe, I would break down again.

One of the female officers, who had her hair pulled back in a severe ponytail, came over to me and touched my shoulder softly. She quieted her chattering CB on her belt.

"Is there someone we can call for you?" she asked.

"My aunt," I muttered, staring off over the darkened sound again, my eyes filling with tears.

One of the other female officers gave commands to Sunny and Brandy and off they went in the direction of the hill. The very same hill I had just come from with Officer White. They were racing off into the distance with the humans following right behind. My mom had been in that area. The dogs caught her scent.

It seemed like hours, but Aunt Vieta finally arrived. Her eyes wide with horror from the scene she witnessed in the parking lot. I couldn't even begin to count how many police and search and rescue arrived. There were divers already out in the ocean, and everywhere I turned, there was activity.

I had shutdown. I was merely operating on autopilot. Aunt Vieta started running toward me and scooped me into her arms.

"We'll find her, Triss. We'll find her," she kept mumbling into my ear, but it did little to comfort me.

"I know we will," I nodded in agreement.

She released me and stood back looking at me.

"Here, I thought you might be freezing." She shoved a coat into my arms that she had tied around her waist.

"Officer White's over there," I said, pointing toward his direction. He was busy getting updates from the teams that had spread in various directions. "He'd be the best person to fill you in. I don't think I could."

I appreciated my aunt's presence, but I would rather just sit on the beach listening to everyone's updates, hoping I would find something out that would bring my mom back immediately. Instead, I was bombarded with statistics about the longer the victim was missing how exponentially the odds of finding them decreased. I doubt that was for me to hear, but I did. And those words would forever haunt me.

"The waters are getting a little rough. We'll start again in the morning," were the first of many sentences that etched a place in my mind, creating a level of despair I didn't think possible.

Awakening Excerpt

The screams shattered my sleep. My heart was pounding seventy miles an hour. I felt for my fleece blanket to throw off, since I seemed to be stuck to my sheets with gallons of sweat. I looked around my blackened room, with only the red glow of the alarm clock displaying 2:00 am to comfort me. My heart sank as I lost the battle for another night's sleep. I heard the gentle snore of my bulldog, Matilda, rattling through the air. She was used to my screams by now. I promised myself with a little whisper that I was safe. It was only a nightmare — another nightmare. That was all it was. It couldn't possibly be real, that kind of terror. The dreams were coming closer together now, and worse yet they seemed to lead to nowhere but sleep deprivation.

I commanded myself to take deep, steady breaths to stay calm. Still shaky from the last images that had blasted into my brain, I tried to rid myself of the awful scene replaying over and over in my mind — my death. The mere thought of the attacks made me want to hide from the world in my closet. The black, swirling creatures were coming at me and through me from every direction. Their mouths open, displaying several sets of teeth with blood dripping from their lips, waiting for me to make a mistake. This was not a world I recognized. How could my mind even create such deadly monsters? The elements of realism spooked me beyond belief. I grabbed a tissue from my nightstand and wiped the dampness from my forehead, unsure of how much longer I could keep this up. Every night and every dream seemed different. They all had similar storylines, to a degree. Sometimes the unfamiliar characters reappeared to haunt me over and over again. It just depended on the night. Part of me felt as if I should know these people or at least the events that kept taking place. Why else would they keep reappearing? However, the events were so fantastical, the thought that I should recognize them made me feel even crazier for thinking it.

Fully awake now and completely disappointed in the prospect of another long and drawn out day without sleep, I trudged to the window and opened my heavy, red velvet curtains to expose the serenity of a dark outside world. The snow was slowly floating down leaving a beautiful pattern on the sidewalk, illuminated only by the streetlight. The sight brought a shiver to my bones. Even though a minute ago I'd had to wipe the wet heat of fear from my body. I couldn't keep chasing and being chased like this. I couldn't go on thinking my life was in danger every time I closed my eyes. I needed rest. I needed sleep. Lack of sleep was making things worse. I was sure of it.

"What is all of this telling me? I don't even know the people in my dreams!" I whined to Matilda.

She responded with her usual snorts and snores, sprawling out even more on my mattress now that I had left a larger area for her enjoyment. I flipped on my nightstand light, which cast its familiar glow, as I attempted to move back into bed without displacing Matilda. A sigh escaped as I grabbed my latest book, which was ready and waiting for another night like all the others.

I opened the book to the third chapter as my mind attempted to identify the people in my dream. Seeing crumpled remnants of humans discarded all over was never something that I could get used to regardless of whether it was a nightmare or not. I was getting used to seeing the swirls appear to attack me, but I was also intrigued by the thought of trying to figure out the identity of the random strangers who appeared time and time again. Sometimes they were the same people. Other times, a completely new set would make an entrance. I always avoided looking into their eyes because, during one of my very first nightmares, all I saw was the dull glow of death staring right back at me. I couldn't stomach it twice, and somehow my subconscious self knew to never look them in the eyes, whoever they were.

Thankfully, the latest batch of characters had seemed kind — as if I knew them from somewhere although that wasn't possible. I'm sure they must have made an appearance in other dreams. I just don't remember them. One stood out in particular. He was trying to save me, but it was too late. The black, soulless swirls got me. My nightmares had never gotten to that point before. Never did I know the conclusion to these nightmarish adventures before tonight.

This time, I saw how it ended. I didn't make it. It wasn't a painful process. I didn't feel tortured. It seemed like I should have felt the attack. I didn't.

What I was left with were horrible feelings of despair and loneliness wrapping their way through every aspect of my life. My soul felt like an empty cavern as I saw myself being blown away into the wind. I remembered looking back at the strangers on the ground. They were looking up towards the sky at me as I left to wherever bodiless souls go. The one guy who was so memorable was staring back at me, tears streaming down his face. He was the one who tried to save me. He'd risked his own life against the monsters for me. He was only a minute too late. My heart now longed for him, this figment of my imagination. I didn't know why.

I couldn't shake the images this time. They were too haunting, too real. And now I was going crazy believing that these things had some sort of significance. Lack of sleep was finally catching up with my fragile state of mind.

The Camp Excerpt

The Cessna 180 engine rumbled through the small six-seat aircraft cabin, but unfortunately it did little to block out the words of the other passengers. I glared at the back of the Captain who was lucky enough to be wearing a headset.

"I'd love to see what's under her jacket." I heard the guy behind me say to no one in particular.

"I'll second that, and I bet we'll get the chance," another one said.

The gnawing in my stomach only grew with every passing minute, but there was nothing I could do. I was stuck in a plane where I could literally touch the pilot. I didn't need to start something that I couldn't finish and have the plane crash because I couldn't handle a little heckling.

I looked out the small, oval window pressing my head against the cold glass covered in water droplets. I couldn't really see anything out the window because the weather was so bad. It was like we were trapped in one continuous rain cloud that was sent from the Gods to mess with me.

Getting tired of seeing nothing but ominous grey, I looked down at the pamphlet hoping the description would magically change, but I wasn't that lucky. My fingers trembled as I silently read the overview once more.

The ReBoot program is a juvenile camp for mid-range offenders who have yet to become established criminals. Youth in their mid to late teen years are often responsive to this type of program which includes occupational training and behavior rehabilitation. We've found that the potential criminals at our work camp for forestry and conservation in Southeast Alaska never become repeat offenders. We generally only accept less dangerous delinquents but all cases are subject for review.

I loved the 'yet to become established criminals' part, as if the first time around didn't really count for these misfits. I so didn't belong here. It wasn't like I needed to be reminded that my newfound campmates weren't savory characters. All I had to do was turn around in my tiny airplane seat to see their predator eyes taking me in.

I couldn't believe my mom let this happen to me. There's no way she could have been fooled into thinking this was a conservation-slash-forestry camp... although I was fooled. I actually thought my stepdad was trying to do something nice for me, for once.

God! I hated my stepfather, and he obviously hated me. This was his last sendoff before I went to college, and it was a doozey. As if living with him since my father's death wasn't horrible enough, he just wanted one more way to stick it to me.

The tin can I was riding in suddenly took a plunge, and all of the instruments went berserk. Gasps and whines filled the air as the high-pitched warning beeps sounded through our tiny capsule. My hands immediately became clammy as my heart raced. There was no calming down in a situation like this, especially when a person was born as jumpy as I was. My fingers gripped the armrest so hard that my nails hurt, and I took a deep breath in and exhaled slowly.

"It's okay, everyone. Just a little turbulence," the pilot told us as the beeps silenced, but the heavy breathing from everyone continued long after his announcement.

I was tempted to turn around in my seat and gloat at all of the guys who were big and tough only a few minutes ago and suddenly turned to pansies, but the Cessna took another huge dip, sounding the bells and whistles again. Man! I hated small planes. Actually, I don't even think this would qualify as a small plane, more like a car that could fly.

As the beads of water continued rolling down the tiny window, I noticed we had begun our descent. *Finally!*

"We'll be landing in approximately fifteen minutes," the pilot said as he continued adjusting controls.

Things were looking up. The dampness on my palms began to evaporate, and I looked back out the window as our plane flew barely above the treetops. The conifers looked like a brightly massed green quilt underneath us. Turning my head in any direction gave way to a completely different landscape. Alongside the deep green woodlands, there were rocky peaks, and monstrous cliffs that trees avoided calling home. If I wasn't so scared to death, I might be able to appreciate the beauty of everything.

I maneuvered my head so that I could see out the pilot's window. Directly in front of us there was a grassy field with small ponds surrounding it, or at least I think they were small ponds. I craned my neck as far as possible searching for the airport. Not only did I not see any buildings, I didn't see any sort of landing strip.

But I did catch a huge bear. I'm sure it was a bear. There was nothing else that big that walked on all fours.

"Whoa, check it out," one of the guys behind me said.

"That thing's huge," the guy next to him said. "I could totally take it down."

I couldn't handle it any longer.

"Why don't you? I'd love to see it," I taunted without looking behind me. There was no way I'd undo my seatbelt in transportation like this even if it meant I couldn't give him my best scowl.

"She does speak," he replied sarcastically.

Gritting my teeth, I watched as we passed by the brown bear with the plane descending at what felt like record speed.

"Please make sure your seatbelts are fastened. I'll make the landing as pleasant as possible," the pilot told us.

What? Landing? There's no runway!

This can't be possible. I've got a bear as an official greeter and our plane was landing on gravel or dirt or something. The only saving grace of this observation was that it kept the other passengers on the plane as silent as me.

I continued to watch the pilot pulling and pushing on things, and realized I really didn't want to see how little control he had over the situation. I'm sure he felt he had it handled, but from this viewpoint it was utterly terrifying. I clamped my eyes shut just in time to feel the plane shudder as the wheels began to touch down.

There was nothing smooth about it as our plane briefly greeted the gravel before pushing back up, only to quickly meet again with the surface below. It felt like a rollercoaster that had no tracks and no intention of stopping. Our plane continued to jump and skip its way down the non-existent runway. I slowly peeled open one eye and watched as we whipped by the tall grass and water finally coming to a slow stop.

The guys' celebratory hollers were deafening. They began throwing off their seatbelts, but I refused to budge. The pilot turned around and I wanted to hug him, but I restrained myself. Instead I looked out the window at the wilderness wondering if I'd survive.

"I'll be around to open the door, and the CLs should be here to greet you any minute. It's best if you don't wander off," the pilot instructed.

"CLs?" I asked, turning my attention back to him.

"Camp Leaders," he responded, his eyes connecting with mine. He opened his door and got out of the plane.

"Newbie. We've got a newbie on our hands," the guy sitting directly behind me shouted, kicking my seat. *What was he, twelve?*

"I wonder if that makes her a newbie in all areas? I can't wait to find out," he continued.

That was it! My seatbelt came flying off, and I leaned over the back of my seat, grabbing the guy's shirt, surprising him and myself. I was gripping the fabric so tightly I raised him slightly off his seat. He looked to be a year or so younger than me with blond hair that was greased back. His clothing was ten times too big for him, but he was still bigger than me.

"If you even look in my direction while we're at

this camp—" I began, but the pilot opened the side door interrupting me. I pushed him back on the seat and turned back around in mine.

"Jeez, chill out," he mumbled under his breath.

"Still gonna get some, Luke?" I heard someone whisper.

Everyone on this plane was so sleazy, except for the poor pilot. I didn't even want to imagine what everyone else at the camp would be like.

I was the last to jump out of the plane, as I looked around the land void of civilization. I couldn't believe my mom fell for allowing my stepdad to send me here.

"Emma Walton?" A girl asked.

I turned around and relief spread through me instantly. The girl looked to be a couple years older than me, so probably twentyish. And she looked normal. Her dark brown hair was bundled into a loose ponytail, and she was dressed in green cargo pants, a black T-shirt and rubber boots. Her smile was friendly, and I knew I'd be sticking around her as much as possible.

"I'm Steph," she said, smiling as she stuck her hand out for a handshake, "one of the CLs here."

Wow! That's formal. I shook her hand quickly.

"Nice to meet you." I grabbed my duffle bag and backpack

"Got everything?" she asked.

I nodded, and she waved at the pilot who was already preparing the plane for takeoff. "See ya in a week," she yelled at him.

A week! I'll be eighteen in a week, and then I can get out of here.

"We're in bear country out here," she began as our

group followed her and the other CLs through the tall grass.

"I saw one on the way in." I adjusted the large strap on my shoulder, hoping we wouldn't be hiking all that far.

"It's all part of being in the backcountry," she replied. "We'll go over everything when we get to camp, but it's nothing to mess with. A ranger went missing a week ago on Baranof Island, and they just found his remains."

A shiver ran down my spine.

"And Baranof Island doesn't have nearly as many brown bears as we have," another CL replied from behind.

Not what I wanted to hear!

BEYOND CONTROL

"Knock. Knock," Brandy hummed, tapping on the door lightly. "You ready?"

"Not really," I replied, pointing at the stack of papers piled on my desk. "But I guess that probably doesn't matter." I smiled and pushed myself away from the desk.

"Not when it comes to your father." She grinned. Brandy stepped into my office, and I gasped when I saw her. She was in the most gorgeous blue dress, and her dark brown hair was piled in loose curls on top of her head. With every movement, her dress shimmered and clung to all the right places, highlighting the beautiful caramel color of her skin.

"Whoa," I said, grinning, suddenly feeling completely underdressed for tonight's function. I looked down at my silver blouse, black pencil skirt, and red stilettos. I was proud of myself for wearing what I thought was a day-to-evening outfit like I always saw in the style magazines... and then Brandy steps into my office, blowing my wishful thinking to smithereens. It must be wonderful to always be so stunning.

"Your assistant cleans up nicely, huh?" she teased. Brandy was my best friend, who I'd met in college, and she knew me better than anyone.

"Your father figured this would happen," she laughed. "So he sent something over. A courier brought it about an hour ago. I didn't even peek."

"You mean my *stepmom* knew this would happen," I laughed.

"Same difference."

I blew the stray hairs out of my face and couldn't help but smile as I thought about my father. He always took such good care of me, especially since my mother's death. Actually, that wasn't completely true. His money always took very good care of me. I only saw him more now because I worked for one of his companies.

"Okay, let's see it," I sighed.

"Don't even pretend you don't want to play dress up." She left my office and returned in a heartbeat with a garment bag and a Nordstrom sack dangling around the hanger.

"I honestly didn't know it was such a big deal," I said, tucking my hair behind my ear.

"That's what black-tie means, dummy." Brandy extended the garment bag toward me and gave an exasperated huff.

I peered nervously through the glass wall that looked over the sea of cubicles. This wasn't something I wanted the rest of the employees to see. I'd already caught the animosity in the air about the fact that I worked here and didn't have to start at the bottom. Brandy saw my apprehension and quickly closed the door and shut the automatic blinds.

"It's not like I got an invitation. I'm his daughter. I

just show up," I replied, unzipping the garment bag to reveal a beautiful flowing chiffon dress. The fabric was soft lavender with tiny pearls stitched at the waistband, and beautiful lace appliques spreading from the hem up the skirt of the dress.

"I wanna see," Brandy whined.

"It's amazing and so... me," I replied, grabbing the hanger from Brandy so she could take a look.

I loved Brandy's dress on her, but it was so not me. Why? Because it was really tiny! One false move and nothing's left to the imagination, but that was exactly how she liked it. I, on the other hand, built a world that kept 'em guessing. That was my motto.

"Suddenly I'm no longer the belle of the ball," she laughed. "Holy. Shit. Is this Valentino?"

I shrugged and felt the familiar heat run up my face. My fingers instinctively ran up the scar along my breastbone as I eyed the neckline. There was no hiding it in this dress.

"Nobody will care what's being auctioned off tonight. They'll all want you," she gushed, noticing where my hand stalled. I could always count on her to make me feel better.

"Oh, please. This covers me all the way up. You'll definitely be the one who everyone's looking at," I assured her.

"Doubtful," she whispered, running her fingertips along the dress. "Let's get you in this. We're running late."

I laid the garment bag across my desk, careful not to knock any of the papers onto the floor, and worked the dress cautiously out of the bag. Brandy unhooked the shoe bag and opened the box up.

"Of course, Jimmy Choo," she said, dangling the

lace pumps from her fingertips.

I glanced at the shoes, and I'd be lying if I didn't admit just how pretty they were. But it was uncomfortable. I'd made it all through college without anyone really knowing about my family's wealth.

"You like them? You can have them after tonight," I replied.

Brandy looked over at me and smiled, shaking her head. "Nope. They're yours and I'm not going to accept them. Never have taken your icky hand-me-downs and never will." She laughed and began unhooking the straps on the Choos.

I kicked off my heels, stripped out of my blouse and wriggled out of my skirt. So much for my bra in this dress. I unclasped it quickly and tossed it on the floor.

"Classy," Brandy said, picking everything up for me. "Oh, I almost missed this," she said, looking into the Nordstrom bag, pulling out a large jewelry box. "Want me to open it?"

I nodded as I slipped the dress over my head and felt the soft fabric cascade over my skin.

"Whoa," she uttered, opening the box. "This is beautiful."

She turned the box toward me, and the knot in my stomach—that I didn't even realize was there—immediately diminished. So much for being cool and confident when it came to strapless dresses. As I looked in the box, a collared, sterling silver necklace with a large stone pendant was perfectly situated in tissue paper. This would cover up most of my scar...

"Nice," I replied, smiling.

I positioned the front slit over my leg as Brandy zipped me up and centered the necklace around my neck, locking the clasp in place.

"You look stunning," she said, stepping back.

The feeling of security the pendant provided as it dangled in the perfect place, gave me an extra dose of courage for the night. Something very few even knew I needed. I'd done a great job over the years explaining to everyone how well adjusted I'd become. Apparently, I hadn't fooled my stepmom or Brandy for that matter.

"Hair okay?" I asked. I had placed it in a loose French knot this morning, and last I looked, it was still holding on.

"Yep. Let's get going." She grabbed my hand and pulled me toward the door. I grabbed my purse out of the chair and followed her to the elevators.

"There should be plenty of cabs at this time," I said, as we wound along the far wall of cubicles and waited for the elevator.

"Umm." Brandy stepped into the elevator, refusing to look at me.

"Oh, no. Please tell me we aren't going in the limo."

"Your father sent it over. He texted me," she replied, trying to hide her smile.

"That thing is such a spectacle, especially in Seattle. I always feel like I should see my high school date inside as it pulls up. Besides, Seattle thrives on bicycles as the main mode of transportation," I protested.

"Sorry," she squealed. "But it sounds like the beast is going to be picking us up. And besides, can you really see yourself peddling on a bicycle in that outfit? Get real."

I rolled my eyes and smiled as we stepped into the

lobby. Sure enough the black stretch sedan was waiting for us beyond the doors.

"Let's just hope we've got some hotties waiting for us at the ball," Brandy said, winking. "Firemen, maybe, or how about some lawyers?"

"Yeah. Because that's what always happens for us," I retorted.

"Maybe we've struck out lately, but I know there's hope out there for you and me. I mean if we can move past the whole blind date fiasco, it would be better for us all. You don't have to keep reminding me. It was bad for us both."

"Yeah. But you weren't the one who wound up with Squiggy for an entire night. I was!" I shuddered at the memory.

"Right. Because my date, Father Time, was a far better choice," she shot back.

"We're screwed, aren't we?" I laughed.

"I don't know. I mean it might not be that bad being roomies forever," she said, pretending to use a cane.

"Watching marathons of the Golden Girls is far different than living it." I narrowed my eyes at her. "Even if we find a couple of *someones* worth talking to, I want to make sure to get home early tonight. I've got a lot on my plate tomorrow," I said, watching Brandy's expression fall.

"You certainly are a fuddy-dud for only being twenty-two."

"Almost twenty-three," I corrected. "And I don't want to let my dad down. He didn't have to give me this position."

She smiled and pulled me through the revolving, glass doors to reveal a beautiful Seattle night. The cerulean sky held very few clouds, and the warm breeze was a nice change from the air-conditioned office building. The city was lively with taxis honking, commuters running to catch buses and trains, and tourists wandering with maps in hand. Bernie, our driver, greeted us. He'd worked for my dad for as long as I could remember. He was like another father to me, and he could actually pass as my dad's brother. They looked pretty similar with strong jawlines and soft brown eyes. The only difference was that my father's dark hair was graying slightly. I reached around Bernie's neck and gave him a big hug, the pumps making me as tall as him. I released my arms, and he beamed.

"Well, don't you two look beautiful," Bernie said, opening the back door for us. He was dressed in his usual dark suit and tie. My father told him years ago that he could wear whatever he wanted, but Bernie refused to ever veer away from the suits. I don't think I'd ever seen the man in jeans.

"Thanks, Bernie," I chimed, crawling inside the limo as gracefully as possible and plunking in the far seat. Brandy climbed in after me, situating herself in the seat next to me as Bernie closed the door. He made it around to the driver's door and slid in the sedan, popping the privacy glass up.

Brandy reached for the bottle of champagne and gave me a huge smile.

"You know, Gabby, this is way better than a taxi," she laughed, as she popped the cork. "No matter how you cut it."

"It's better with my best friend in here, no doubt," I said laughing, while I steadied my glass for her to pour in some of the pink bubbly.

"Agreed." She poured some of the pink liquid into her glass and took a taste.

I sat back and drank a few sips of the champagne, hoping it would relax me before we got there. My stepmom and dad were throwing a fundraiser at one of the local wineries in Woodinville. I think it was at Chateau Marx last I heard, but I tended to dismiss these things as quickly as I heard about them because it felt like these events were endless, always some cause to sponsor or some reason to celebrate.

"Since you got the invitation, do you know what this one's for?" I asked, raising a brow.

"I think it was to help with medical bills for that little boy who was struck in the hit-and-run accident. I think that's where I recognized his name from, anyway."

"Shit. Now I feel like a complete d-bag," I muttered.

The car continued to lurch and crawl as Bernie made his way through the downtown traffic, and my stomach wasn't feeling so great with the bubbles sloshing with each pause.

"You're looking a little green," Brandy noticed. "Want me to finish that for you?" She wiggled her brows and pointed with her free hand.

"Actually. Yeah." I smiled and handed her my flute and leaned my head back to focus on breathing, staring at the nip and tuck upholstery of the ceiling.

"So this is the real reason you don't like the limo," Brandy chuckled. "Now it makes sense. Does anyone know?"

"I told them I outgrew it. I was tired of getting teased endlessly," I whispered, steadying my breathing as the sloshing continued. "Besides, it only happens in traffic."

Brandy continued to laugh all the way to the onramp of the highway, and I immediately perked up as the car began to steady its speed.

"Traffic doesn't look too bad," she said, sipping from one glass and holding the other.

"Things are looking up," I said, watching the downtown corridor flash by on our way to the floating bridge. The silvery, pink, and blue skyscrapers gave way to brick homes and condominiums lining the highway.

The traffic on the highway was nonexistent, which made the commute a breeze. I grabbed my empty flute back from Brandy and filled it halfway up as the nausea subsided. Our car glided onto the ramp of the 520-floating bridge, and I took a triumphant gulp of the fizzy stuff as we made our way across the water. I prevailed.

"This place is always so beautiful in the summer," Brandy replied, looking out the window.

She was right. The calmness on the one side of the bridge allowed for the sun to dance off the glistening water, whereas the other side of the bridge presented the choppy whitecaps, which bounced off the worn cement of the bridge. I always wondered why there was such a difference between the two sides. There was always the calm side and always the choppy side, kind of like my life.

The car began to slow again and my stomach tightened. Just as I was about to take another sip of champagne, my entire body lunged sideways onto Brandy's lap as our limo hit whatever was in front of us. I braced myself for a vehicle to crash into us from behind, but thankfully it was only the one hit as the sound of brakes and tires squealing behind us stopped. Bernie immediately rolled down the partition and looked panic stricken, checking us for injuries.

"You girls, okay?" he asked, breathless. "I'm so sorry. I don't know what happened." His face was ashen and his brown eyes wide.

I hoisted myself out of Brandy's lap and straightened up to see out the windshield.

"We're okay, Bernie. Are you?" I asked.

"Yes, ma'am," he muttered, clearly shaken.

"Not a drop spilt," Brandy offered, trying to make him feel better with her usual dose of humor.

I shook my head and looked through the windshield. It looked like we'd hit some sort of white utility trailer. I couldn't see what kind of vehicle was towing it, but judging by the size of the trailer, it would have to be something beefy. All I knew was getting in an accident on the bridge was every commuter's worst nightmare. Bernie quickly opened his door and jumped out. I hoped they could quickly trade information and we could move on.

"Whoa. Sometimes things are meant to be," she sang, squeezing my elbow.

"What are you talking about?" I asked. There was nothing worth getting in an accident over, especially as the horns blared behind us.

"*That's* what I'm talking about," she purred, yanking on me to look outside. "Did you know such perfection was possible?"

Clearly the bubbles had already gotten to her.

I craned my neck and saw Bernie hustling over to someone, and that's when I saw him. I didn't believe my eyes. Men like this didn't exist in Seattle. We were a city full of hipsters and techies, but here he was...

standing right next to our car. I felt as if my world had done a pause. Just the mere sight of him made my heart flutter like I was back in grade school waiting to open my very first Valentine.

This was crazy!

As he exchanged information with Bernie, I watched his every move. From his dark hair that the breeze mussed up slightly to the lopsided grin that he wore, I simply couldn't look away. There was something so intriguing about him. I mean there was no denying it. The guy was completely built, but there was something more.

It didn't hurt that his smile was out of this world, but any guy who just got rear-ended and had the decency to smile about it was unusual. The dark shadow along his jawline signaled a morning without a shave, which complimented his rugged appearance and I just...

"You stopped breathing," Brandy mumbled and all I could do was smile.

He was dressed in a pair of ripped jeans, and his shoulders were broad, filling out his charcoal t-shirt. As my eyes fell back down to his jeans, my insides clashed madly as I glimpsed bronzed skin where his shirt had tugged up slightly. I looked over at Brandy who was in the same zone as me.

The way the sun was setting, I didn't think he could see inside, but it somehow felt like his eyes were on me, watching me fidget. Okay. That was probably wishful thinking, but it really did feel that way. So much so that I refused to look in his direction, even though it was killing me not to check him out.

"Can he see through the windshield, do you

think?" Brandy mused.

"Why?" I asked. "I don't think so, but I'm not sure since the privacy glass is down."

"Well, it looks like he's captivated by someone back here and it's not me," she stated.

"Yeah. Then he definitely can't see back here," I said, feeling the heat run up my body.

"I'm pretty sure he can, and all I can say is lucky you."

I turned my attention back to him and saw him speaking with Bernie, but I will admit his gaze did manage to gravitate in this direction.

"I think I'd trade my soul for one night with him," I whispered.

"That's my Gabby," Brandy chuckled. "You just needed a Mr. Perfect to show up."

"He's completely unattainable," I replied, daring myself to look at him once more. "That's why I can say it. He'll drive off, so will we, and I won't have to worry."

His hand gripped a leather wallet, and my gaze followed up his long, muscular arm as I watched him stuff it back in his pocket. How could a slight movement do this to me? His laughter echoed all the way to the car as he patted Bernie's shoulder and dipped his head to peek through the windshield. This time there was no doubt who he was looking at as our eyes locked, sending a shiver up my spine. His long lashes outlined his amber eyes, and they were like liquescent gold as the sunlight caught the bronze flecks just right. I didn't even think that was a possible eye color, except maybe in a little movie I happened to love back in high school and college, but still those were contacts. These weren't. His lip quirked up, and he gave a slight nod. So slight, I wasn't even sure it happened.

Brandy squealed and tightened her grip. "He's coming this way," she said.

"Quick. Sit over there." I pointed to the backseat, and she dove toward it. I started laughing but followed right behind her. I felt the giddiness of high school fill me to the brim, and I had no idea why.

"How come we just did that?" she muttered, ready for the next commandment as she adjusted her dress.

"I have no idea," I confessed.

I pointed at the Grecian God as he peered into the darkened glass next to us. He did a double tap on the window with his knuckles as his lips twisted into a cocky smile. When he stood back up, I noticed his shirt hugging his flat stomach and began dreaming about my fingers skating across it and started chuckling.

"What's so funny?" Brandy quipped and I shook my head.

"I have no effing idea, but this mirage of a man is turning me into a mess."

"He's no mirage," she replied.

I watched as the man threw us another lopsided smile, but I also knew this time he couldn't see us. He just seemed to like the idea of messing with us.

"So, you got the President inside here or a bunch of giggling high school girls on their way to prom?" His voice low, scalding my insides.

Brandy looked at me horrified. "This is why you hate riding in this thing," she stated.

I nodded quickly, keeping my eyes on the guy who was slowly moving toward the door.

"Completely pretentious modes of transportation

will never lead to good things." I took a deep breath in.

"Yep. My bet is that it's a bunch of sixteen year olds," he said coyly, arrogance filling his every word and gesture. "Waiting to get—"

Brandy's breathing stopped at about the same time mine did.

My heart fell to my toes as he opened the door and ducked his head inside the limo. He was gorgeous. No. That's not true. He was beyond gorgeous. His amber eyes filled with mischief as he looked at Brandy and then at me.

He looked to be in his late twenties. I heard Bernie talking, but I couldn't decipher what he was saying. All I could do was look at this piece of perfection as he toyed with us and obviously enjoyed it. My hand slid up by my necklace as I attempted to block my scar from his view, but all that did was make me more self-conscious.

"Are you two okay?" he asked.

I nodded, speechless, and looked away.

"That was quite a hit," he continued. "I'm an EMT if…"

I whipped my head around, intending to give him a mocking glance, but instead I wound up blushing as his smile turned to a wonderfully wicked grin with his eyes capturing my discomfort.

"If he can do that with his eyes, I can't even imagine what he can do with…" Brandy whispered in my ear.

"What was that?" the man's voice rumbled, eyeing me, not Brandy.

"Okay, you've had your fun," I told him, flushing from the inside out. "We've got an event we're late for." I watched his eyes follow my lips as I spoke, which did nothing but create a hornets nest inside of me. How could his eyes do that to me, penetrate me like that?

"You're right. What was I thinking? You're the only ones who have a place to be." He flashed me another wide grin. The intensity in him shifted only slightly as he pretended to be annoyed. "I wasn't on my way to anywhere in particular. In fact, I had only planned on driving back and forth on the bridge all night. One side... Then the other..."

"I didn't mean that where we had to go was more important than you," I sputtered out. This is what I hated about riding in these things. Limos automatically put people in the ass-hat category. However, wanting to live up to the already laid reputation, my lips pinched together, and my arms crossed automatically.

"Maybe we're headed to the same place," he replied, his eyes carefully reading my actions, teasing me. "Although, judging by how you're dressed, it's doubtful."

I frowned and looked away from the guy and mumbled, "You really should drive more carefully."

The guy laughed and my eyes flicked back to his. "That's what most people hear when they've just gotten rear-ended," he replied. "Well, I think I struck out here so my insurance will be in touch." He gave me a wink and ducked out of the car.

I watched Bernie and the guy trade goodbyes quickly before he jogged back to whatever vehicle was pulling the trailer.

Brandy reached for the bottle of champagne and replenished both of our flutes. "I think someone's got a crush on the mystery man."

"I do not."

"You always get this way when you do," she continued laughing.

"What way?" I demanded.

"Snippety." She smiled as if she'd won the battle.

Bernie climbed back into the car, apologizing profusely, and Brandy and I both resituated back to the side seat. I watched as the utility trailer pulled away and we followed.

"It looks like it did more damage to this car than his trailer," Bernie said. "It's gonna be in the shop for awhile."

"That's a shame," Brandy replied sarcastically. Finally the woman was on my side about riding in this car.

"So what's that guy's name?" Brandy asked Bernie. I jabbed her in the ribs, and all she did was laugh.

"Jason something or other," Bernie replied. "I've got it written down. He certainly got a kick out of you two, didn't he?"

"Jason," Brandy repeated it for me as if I didn't hear it the first time. "That's a nice name."

She was about to get on one of her 'pair up Gabby' kicks so I quickly deterred her, hoping her champagne consumption would aid in my rescue.

I turned to her and asked, "You wanna know what's more ridiculous than showing up to places in a limo?"

"What?" she asked playfully, batting her lashes and forgetting about setting me up with the stranger.

"Pulling up to a place in a busted-ass limo," I replied, and we both started laughing. Dating crisis averted once again.

BOOKS BY KARICE BOLTON

THE WITCH AVENUE SERIES
LONELY SOULS
ALTERED SOULS
RELEASED SOULS
SHATTERED SOULS

THE WATCHERS TRILOGY
AWAKENING
LEGIONS
CATACLYSM
TAKEN NOVELLA (A Watchers Prequel)

THE CAMP

BEYOND LOVE SERIES
BEYOND CONTROL
BEYOND DOUBT
BEYOND REASON

AFTERWORLD SERIES
RecruitZ
AlibiZ-Coming Soon

ABOUT THE AUTHOR

Karice Bolton lives in the Pacific Northwest and is a writer of Young Adult and New Adult books. She loves to read anything and everything. She also enjoys baking, skiing, and spending time with her wonderful husband and two English bulldogs.

Karice would love if you stopped by her blog or FB page to find out the latest news on giveaways and upcoming releases, or you can just send her an email. She loves hearing from her readers and responds as soon as she can.

Contact the Author

To contact the author, please visit her online at http://www.karicebolton.com or via Twitter/Facebook @KariceBolton.